R.L. PEREZ

OAK & EMBER

WILLOW
HAVEN
PRESS

OAK & EMBER

www.rlperez.com

Ares Jungle

Fulcrum

✦

Realm of Elysium

Portal

Amara

Portal

CONTENTS

"From Pandora's box, where all the ills of humanity swarmed, the Greeks drew out hope after all the others, as the most dreadful of all. I know no more stirring symbol; for contrary to the general belief, hope equals resignation. And to live is not to resign oneself."

— Albert Camus, *The Myth of Sisyphus and Other Essays*

PROLOGUE
GAIA

THE TREES STIRRED WITH THE WIND AS A MURKY haze formed in the sky. Swirling clouds and flashes of lightning indicated a storm approached.

But Gaia knew this was no ordinary storm. The current of energy spiraling in the air had a familiar scent to it.

The scent of earth magic. *Her* magic.

"Pandora," she whispered, gazing up at the granite sky. At last, her third daughter was free.

From behind her, the front door of her home swung open, and Sybil strode down the path, carrying a wicker basket full of books. She stopped at Gaia's side and followed her gaze.

"It's the gods," Sybil said sagely. Gaia always admired

that about her; she had a godly sense, even if she had no god blood.

"Yes," Gaia agreed solemnly, turning to look at her beloved. "It is."

Sybil met her gaze with a hardened expression. Ever since she'd discovered Gaia's true identity—and learned she had been lied to for years—their relationship hadn't been the same. Gaia understood that it would take time for Sybil to forgive her, if she ever did at all.

But with Pandora unleashed, she felt a sense of urgency.

Either her daughter would come for her... or the magic from her box would.

One way or another, Gaia would face a battle like no other.

"I have always loved you, Sybil," Gaia said softly. "Even with the foolish choices I made, it was all out of love."

"I knew there was something different about you," Sybil said. "I should have asked. Should have urged you to tell me. Instead, I respected your space, trusting you would tell me in time." She heaved a sorrowful sigh. "But you never did. I found out when you were *summoned* by Prue. If you had only told me—no matter how long it took—I would have accepted you."

Gaia's heart twisted at her words. There was nothing

she could say. No magic words, no powerful spell that could heal this rift between them.

Only time.

But that was what Gaia feared she had little of: time. Pandora's magic might come for her today or tomorrow.

She drew closer to Sybil and placed a hand on her shoulder. She would have gathered her in her arms if she'd let her. Or if the basket full of books wasn't in the way.

"I am truly sorry for letting my fear come between us," Gaia said, pouring as much earnest affection into her voice as she could muster. "Despite what I am, when it comes to you, I am weak. I feel as pathetic and frail and insecure as a mortal. Around you, I..." She shook her head, unable to find the words. She swallowed and tried again. "Nothing makes sense except when I am around you. And I was so desperate to preserve that, to keep you by my side, that I let this secret come between us. You're right. If I had seen reason, I would have *known* you would have remained by my side. I am sorry for doubting that. I know it may be too late, Sybil, but you are my life. My entire *being* belongs to you."

Sybil's eyes glistened with tears. She sniffed and ducked her head, her eyelids closing as the tears pooled over, spilling down her face. "Polly, you always had a way with words."

Polly. For years, Gaia had lived on this tiny island as

Polina, the Mother of the coven. Even though it wasn't her true name, she hoped Sybil would continue to use it. It made her feel normal again. Like nothing had changed between them.

"But I am *not* your life," Sybil said, raising her gaze to meet Gaia's. "You have two daughters who need you."

Gaia inhaled deeply. She needed to prove to Sybil that she would do better. So, it was time for the full truth. "I have three daughters."

Sybil stared at her. "Three?"

"I bore triplets. One was taken from me, and I have sensed her bitterness growing all these years." Gaia gestured to the sky. "This darkness is her making. She will come for me, Sybil. And I'm not sure I will survive her wrath."

Sybil blinked, her mouth opening and closing. "But... you are *Gaia*. The creator of the realm. The mother of all the earth."

Gaia smiled sadly. "Yes. But my powers have been stripped. I am only a shadow of who I once was."

Sybil's brows knitted together, her expression conflicted, as if she didn't quite know how to respond. "This third daughter... Where is she?"

"I do not know. It was part of my curse that she was hidden from me. Otherwise I would have found her. I would have done anything for her."

"And yet she seeks your destruction?"

"Yes. The years without me have stoked her fire. And I fear my words alone will not be enough to convince her that I have loved her and yearned for her all these years."

Sorrow filled Sybil's eyes. "Polly... That is devastating. I—I'm so terribly sorry."

Emotion stuck in Gaia's throat, and she nodded, unable to speak.

"Where will you go?" Sybil asked.

Gaia's gaze shifted to the horizon. The sky above them was gray and dismal, but the skies beyond only darkened with rage and foreboding. "I will meet her where the darkness is thickest."

"You will offer yourself up, like a lamb to the slaughter?" Anger tinged Sybil's voice.

Gaia fixed a defeated look on her lover. "She is my daughter. I will not fight her, nor will I hide from her. This is my penance."

She turned to leave, prepared to stride down the road and make arrangements to board a vessel before the seas became too perilous to travel. But Sybil's words stopped her.

"I will always love you, Polly."

Gaia turned then, her dark hair whipping around her face. Sybil still held the wicker basket, and Gaia had the sense the weight of her books was grounding her; that if Sybil released it, she would collapse or float away.

And perhaps it was for the best that this barrier stood

between them. If Gaia was able to hold her, she might never let go. She might never have the strength to walk away.

"If I survive this," Gaia said quietly, "I swear I will find you. I will do whatever it takes to earn your trust again."

Sybil's lips pressed together in a tight line as more tears streamed down her face.

With her heart heavy and her eyes moist, Gaia turned from the one woman she loved more than anything. The one soul who had captured her heart so fully.

The one she might never see again.

ELYSIUM

PANDORA

THESE DAMNED GODS AND THEIR PRETENTIOUS nature would be the death of Pandora. She was certain of it.

She sat in a large receiving room within the gleaming palace of Elysium, and everything around her screamed of elegance and finery. She smoothed her skirts for the hundredth time, the cold marble hard and unyielding at her back. Her gaze wandered to the open veranda before her, which boasted a wide coast and a cerulean sea.

Pretentious indeed. At least the illusion of the Underworld had been a humble forest. It was one of the things Pandora loved most about the place where she'd grown up. It was simple. And the simplicity had felt so *real*.

But this? This felt as false as Pandora's persona. As false as the mask she would wear during her stay here.

The waves lapped, the rush of the ocean surrounding her. *Look at this paradise,* it seemed to say. *Isn't it wonderful? Everything here is absolutely perfect.*

The whole notion made Pandora want to vomit. Did no one see through this facade? Were all the deities here complete morons?

She would see for herself, she supposed. Assuming *anyone* would come and greet her. She had been escorted to this chamber, left to wait for hours. As if the gods had anything better to do than sip wine and lord over their elegant lifestyle.

Pandora balled her hands into fists as her rage bled through her thoughts, triggering the memories that often plagued her. Anguished screams. Agony pulling at her, flaying her inside out. The gods ignoring her cries and pleas, looking on with cold apathy as her magic was stripped from her, ripped violently from her very soul, her very *being.*

Pandora's fists began to shake. *You are in control,* she told herself. *You are in control.*

But the screams still rang in her mind, an echo of the past. A life she never knew, but was cursed to remember.

"Ah, Hecate."

Pandora's fists relaxed, and in an instant, she had donned her persona—a humble, lesser goddess of the

Underworld. The name she had taken as a child of the Underworld, to conceal the identity of the soul residing inside her. For most of her life, she had been known as Hecate, or Trivia, the goddess of three paths.

She rose to her feet, clasping her hands in front of her, and sank into a curtsy before inspecting the deity before her.

Her lips puckered into a scowl.

It had been an age since she'd last seen him. An age since she'd been to Elysium, really. But she remembered their last encounter with irritation and loathing.

Sol, the sun god.

His warm brown eyes were as alluring as ever, tainted by the smug smirk of his lips. His blond hair had grown since she'd last seen him, now falling to his shoulders. And his face, once clean shaven, was now covered in neatly trimmed facial hair that, Pandora begrudgingly admitted, suited his face quite nicely.

In fact, everything about him was attractive. Had he always looked like this? Surely not. The last Pandora had seen him, he'd been tall and scrawny, cold and distant. Nothing impressive.

Or perhaps she'd been too young to appreciate his lean, muscular form.

He had the body of a soldier—broad shoulders and firm biceps that she could easily see beneath the royal blue tunic of his apprentice uniform. Gods above, she hated to admit it, but he was *gorgeous*.

This didn't change the fact that Sol, the sun god, was an absolute ass. Every time Pandora had visited, he'd made her life a living hell, constantly reminding her she was no better than the dust at his feet.

She lifted her chin. She'd been prepared to grovel at the feet of a prestigious god. Apollo, if she'd been lucky. Instead, the almighty god of sun and time had sent his lackey. As if Pandora wasn't worthy of being greeted by the king himself.

"Actually, I go by the name Trivia now," Pandora said with a sniff. She wasn't sure why she said it; she was fully intending to adopt her Hecate persona. But ever since Prue had referred to her as Trivia, the identity had seemed more fitting. It felt a bit more true to who Pandora actually was. Her whole life had been a spiral of deception. It made her yearn for something real.

Prue. Her sister.

Anger and sorrow warred within Pandora at the thought of her lost sister. She didn't care what became of her. If she had been destroyed along with the Underworld, it didn't matter.

At least, that was what Pandora told herself.

Sol's eyebrows lifted, his smirk widening. His eyes dragged over her body from head to toe, and she was torn between fidgeting under his scrutiny and punching him in the face. "Is that so? I didn't realize you were *grand* enough for two names."

"Most gods have two names, you imbecile," Pandora said lightly.

"Very true," he quipped, his eyes gleaming. "It *has* been a while, hasn't it, Hecate? Or should I say, *Trivia?* I must say, you look simply radiant. From the scrawny girl I saw before, I never would have thought you would blossom into something so... beautiful." He murmured the word, low and deep, as if that was meant to send her swooning.

Pandora snorted. "Is that supposed to be a compliment?"

"It's supposed to be whatever you want it to be," he said with a wink.

She rolled her eyes. "So, what, am I not to be greeted by the great god himself?"

"He sent me to fetch you."

Pandora bristled at that. *Fetch.* Like she was some item to be retrieved.

"You'll be given a room and the finest food you could ask for," Sol said. "His Majesty will see you in the morning."

Pandora scoffed. "In the *morning?*" Her voice rang in the resplendent walls around her.

Only when Sol's eyebrows lifted further did she realize how loud her outburst had been. Her mouth clamped shut, her teeth grinding together. Damn this god. He evoked her wrath, and now her entire plan of portraying herself as a humble deity was unraveled.

She sighed and said more quietly, "What could he possibly be busy with that would keep him from greeting a guest?"

Sol's expression sobered. "He's rather busy. In case it escaped your notice, Pandora's box has been opened."

For some reason, the sound of her *true* name sent prickles of awareness along Pandora's flesh. So few ever used her true name that it jolted her every time. She had to forcibly remind herself that he wasn't referring to her —only the box that had housed her magic.

Screams reverberated in her mind once more as the memory resurfaced again. The magic, tearing her soul apart, ripping her into pieces, consumed by agony and fire...

"Trivia?" Sol asked.

Pandora stiffened, snapping out of her reverie and fixing a glare on Sol. "What?"

"Did you hear me?" His voice was slow, as if she were dim-witted.

What an ass.

"Of *course* I heard you," she snapped. "And no, it didn't escape my notice. My realm was destroyed by this magic, so I'm *well* aware of what has transpired."

Sol's mouth fell open. "The Underworld is..."

"Gone, yes. The magic swallowed it up."

He shook his head. "No. It can't be. We would have felt it. An entire realm destroyed? That would have impacted our realm, too."

Pandora rolled her eyes. "You lot are so consumed by your revelry and festivities that I doubt you would even notice if *all* the realms were ripped apart."

"Our gods' blood is linked to that realm," Sol said, his tone taking on a harsh edge. "Whatever you may think of us, you cannot deny that connection."

"*Me,* deny that connection? Well, that's rich, since you *glorious* Elysium gods never deigned to grace us with your distinguished presence. Not once."

Sol groaned. "Don't start with this, Trivia. You know full well that we cannot safely dwell among your kind for too long."

Your kind. Like she was some demonic species. She opened her mouth to argue, rage mounting within her, when he raised a hand to silence her, as if she were a servant he could command.

"I need to see Apollo," Sol said, all business now. "He must know about this development."

"It's not a *development,*" Pandora snapped. "It's a realm full of people and creatures that don't exist anymore."

She didn't have to force emotion into her voice; it was already there. Inside, her heart twisted at the thought of the innocent lives that had been taken because of what she'd unleashed in the Underworld. She'd grown up there; she'd known firsthand that it wasn't all bad. There had been people there—human souls, even demons—who had been kind to her.

Including her own sisters.

But the Underworld also represented the cage she'd been forced into. The prison where her mother had abandoned her. The loneliness and solitude of growing up as an unwanted, unloved, and insignificant goddess.

Not to mention it was Aidoneus's home. And the former god of the Underworld had played a key role in the suffering that plagued her memories—the trauma of another life.

She owed it to those memories to seek retribution. If destroying Aidoneus's home resulted in the loss of other lives, then so be it. There were always casualties in war.

But Sol and Apollo and every other damned god in Elysium didn't give a shit about any other realm or person or god besides themselves. And it infuriated her when they pretended otherwise.

That was exactly why this place had to burn, too.

Sol waved a hand as if this didn't matter. The motion only stoked Pandora's ire.

"I'll send a servant to prepare a room for you," Sol said, venturing back the way he'd come. "Someone will fetch you shortly."

"Don't you *dare* walk away from me, you pretentious bastard," Pandora hissed, stomping after him, her shoes echoing against the marble floors. "I have come here with no allies, no home to return to, and no patience for your pompous bullshit. I know I'm not a god who is *worthy* of your attention, but dammit, I've come a long way and spent a lot of magic to get here. You will *not* leave me to sit on this damn balcony for hours. I'm done waiting. So, either take me with you to Apollo, or take me to my room this instant."

Sol turned to face her fully. His eyebrows lifted, and a quirk turned the corners of his lips. His expression almost seemed... amused.

He was *amused* by her insults?

When he merely watched her for another moment, Pandora felt her resolve falter. She lifted her chin and added, "And if you decide to walk away from me, I will simply follow you."

Sol huffed a laugh. "I have no doubt. Gods, you certainly are formidable when provoked."

"You haven't seen even *half* of my wrath. Trust me." Her mind turned to Evander, the poor death god she had left stranded in Elysium. He was likely dead now. He hadn't stood a chance against the power of her earth magic, and with his demonic nature, the atmosphere in Elysium would devour him completely.

Guilt nibbled in the pit of her stomach, but she

pushed it away. Her plan would never work if she let feelings like this get in the way.

Like with the Underworld, it had to be done. Only then could the restless agony roiling inside her be set free.

Sol jerked his head toward the hallway. "Follow me, then."

"To Apollo?"

He fixed a flat stare at her. "To your room. Your tantrum will only take you so far, my lady."

Tantrum. What was she, a screaming toddler?

Her hands balled into fists as he chuckled at her scowl. She had a fierce desire to punch him directly in his perfectly shaped nose. It would look so much better if it were a bit more crooked. And bloody.

Before she could, however, Sol turned on his heel and strode down the hall. His long legs kept a brisk pace, and she hurried after him, muttering curses under her breath.

CHASM
CYRUS

CYRUS WAS CONSUMED BY DARKNESS AND nightmares. A dizzying array of horrifying images flooded his mind: dismembered body parts, Prue's lifeless body, a feral caged animal with blood dripping from its mouth...

Screams rang in his ears. He was nothing but a disembodied spirit, floating aimlessly, with no direction or control.

Am I dead? he thought. He must be.

Either that, or Tartarus had completely taken hold of him.

"Prue," Cyrus moaned, his voice a weak rasp.

The rumble in his throat and the sound of his own voice in his ears sent a bolt of clarity through him. Followed immediately by the most intense pain he had ever known. An anguished scream ripped through him as white-hot fire pierced his flesh, boiling his blood and tearing him apart from the inside. His skin felt like it was melting off his body, his bones weak and fragile, leaving nothing but broken shards within him.

He was dying. Surely, he had to be.

Each second was torture. Pure agony. He tried to move, but even the mere *thought* of motion sent a fresh wave of pain through him. For several long, tedious moments, he did nothing but exist in this space of misery. No movement. No thoughts.

He was nothing. He would never be anything ever again.

"Prue," he said again, his throat dry and numb.

The thought of her broken body, her severed limbs, her horrified scream...

I need to move, he thought urgently. *Now.*

Another roar of fury burst from him, but this was filled with determination instead of pain. He would do whatever it took to get to Prue—even if it meant ripping himself apart.

Gradually, feeling returned to his body, but gods above, it was the most exquisite torture he had ever endured. His limbs weighed down heavily, his skin burning, his insides throbbing...

Then he realized why. There was, quite literally, a heavy weight pressing him down.

Boulders. Rocks. Dirt, dust, and granite.

He was *buried*.

He blinked, the particles stinging his eyes, but he still saw nothing but darkness. How far deep was he?

And where was Prue?

"Prue!" he bellowed, his voice echoing in the vast chasm.

Gods, please answer me. Please tell me you're still alive.

She may have been the daughter of Gaia, but her god's blood wasn't made of this realm. He had no idea if she could survive a fatal wound down here like he could.

Gritting his teeth, he summoned every ounce of strength, all the magic he had left inside him, and *pushed*. Agony sliced through him, swift and brutal, cutting deep, piercing through skin and bone as he pushed harder. White spots floated in his vision, and he nearly blacked out from the pain, but still he pushed.

Rocks shifted, and more dust burned his eyes. Light filtered through the gaps in the boulders, and he reached for it, stretching outward, grasping for freedom...

His cry echoed around him as he finally dug free from the rubble. Dirt coated every inch of him, obscuring the tattoos that covered his flesh. He coughed, his throat itchy and dry, the taste of earth and dust sticking in his mouth.

He surveyed his surroundings, squinting against the haze of ash and fog. He tried to make out the caves he knew so well, or the illusion of the forest and rivers of the Underworld. But it was no use.

There was nothing but fog.

"Hello?" he called out. His voice rang and bounced back to him, surrounding him with the emptiness of *nothing.*

Good gods, what had happened? His aching mind struggled to recall the details.

Pandora's box had been opened. The dark magic had been unleashed. And the caves had collapsed.

His heart racing, Cyrus scanned the area with greater urgency. Prue—where was she? He called out for her again, but no one answered. It was as if nothing existed in the universe except for him.

The thought nearly drove him mad.

Prue was here. She *had* to be.

One by one, he started shifting boulders, digging through the rubble in search of her. A hand. An arm. A body part. *Anything.*

He wasn't sure how much time passed, but his mind was so consumed with the task of finding his wife that he didn't allow any other thoughts to distract him. One rock after another, he lifted, then cast aside. His hands were soon covered in scrapes and cuts, but he paid them no heed.

All that mattered was Prue.

After an eternity of searching, he caught sight of her

brown skin, stained with dirt and... blood.

"Prue. *Prue!*" Cyrus shoved aside the boulders, panic coursing through him, rage and shock and denial burning and coiling tightly in his chest. *No, no, no.*

When he'd lifted the final boulder off her, he stared, frozen and stunned. Bruises and bloodstains marred her beautiful body. Her dress was torn and covered in dust. A large, bloody gash still oozed blood on her temple. Her eyes were closed, her mouth slightly open.

She wasn't breathing.

Carefully, his movements ever so tender, Cyrus gathered her in his arms, bringing her fully against his chest.

"It's all right," he told her, shutting his eyes against the agony that threatened to consume him. "You'll be all right, my love."

He didn't speak the truth he was afraid to face. That his wife was dead. He had heard her scream, felt her magic unleash itself to shield them both.

But it had failed... because it had taken too much from her. That was why they were both buried.

Because it had killed her.

"No," Cyrus whispered, shutting out the horrific thought. No, she was his wife and the goddess of this realm. He would find a way to save her. He swore on his own life he would.

His own life...

Gods above. Could he use his soul magic to revive

her, like he had in the mortal realm when she'd fallen down the mountain?

Did he even have enough to do it?

It didn't matter. He had to try. But first, he needed access to his vault to retrieve the spell ingredients. His soul magic was too far spent and Prue was too far gone for normal magic to work.

He would need something much more powerful. And fast.

EXTRAVAGANCE
PANDORA

SOL LED PANDORA UP A WINDING SPIRAL staircase lined with a maroon velvet carpet. She tried to keep her derision to herself as she took note of all the excessive grandeur Apollo had put into this castle, but a scoff escaped her when she noticed the intricate carvings in the mahogany banister.

Sol glanced over his shoulder with a smirk. "Something wrong?"

"Extravagant," Pandora muttered.

"Sorry, what was that?"

"Everything here is overly extravagant," she said more loudly. "It's like you all want to flaunt your grand lifestyle to those who aren't as fortunate."

"Or maybe we don't care at all what others think and just want a grand place to live. Others be damned."

Pandora balled her hands into fists. "It's exactly that kind of thinking that leads to a division between realms. A division that would *prevent* you from even knowing the Underworld was destroyed."

Sol sighed. "What would you have me say, Trivia? That we acknowledge your realm exists but don't wish to associate with it? This is true. It's also true that we don't trouble ourselves too much with your realm because, let's be frank, it's rather dismal down there. Aidoneus could have cheered the place up a bit, and maybe more of us would have visited." He shrugged. "I suppose it doesn't matter anymore, does it? The realm is gone. So why are you fretting so much about it?"

Fury burned in Pandora's chest. It was only thanks to her years of deception that she refrained from striking Sol in the back of the head.

He'll perish, along with the rest of these arrogant assholes, she reminded herself. *Just be patient and stick to the plan.*

To keep her anger at bay, she changed the subject. "Where is my room located? I'm surprised you're not taking me to the servants' quarters."

"Come now, we can be perfectly civil despite our differences. We're giving you one of the best rooms in the castle. It overlooks the sea."

"The *fake* sea."

"Of course it's fake. Would you prefer to be in the wretched mortal realm where it's *real*?"

"Have you even *been* to the mortal realm before?"

A pause. "No."

Pandora snorted. "Then, how do you know it's so wretched?"

"Why would I have need to travel there? We have everything here."

"Yes, you have everything, leaving the rest of us with nothing."

Sol huffed a laugh as they finally reached the top of the staircase. "I'd forgotten how unpleasant it was to converse with you, Trivia. Thank you for reminding me."

Pandora offered a simpering grin. "My pleasure. I'd love nothing more than to shit all over your good mood."

Sol rolled his eyes and faced forward, leading Pandora down a long hallway lined with an onyx rug. Sconces on the walls illuminated several large oil paintings depicting fallen gods and goddesses that had reigned before Apollo. Pandora glanced over them, idly wondering if any of these deities would have done a finer job of ruling than Apollo. Some, perhaps. But others had been much, much worse, according to the tales Pandora had heard as a child.

When Sol reached the end of the hall, he turned and gestured toward a set of double doors with brass handles carved with swirling embellishments. He bowed low with a sardonic smile on his face.

"Your chambers, my lady."

Pandora had the strongest urge to kick him. Without a word, she turned the handle and stepped into the room.

"Your supper will be brought to you shortly," Sol said from the hall. "You've been through quite an ordeal, so we'll let you rest."

"What you're *really* saying is, Apollo doesn't have time to see someone as unimportant as me, so I'm to keep to my rooms like a good little girl." She wrinkled her nose at him and adorned a false smile.

Sol grinned. "Your words, not mine."

With a growl, Pandora removed her sandal, prepared to thwack Sol over the head with it, but he slammed the doors shut with a chuckle, leaving her alone in the room.

"When your golden castle crumbles and your flesh turns to ash, I'll simply look on and laugh," she whispered before replacing her sandal. She had to keep reminding herself that soon *she* would triumph over these fools. And they would wish they had treated her better.

They would beg for mercy. And she would gladly refuse.

With a deep breath, she turned and faced her

bedchambers, unable to keep her eyebrows from lifting in surprise at what awaited her.

A four-poster bed took up half the room, with delicate white drapes and a dozen fluffy pillows adorning it. Opposite the bed was a set of open doors that led to a balcony overlooking the glittering blue sea. Already, the sound of the waves provided a soothing rhythm that echoed in the vast chamber. On the other side of the room was a small seating area where a tray of tea and biscuits waited. Behind that were the bathing chambers. Pandora nearly groaned with relief at the thought of taking a proper bath. The castle in the Underworld hadn't been drab by any means, but lately she had been masquerading herself as Prue's lady's maid, which left her confined to the servants' quarters. Despite her barbed comment to Sol about where her chambers were located, she *did* appreciate the luxuries afforded to her because of her status as goddess.

Her thoughts turned to Prue, and a twist of emotion wrenched through her. She had expected someone pretentious and cruel and cold, just like Cyrus. But she *hadn't* expected someone like Prue. Someone who cared about the people of the Underworld, who sought to make a difference.

In truth, Pandora hadn't expected to actually like her sister.

She shook her head to rid herself of these useless

thoughts. It didn't matter. It had to be done. The agony burning in her chest demanded it.

She could not rest until her revenge was complete. Only then would she find peace.

"Time to get to work," she muttered, smoothing her hands along her skirts and striding toward the balcony. She was here for a reason, and she couldn't forget it.

She would bring down Elysium from the inside. But she needed to infuse her magic in this realm first. Only then could the darkness from her box be drawn in.

This place would crumble, just like the Underworld. But the Underworld's demise had been much easier. The area had been enriched with death magic, which was like kindling to a flame, only igniting her darkness and feeding it with fuel.

But here? Sol had a point—the gods of Elysium did not often associate with those of the Underworld because of the differences between realms. Even the very air was different. The magic here was foreign to Pandora and would be foreign to her powers as well.

She needed to change that. To acquaint herself with the energies in the air so her magic would recognize it and eventually bring it down. But she had to do it discreetly; if anyone caught wind of her earth magic, she would be cast out in a heartbeat.

Just like Gaia.

No. Pandora forced out all thoughts of the earth

goddess before they boiled her blood and caused her to do something reckless. She would deal with her dear and loving mother later.

Ending Gaia would be the third and final step of Pandora's revenge. Only then would she finally be free of the weights dragging her down.

The weight of abandonment.

The weight of torment.

The weight of endless agony and suffering.

Oh, yes, she would make *all* of them pay.

Pandora gasped, only then realizing her hands were clutched so tightly that her fingernails broke skin on her palm, carving bloody crescent marks in her hand. Hissing, she flexed her hand, inspecting the wounds.

Red. Her blood was red, despite her lineage. The gods bled silver. And yet, here she was, bleeding like a godforsaken mortal.

Inferior. That was what gods like Sol thought of her. She was *less than* worthy of the status of goddess.

Fresh anger brewed within her as she clenched her hand once more, steeling herself with another breath. The memories of anguish threatened to consume her, but she held them at bay with the promise that soon—*soon*—all would be hers once more.

She stepped onto the balcony as the wind whipped at her, tousling her scarlet hair around her face. The salty sea air filled her nose, mingling with the soothing rhythm of the waves around her.

Gods, she had to admit... this *was* quite pleasant.

Which only made her angrier. How long did the gods here lord over their paradise and treasures while they left everyone else to suffer?

Pandora lifted her hands and thrust them, palms out, toward the sea. Tendrils of her earth magic swirled forward, twisting in the air and vanishing among the clouds. She closed her eyes, following her magic with her senses as they stretched out, out, out...

Gods above, how far did this realm go? Minutes passed, and her magic was still reaching, searching for the walls of Elysium, digging through the illusion to find where the realm began and ended.

At long last, her magic connected with something. Frowning, Pandora extended her awareness, eyes still closed, as she searched mentally for what she was looking for.

"Ah," she murmured, then stiffened. "What the hell?"

There was *magic* lining the outer walls of Elysium. Her own powers hesitated, worried she would trigger some sort of alarm and end her plans before they even began. Gingerly, her magic crept forward like the brush of a fingertip along the surface of the outer walls.

She gasped, then withdrew her magic before she alerted anyone.

Damn it all. Elysium was *warded*. Thick, heavy defensive magic surrounded the entire realm like an impenetrable breastplate.

Each realm had its own level of protection built into it as part of the magic of the land. But on top of that natural barrier, it seemed Apollo had infused his *own* magic as an added layer. Aidoneus had never done such a thing with the Underworld; he had always relied on the magic of the land itself.

Why would Apollo add his own magic to the walls of the realm?

She thought of what Sol had told her when she'd conveyed the news of the Underworld's demise: *We would have felt it. An entire realm destroyed? That would have impacted our realm, too.*

"Not if this place is warded," Pandora muttered, her eyes narrowing as she surveyed the expansive shore before her: lapping waves, pearly white sand, swaying trees, and an array of cerulean roofs that indicated a village rested below the castle.

A village! Perfect. The wards would be strongest surrounding the palace. But the outer city? Apollo would be much less concerned with the welfare of civilians. If she was to find a flaw in the wards of Elysium, it would be there.

That was where she would make her move.

Itching to get started, Pandora strode purposefully toward the double doors, prepared to do some exploring, before she stopped short.

"Keep to my rooms like a good little girl," she said through clenched teeth. If she wandered the castle, people would notice. Word would spread that Hecate, the lesser goddess of the Underworld, was roaming as she pleased among the glistening halls of Elysium.

She had to play her part. She had to wait for Apollo. Only after she'd gained their trust could she search for a weakness.

"Patience, Pandora," she whispered to herself, massaging circles along the back of her hand to soothe the roiling tension within her. "You've waited this long. You can wait a few more days."

But so much tension had built in her over these past years, and meeting her sisters for the first time had ignited something wild within her. It was part sorrow, part anger, part devastation at the family she'd never have. The family that had been stolen from her.

With an exhausted sigh, she sank onto the edge of the bed, closing her eyes against the agony. Oh yes, she would certainly have nightmares when she slept. Memories of Gaia and Apollo and her sisters were fresh in her mind, and the consequences were inevitable.

She would not sleep tonight. She found herself

missing Cerberus, the lovable dog who had followed her around in the Underworld. He had been such a good listener... always willing to cuddle with her no matter what despicable acts she'd committed.

She hoped he'd somehow survived. He was a creature born of death magic, like all the demons in the Underworld, so she couldn't have brought him with her. Perhaps he *had* survived somehow, and she could return and find him. He was a resourceful dog. He had no power, so the magic from her box would have no reason to attack him.

With this comforting thought, Pandora fell backwards, allowing her head to hit the soft pillows as she waited for oblivion to consume her.

APOLLO
PANDORA

FOR THE TENTH TIME, A HEAVY SIGH ESCAPED
Pandora's lips. Her eyes surveyed the grand surroundings with bitterness and resentment. Fourteen ivory
pillars supported the curved, dome-shaped ceiling of the
throne room. Large braziers at the bottoms of each of
the pillars illuminated the marbled flooring, shrouding
the hall in warm oranges and dancing shadows. Intricately carved marble icons and sculptures glared down
upon her from the ceiling as she sat on one of the many
birch benches surrounding the inner perimeter of the
throne room.

Those expecting an audience with the almighty King
Apollo were required to wait on these benches for the
great god of sun and time to deign to grace them with
his magnificent presence.

Pandora scoffed and crossed her arms, becoming more irritated by the minute. This place was too much. Every adornment seemed to make a mockery of Pandora's life and upbringing, as if to say, *Look at all this lavishness* you *were not allowed to have.*

Soon, it wouldn't matter. Soon, this place would be nothing but ash, just like the Underworld.

At long last, after making her wait an eternity, the double doors burst open, and a squadron of soldiers appeared. Pandora rose to her feet but kept the scowl on her face. Dozens of armed men marched inside and formed a line at the back of the throne room.

Last of all was Apollo himself.

Pandora held her breath. She had not laid eyes on the loathsome god in several years, but he hadn't changed much. He wore a gleaming white tunic with intricate gold embroidery. A sword was belted at his waist, and a crimson robe was half-draped over one shoulder, giving an air of casual elegance. His brown hair was neatly slicked back, his beard short and trimmed, and his dark black eyes scanned the room with smug indifference. When they settled on Pandora, a smirk formed on his lips. He approached, his sandaled feet gliding smoothly along the vermilion carpet that ran down the length of the room.

"Hecate," he said, his voice rich and smooth. "Such a pleasure to see you once again."

Pandora offered a curtsy, quelling her hatred and rage to adopt the persona she had so carefully created for this very purpose. "My lord and king, you are so kind to accept me and provide me with hospitality. I'm sure Sol has informed you that my home has been destroyed."

Apollo's face sagged, his eyes closing briefly. "Ah, yes. I was devastated to hear of the realm's demise."

"You were not aware of it?" Pandora asked. "Sol seemed quite surprised when I brought the news."

Apollo hesitated for only a moment before he replied, "I have sensed some disturbances in the Underworld for some time now. At first, I thought nothing of it, but now that this tragedy has befallen us, I am full of remorse that I did not investigate early on."

Befallen us. As if he were in any way affected by this. Pandora wanted to spit in his face.

But his reply answered her question. He did *not* know; his claim of sensing "disturbances" was utter shit.

Which meant his wards were fully intact. Her work would be much harder than she'd originally anticipated.

It was time to initiate her back-up plan.

Clearing her throat, Pandora said, "In truth, I am here for more than just refuge. I have come to offer my services."

Apollo arched an eyebrow, his expression full of doubt. "Oh?" His gaze raked over her as if to say, *What could you possibly offer?*

Biting back a nasty retort, Pandora dropped her gaze so he wouldn't see the ire in her eyes. "As far as I'm aware, I am the only survivor from the Underworld. I am intimately familiar with death magic. I can help you fortify and defend this realm against the darkness in Pandora's box."

Apollo waved a hand. "I'm not concerned with that."

Pandora faltered. "You aren't?"

"We are safe here. I have made sure of it."

Pandora swallowed down her frustration and tried again. "With all due respect, my lord, this magic has already wiped out an entire realm."

"Yes, but I have measures in place that will ensure what happened in the Underworld will not affect us here."

Ah, yes. Because of the wards. "My lord, I have seen this dark magic firsthand. It is hungry, and it will not stop. I'm sure in all your years of wisdom, you have experienced some of the consequences of this particular type of magic. Was it not this same magic that defeated King Jupiter?"

Apollo stilled, his expression rigid and his eyes darkening for a brief moment. Jupiter had been his predecessor. There were whispers that Apollo had a hand in his demise, and his reaction only confirmed this for Pandora.

"In addition," she went on, "I have heard that

Neptune is missing, and I fear the magic may be behind his absence as well."

"I do not fear for Neptune," Apollo replied, the firmness of his voice returning. "He is strong and capable. He will not fall prey to this darkness like his brother did."

Pandora had to refrain from rolling her eyes. Neptune had helped *create* some of the darkness in her box. The memories trapped inside her told her as much.

She didn't know if the magic had killed him or not. But the disappearance of a powerful sea god would certainly cause rumors to spread, and Apollo knew this.

"*You* may not fear for Neptune, my lord, but the people might," Pandora said. "And despite your reassurances, I am certain your subjects would appreciate extra efforts to keep them safe." She paused, then added a layer of flattery to her argument for good measure. "As a *lesser* goddess myself, I know it would make me feel safer, since my magic isn't nearly as strong as yours is."

If anything, announcing to the court that Apollo would be working with Hecate of the Underworld to put a stop to this darkness and keep it from spreading would put the rumors at ease. And it would cast Apollo in a good light, making him appear to be a concerned king who would do anything to ensure the safety of his people. Even adding protections that he found unnecessary.

She could practically see these thoughts flicking through his mind, calculating any risks that might be associated with her offer. After a long moment, a wide smile spread across his face, and she knew she'd won.

"You make an excellent point, Hecate. You are quite right; we can never be too careful, and with the demise of the Underworld and our dear Neptune's mysterious absence, we must take every precaution. I will assign you to work alongside my apprentice to take the appropriate measures. Whatever resources you need are at your complete disposal."

Alarm flared in Pandora's chest, and she sputtered, "Uh, apprentice? My lord, this is a daunting task that will require a powerful amount of magic."

"No, no, Sol is more suited to your, uh, *position* of power." Apollo offered a false smile that Pandora knew too well. It was one she often wore.

Position of power. Which was his way of saying she wasn't worthy of working directly alongside him.

Wait a moment... *Sol?*

"Sol is your apprentice?" she asked hesitantly.

Apollo's expression brightened. "Yes indeed. He hails from the same sun magic as me and would make an excellent god of the sun when it is time for me to step down."

Pandora's eyes narrowed. "You intend to step down from the throne?"

"From the throne? Gods, no!" Apollo barked out a laugh. "No, no, I intend to rule for a long while. But with my responsibilities to the crown, my duties to the sun have been neglected, and Sol will do a fine job replacing me in that respect."

Pandora's mind worked furiously to keep up with what he was implying. If he was stepping down as god of the sun, then that could only mean he had bigger plans in mind. Expansion perhaps? Did he intend to rebuild the Underworld as part of his own domain? Or was there something else at play that Pandora wasn't seeing?

"No, this will be an excellent task for Sol," Apollo went on, stroking his chin in contemplation. "I have been meaning to elevate his rank, and this is the perfect opportunity for him to prove himself." He gave a sure nod. "It's settled, then. You and Sol will be the new defenders of Elysium! Doesn't that sound grand?" He beamed as if he'd just bestowed Pandora with a marvelous gift.

Working alongside her childhood nemesis? The god who had tormented her relentlessly the last time she was here? This seemed more like a scene from one of her nightmares. But she forced herself to curtsy and say, "Yes, my lord. Grand indeed."

STRANGER
MONA

MONA AWOKE TO THE SOUND OF RUSHING WATER, and for a moment, she thought she'd returned to Cocytus, where a dark and handsome prince of Hell awaited her.

Her eyes flew open, a smile already on her face. With a jolt, she realized she was *not* in the Underworld but on a beach in a foreign place. Her head was half buried in the sand, her black hair drenched in salty ocean water. Sand coated her arms and legs, and her dress was a sopping wet mess around her body.

Peeling back the hair out of her face, Mona rose on shaky legs and staggered forward, trying to get her bearings. What had happened? The last she remembered, she and Romanos had dived through the portal to Elysium because the magic of Pandora was about to devour them.

Mona had been intent on saving Evander. Trivia had abducted him, bringing him through the portal. With Typhon, his demonic alter ego, this was essentially a death sentence. Typhon couldn't survive in any realm but the Underworld.

Urgency quickened her pulse, and she whirled around, looking for Romanos. But she was utterly and completely alone on the beach.

"Romanos?" she called. Worry wriggled through her stomach. Where had he gone? They had jumped through together. Romanos claimed to be cursed, unable to travel through different realms. What if he were dying somewhere? He would need Mona's help.

"Romanos!" Her voice echoed in the vast space. What *was* this place? Was this Elysium?

Squinting against the burning sun, Mona surveyed her surroundings. Trees lined the shore, behind which rested dozens and dozens of white buildings that gleamed in the sunlight. A great hill rose up on the left side of the beach, upon which a magnificent pearly castle rested. Golden statues glinted, reflecting the sun, and waves crashed against the cliff side underneath.

Mona's breath caught in her throat. This was definitely Elysium.

Either Romanos had arrived in a different location, or he had entered another realm.

Low voices echoed nearby. Mona's heart slammed

against her rib cage as she gathered her skirts and bolted for the trees, not wanting to be spotted. She doubted anyone would take kindly to her presence. She was a stranger, and she had come from the Underworld, which had been consumed by Pandora's magic. From what Evander had told her, the gods of Elysium weren't too fond of the Underworld.

Leaves crunched as Mona used the shade of the trees for cover, hiding behind a wide trunk as the voices drew nearer. The sound of the waves made it difficult to understand them, but as they grew closer, Mona made out the word *portal*.

She froze, listening hard. Soon, the voices were so close that if she emerged from her hiding spot, she would most certainly be seen.

"I felt the magic of this portal," insisted a female voice. "I'm certain of it."

"Well, clearly you're mistaken. There's no one here." The second was a male voice, and he sounded irritated.

"Perhaps they ran off. We may have just missed them."

"I've heard rumors that Hecate from the Underworld is here. I'm sure it's just her presence you felt."

Mona inhaled sharply. Hecate. That was another name for Trivia, the goddess of pathways in the Underworld.

Trivia was here. And the people knew it.

So where was Evander?

"She arrived on the *other* side of the realm," the woman said impatiently. "From what I heard, the guards already escorted her to the castle."

The other side. So there were two entrances to Elysium: the shore, and the one that Trivia came through.

Evander was likely there. Possibly Romanos as well. Mona *had* to find this other portal.

But how? This was a strange new place, and she had no one to help her. She was on her own.

Her thoughts turned to Prue, and anguish ripped at her heart. She had no idea if her sister had survived. Last she'd seen, Prue and Cyrus had been in the caves of Tartarus when the dark magic had consumed everything.

She's not dead, Mona assured herself. *She's a goddess. If anyone can survive, it's her.*

All Mona had to do was find Evander and Romanos, get back through the portal somehow, and then she could help Prue.

It all sounded impossible.

Oh Goddess, I can't do this. Fear ate away at her chest, threatening to devour her. For a moment, her vision blurred, and she couldn't breathe. Terror clutched at her throat, blocking her airway. Panic seized her limbs, freezing her in place.

I can't do this I can't do this I can't do this.

In the deepest recesses of her mind, a song burned to life, warming her blood and bringing breath back to her lungs. She inhaled deeply, clinging to the melody, allowing it to wash over her, to soothe her, to chase away her fears...

Only when her vision returned and she was breathing normally did she realize she was humming her death song.

The song she used to sing with Evander.

"I've already died," she whispered to herself. "I've endured the worst. I can endure this, too."

What she didn't say was that dying was far easier than watching the ones she loved die.

You are not a coward, she reminded herself. The voice in her head sounded like Prue, tinged with impatience and a ferocity she admired and often envied. *Snap out of it, Mona. You can do this.*

With a sure nod, Mona peered around the thick tree trunk one last time to ensure the people she'd overheard had vanished. Then she slipped out of her hiding spot, adjusting her dress and dusting sand off the fabric, hoping she would be able to blend in. She possessed god blood, after all. *Gaia's* blood. And Gaia had once been a goddess of Elysium herself. Perhaps this would be easier than she thought.

Feeling more optimistic, Mona weaved through the

trees, emerging to find a cobbled path that wound around the beach. She followed it, not quite knowing where she was going, just knowing that movement was progress.

Mona's footsteps quickened, and she rounded a corner and collided with another figure. With an ungraceful grunt, Mona staggered backward, practically collapsing in a clumsy heap on the ground. Her feet slid on the walkway, and she caught herself just in time, prepared to cry out in indignation at whoever stood in her path.

The protest died on her lips as she took in a tall, regal figure with flaming red hair and identical crimson eyes. A shimmering golden gown was draped over one shoulder, accentuating the thick muscles in her arms. A sly smile spread across her full lips as she looked Mona over.

"Ah, now, what have we here?" she crooned. "You don't belong here, do you, little witch?"

TALENTS

PANDORA

PANDORA SAT IN THE FINEST LIBRARY SHE HAD ever beheld, sifting through her notes for the tenth time. The night before, she had painstakingly written out an elaborate outline that she intended to give to Sol to convince him her ideas were sound.

If she wanted the freedom to put her plan into motion, she first needed to gain his trust. And if anyone needed convincing that Pandora's ideas were worth hearing, it was Sol, the nuisance who had belittled her for years.

"Bastard," Pandora muttered, glancing out the massive floor-to-ceiling window once more. The sun was now high in the sky, leaving ripples of dancing light swirling among the ocean waves below. It was close to mid-morning. Where the hell *was* this sun god? She had sent him a clear message the day before that they were to get to work at sunrise. Wasn't this important enough to warrant his attention? Regardless of how much he despised her, she would have thought that saving the realm actually meant something to him.

Pandora angrily shoved the table in front of her and jumped to her feet, seething. She had only been here a few days, and she had already had enough of these gods-damned idle gods and their lazy schedules and frivolous lifestyles. She rolled up her notes and tucked them into the bodice of her black dress, then ensured her ruby necklace was in place at her collarbone.

It was for more than just an accessory. It contained a fragment of death magic. Pandora always kept a few vials of pure, untainted death magic on her person, but since the Underworld was destroyed, she had limited access to it. Infusing it in a piece of jewelry had been inspired by Prue's pomegranate necklace. Pandora had immediately known there was magic contained in the necklace, and it had been a genius idea, really.

If she hadn't despised her sister, she might have complimented her on it.

But Prue was probably dead, so it didn't matter.

Pandora tried to ignore the twinge of guilt that flared in her chest at the thought of her dead sister.

With an irritated huff, she strode forward, fed up with waiting around for these useless gods. Her feet glided along the soft velvet carpet that lined the library as she stormed past the crackling fire and the high-backed armchairs surrounding it, scowling at the towering bookcases as she walked.

When she exited the library, she approached a servant who held a pile of folded silver curtains in his arms.

"Pardon me," she said, adopting her humble Hecate persona.

The servant jumped, then turned to face her, his eyes wide with surprise. Upon noticing her, he dropped into a short, polite bow.

Pandora offered a small smile. She had great respect for the servants of Elysium; they were not powerful gods like Apollo, but they were still descendants from deities. Their bloodlines were watered down by humans, making them far less powerful than the nobility who lived in the castle.

Pandora herself might have been close to such a bloodline, if she hadn't been raised by Aidoneus himself. "I have a message for Lord Sol. Would you be able to deliver it for me?"

The servant inclined his head, and a tangle of bouncy curls momentarily obscured his eyes. "Of course, Lady Hecate."

Ah, so he knew who she was. The title he addressed her with, and the show of respect to her as a goddess, only made Pandora like him more. Her smile widened as she said, "Could you please inform him the Lady Hecate anxiously awaits his arrival in the library?"

The servant nodded. "Yes, my lady. Right away."

He bustled away, and Pandora smirked at his departure. She bent over and removed her shoes, dangling the straps from her fingers. After waiting a few moments, she soundlessly trailed after him. The cool marble floor was brisk against her bare feet, but it was much more inconspicuous than the loud clopping of her sandals.

She rounded the corner and immediately backed up a few steps so she wouldn't be seen. The servant was now depositing the drapes into the arms of another attendant before hurrying off, no doubt to relay Pandora's message. After ensuring the hall was empty, Pandora emerged and hastened to catch up with the servant.

It wasn't difficult to follow him. She wagered he wasn't accustomed to deities following him around. But she didn't care. She had stooped to much lesser roles to achieve what she wanted.

The few servants Pandora passed didn't give her a second glance, nor did they notice that she crept around the castle barefoot. They bowed their heads as they passed, acknowledging her as a goddess.

For once, she had their respect. She wasn't sure if it was something Apollo had said, or simply that she was a woman in fine apparel that made her seem more god-like. But she felt her chin lifting and the corners of her mouth rising in satisfaction.

She had never been respected before. Not here, not in the Underworld... Nowhere had she been given the treatment she deserved.

She would enjoy it. While it lasted.

The servant climbed a winding staircase and followed a long, narrow hallway on the second floor. Pandora followed, lingering at the end of the hallway by a table boasting a white marble bust of Apollo. She counted the doors to figure out which one he would approach.

The servant reached the seventh door on the left and tapped lightly on it. A loud, obnoxiously familiar voice called, "You may enter!"

Pandora rolled her eyes. Even the way he spoke to servants was pompous. What an ass.

The servant muttered something incoherent, and she heard Sol's boisterous laugh. "Ah, yes, I'm sure she is. Thank you for relaying the message, Alexander."

Pandora hid behind Apollo's bust as the servant hurried past her, oblivious that he had led Pandora right to Sol.

When she was certain the servant was out of sight, she replaced her shoes and stomped down the carpeted hallway before pounding her fist on Sol's door.

"Oh, what now?" he barked.

Instead of answering, she threw open the doors and strode inside.

The room was twice as big as hers, with a massive bed on one end and several lush sofas on the other. A large platter of fruits, cheeses, and breads rested on the table between the couches, and hanging on the walls were dozens upon dozens of the most breathtaking paintings Pandora had ever seen. Sunsets with swirls of amber and gold, ocean waves of pure amethyst and turquoise, palm trees in a storm of icy blues and grays, a vibrant forest of emerald and jade... All the paintings depicted various forms of nature, and the colors were as luminous as if the art had been crafted by magic itself. The paintings took up the entire wall, completely obscuring the wallpaper. Pandora had to forcibly tear her eyes away from them and remind herself why she was here.

Finding her resolve once more, she spotted Sol standing by the open balcony doors with a canvas before him, a paintbrush in his hand as he faced away from her.

And he was wearing nothing but a pair of loose, tan trousers.

Gods above, Pandora thought, her throat filling with heat as Sol turned to face her. Several splotches of cerulean paint stained his hairy chest, and there was one on the left side of his nose as well. Pandora couldn't keep her gaze from straying to the sculpted muscles of his chest and abdomen. His tan, golden skin glowed with the rising sun behind him. Goddess, he was breathtaking. Like a piece of art himself.

Sol's eyebrows lifted, though he showed no other sign of surprise at her sudden entrance.

"Ah, Hecate," he said idly. "By all means, show yourself in." With that, he turned back to his painting.

Pandora's mouth opened and closed, but she couldn't figure out what she wanted to say.

So, you're a painter?

Would you put a shirt on, please?

Why didn't you bother showing up at the library?

Why are you so godsdamned gorgeous?

After a moment of utter stupidity, with her standing in the open doorway like a fool, she cleared her throat and lifted her chin. "You've kept me waiting because of some *paint*? I don't know about you, but when Apollo gives me a task, I take it seriously. And it's Trivia, by the way."

At first, Sol said nothing. He merely continued to paint, his fingers moving in lithe strokes that told Pandora he had done this many times before. With a new perspective, she glanced at the paintings hanging on the wall once more.

Had he painted all of these?

At long last, Sol set his brush down and wiped his paint-stained fingers on a nearby rag, then turned to face

Pandora once more. "The sun is perfect," he said. "I knew the scene wouldn't last long, so I had to act." He shrugged and offered her a cocky smile. "I figured you wouldn't mind."

Pandora opened her mouth to say that she *did* mind, but then her gaze snagged on his painting, and the words died in her throat. Pinks and oranges and reds mingled to form a burst of color surrounding the morning sun that filled the sky above the ocean.

It *was* stunning. She couldn't deny it.

Somehow, the idea that Sol, the arrogant ass she'd always loathed, loved to paint beautiful nature scenes made her anger ebb slightly.

Only slightly.

"So, what do you think?" Sol spread his arms, indicating the paintings that surrounded him. That infuriating smirk still rested on his lips.

Pandora squared her shoulders. "Do you use your magic when you paint?"

His smile faltered. "No. Of course not. That's not how my magic works."

"Really? Because I see an awful lot of paintings of the sun. I just assumed..."

"You assumed I have no talents besides my sun magic?"

"Oh, no, I'm *well* aware of your non-magical talents," Pandora said, rolling her eyes. "Snobbery, condescension, rudeness, lack of consideration for any being except yourself..."

Sol frowned, but nodded. "All true." He leaned against the balcony door frame, bracing one arm against it, drawing Pandora's eyes to the way his bicep flexed with the motion. "You are only describing the talents you've seen firsthand. There is *so* much more to me than just that."

Pandora scoffed. "Gods, you truly are a self-absorbed bastard, aren't you? Just because you can wiggle your fingers and fling paint on a canvas doesn't change that."

Sol arched a single eyebrow, his eyes taking on a dark, heady glint that Pandora didn't like one bit. "My point exactly. You've only scratched the surface of Sol, the sun god. There are *far* more interesting things I can do with these fingers." He flashed a wide grin and flicked his tongue along the length of his lower lip.

A jolt rippled through Pandora's body at the sight of his tongue and that intoxicating look fixed on *her*. Heat coiled low in her belly, and her cheeks flamed. It was too hot, too stifling in this room. His shirtless torso, the paint stains along his bare skin, the flex of his muscles, *that look...*

Gods above, what was he doing? Was he flirting with her?

And... was her body responding to it?

Stop it, she chided herself, forcing a look of disgust

on her face. *You have work to do. Remember?* "Is that supposed to impress me? Put some clothes on and meet me in the library. We have more important things to do."

Without waiting for a response, she turned on her heel and strode from the room, her face on fire. From behind her, Sol chuckled, and said, "I'm sorry my lack of clothes makes you uncomfortable."

The humor in his voice told her he was not sorry about it in the slightest.

PARTNERS
PANDORA

PANDORA MANAGED TO COMPOSE HERSELF ONCE she'd returned to the library. She had been caught off guard; that was all. The last time she'd seen Sol, he had been different, and... well, less handsome.

And Pandora had been younger. Too young to notice his appearance.

But just because he had a gorgeous body didn't make him any less terrible. And she had to remind herself of that if she was to accomplish her goal.

Prue and Mona had also seemed likable, but she had still betrayed them.

Nothing would stop her. Nothing.

When footsteps echoed nearby, Pandora straightened in her seat, smoothing her hands along the black silk of her dress.

Focus on your task, she silently reminded herself.

Sol swaggered into the library, his steps slow and leisurely, as if he was in no hurry. Though she knew he did it to provoke her, it still set her teeth on edge. At least he was dressed this time. He wore a fine navy tunic with gleaming gold buttons and embroidery. He was fastening his wrist cuffs as he approached, shooting her a glance from under his lashes.

Pandora tapped her foot loudly under the table as he took his time seating himself in front of her.

He chuckled. "So impatient. Another reason why we never got along, I suppose."

"Because you prefer to laze about all day while I actually do important things?" Pandora raised her eyebrows.

"You take yourself too seriously, Trivia. You always have, even when you were a child and nothing more than a nuisance following Aidoneus around. This *dark magic* we are defending against—is it here right now? Is it at our very doorstep?" He frowned, hands spread, as he looked around in mock curiosity. "No? Then, what is the rush?"

Pandora splayed her hands on the table and leaned forward, giving him a lethal look. "The dark magic isn't here yet, but the urgency is we don't know *when* it will get here. Yes, it could arrive right now! And we would be woefully unprepared for it."

Sol clapped his hands. "Very well. What do you propose?"

Pandora exhaled in relief. At least he was cooperating. For now. "I've outlined a list of tasks for us to work through that will strengthen this realm's defenses." She slid the paper with her notes across the table to him.

Sol didn't even glance at it. "What's first on the list?"

Pandora's eyes narrowed. "Why don't you read it?"

He grinned. "Why would I do that when you're so good at explaining it? I do love to watch that pretty mouth of yours."

Ignoring the heat rising in her chest, Pandora hissed, "You're insufferable. Are you even paying attention?"

"Yes. You've compiled a list, which I'm sure is very thorough and dull."

Pandora scoffed and let her hands fall on the table. "This is impossible. *You* are impossible. How am I supposed to do what Apollo asked when you behave like this?"

"He asked us to work together. He didn't ask us to complete a list of tasks *you* created. I'm not your subordinate; you cannot force me to work for you." He crossed his arms. "Technically, I outrank you. So *I* should be compiling a list of things for *you* to do."

Pandora groaned, throwing her head back to glare at the ceiling. Like hell would she let him tell her what to do. "All right then, *oh great and mighty Sol*, what would you propose we do?"

He grinned, leaning back against his chair with his hands behind his head. "Relax! Trust the wards to protect us. Be at ease."

Pandora scowled at him. "Meaning, disregard what Apollo has asked us to do?"

Sol sighed and dropped his hands. "All right, then. How about you tell me what you propose we do first, and I'll tell you if I agree or not?"

"Fine. My suggestion is to travel to the lower towns, where the wards are weakest."

Sol frowned. "The wards shouldn't be weak anywhere. Apollo and Hestia created them, and they are the two strongest gods in all of Elysium." He shot her a lopsided grin. "And, as Hestia's son, I can tell you first-hand that the magic of her bloodline is *quite* powerful."

Pandora rolled her eyes. "As infallible as you believe your Elysium borders to be, they will likely be strongest surrounding the palace, correct? Because that's where you *mighty* and *important* gods live?"

"Yes," Sol said slowly, oblivious to her sarcasm.

"So, I want to inspect the magic surrounding the village. If Pandora's magic is looking for a way in, it would likely be in a location no one would expect."

Sol stroked the beard on his chin and nodded. "Yes, that *does* make sense."

Pandora blinked, unsettled by this reaction. "Um. Thank you."

"Oh, calm down. That wasn't a compliment."

Pandora rolled her eyes. "So, what do you think? Can we move forward with my idea?"

Sol only continued to stroke his beard, his expression twisting in a grimace. She just *knew* he was going to find another reason to argue with her.

She needed to try another tactic. They were butting heads too much on this.

She needed to become the humble Hecate, as much as she despised pandering to the whims of someone like Sol.

With a deep breath, she said, "Look. We've been assigned to work together. We may not like each other, but this is important. You love Elysium, don't you?"

Frowning, Sol nodded.

"Good. So, I imagine you don't want it destroyed like the Underworld. Well, I don't, either. Watching one realm die was traumatic enough. I'm here to make sure the same thing doesn't happen here. Can't we just agree to be civil to one another, at least until this task is finished? Then we can part ways and go on hating each other for as long as we desire."

Sol didn't answer for a long moment. His dark eyes were contemplative as he considered her offer. She honestly didn't know what she would do if he argued further. She wasn't sure she had any kindness left in her for this despicable man.

At long last, he said, "I don't hate you."

Pandora's head reared back. She hadn't expected that. "You don't?" Well, he certainly had a funny way of showing it.

"No. I may dislike you... But it's impossible for me to hate a beautiful woman."

It took Pandora a full minute to register his words. He found her beautiful? Her cheeks warmed from the directness of his words.

But indignation quickly followed. How vain was he to let a person's looks influence his opinion of them?

A slow smile spread across his face. "Ah, I've rendered you speechless. Another one of my talents."

Pandora groaned. "There he is. I was worried the real Sol had vanished and been replaced by an imposter."

Sol laughed, his eyes crinkling with warmth. "See? If you didn't take yourself so seriously, Trivia, you might actually have a bit of fun."

"The magic of Pandora has already destroyed one realm, and you want to have fun?"

He shrugged. "If we die tomorrow, that's all the more reason to seek enjoyment while we can. Wouldn't you like to do something bold and exciting and... passionate in your last hours?" That dark, heady look returned, the one that made Pandora's knees go weak.

She tried to take a steadying breath, but her inhale was shaky. Sweat collected on her palms, and she wiped them on her skirt once more.

He was toying with her because it unsettled her. Why was she allowing him to do this? Toying with people was *her* specialty.

She forced a chuckle and shook her head, as if she found his flirting to be endearing. "Ah, Sol, as flattering as your proposition is, if I were to take a tumble with someone in this castle, it would certainly not be you."

His eyebrows lifted as if he were merely curious instead of insulted. "Oh? And why is that?"

"I prefer to spend my passionate nights with someone who doesn't treat me like a cockroach under their shoe."

Sol huffed a laugh. "I've been perfectly civil toward you since you arrived."

"Well, *that's* certainly untrue, but I'm referring to before." When Sol frowned, she added, "The last time I was here? Do you not recall?"

Sol's gaze turned distant, and he tilted his head back, his expression thoughtful. After a moment, his eyes widened. "Oh! Yes, I recall. You asked if you could accompany me with my apprentice work, yes?"

"Yes. And you replied, *I would no sooner let...*"

"*Let vermin live in my wardrobe.*" He laughed loudly,

as if he'd told a hilarious joke. "Gods, Trivia, that was ages ago. Are you still upset about that?"

"No, I'm hardly upset. But it did paint an accurate picture of the kind of person you are. And the kind of person I'd rather not associate with."

Sol shrugged. "Unfortunately, you're stuck with me. At least until this obscenely long list of tasks is accomplished." He wrinkled his nose at the paper on the table. "I agree with you. We can be civil to one another, at least for a short time. But you are *not* my superior."

Pandora gave him a cold smile. "And you are not mine."

"Partners, then?" Sol extended his hand across the table.

Pandora scrutinized him, searching for the telltale glint of his eyes that indicated he was mocking her. All she saw was sincerity and a half smile quirking the corner of his mouth. He still looked smug and arrogant, but his eyes weren't dancing with laughter. He was being earnest. Or as earnest as someone like Sol could manage.

After a moment, she took his hand in hers, and they shook. His palm was warm and smooth and dwarfed hers completely. She wanted to cling to him, to keep her skin flush against his. Far too soon, he released her hand, and she forced herself to withdraw her arm.

Sol rose to his feet and stepped around the table. "Come. I'll show you the way to the village."

She stared up at him. "So, we're going with my idea?"

He shrugged one shoulder. "For now. I think it's worth investigating. But don't you fret. I'll be thinking long and hard about my own exhausting list of tasks to work through." He winked at her.

With a long-suffering sigh, Pandora stood, following Sol as he led her out of the library.

SURVIVORS
CYRUS

IT WAS PERILOUS WORK, CARRYING PRUE'S BODY across the jagged rocks and boulders. His feet kept slipping on shards of rock, the movement jostling Prue as he scrambled to keep a firm grasp on her. The dirt particles in the air stung Cyrus's eyes, and he coughed frequently from the thick dust swirling around him. He wasn't sure which direction he was going; he couldn't even see the sun in the sky, although the magical illusion of the Underworld had started to break, even before Pandora's magic had been unleashed.

Without the illusion, what would the Underworld look like?

His body aching and his throat parched, he finally reached the smooth, flat ground that indicated he had emerged from the rubble. He took a moment to catch his breath, his shoulders and back straining from carrying Prue's weight. But he refused to put her down. Her beautiful body would not touch the ground again. Not until she had been revived.

Blinking sweat from his eyes, Cyrus squinted through the fog, trying to get his bearings. But he saw nothing but murky, muddy gray.

Despair washed over him, and for a moment, he closed his eyes, unsure of how he would get through this. His chest constricted so tightly that he couldn't breathe. The reality of his circumstances cut through him like a sharp knife. He was alone. He was wounded. And he didn't know where he was. His magic was completely depleted. His wife was...

No, he thought angrily, his eyes flying open. *Don't think it. This isn't over yet. Just keep moving.*

He had to find the castle. Or whatever was left of it. Even if his once glorious palace was nothing more than ruins, he knew there was a powerful spell book in his vault that had what he needed to save Prue. Even with the destruction around him, the strength of the magic contained in the book would have protected it.

Obediently, his feet shuffled forward, until he caught a whiff of something familiar. A scent that tickled his nose and stirred his memories.

Demons.

His eyes grew wide. There were demons nearby. Which meant he wasn't the only one who had survived.

His pace quickened as he darted forward, following his nose. Why hadn't he thought of it before? When he and Prue had been in Tartarus, he had coached her on how to rely on her divine senses instead of her mortal ones.

He needed to do the same.

So he closed his eyes. His steps slowed on instinct. The last thing he needed was to trip on a tree root and injure himself further—and Prue.

But the ground remained smooth and flat. No hills. No tree roots. Not even a snapping twig or crunching leaf.

Yes, the illusion was certainly gone. There was nothing left.

Focusing on his breathing, Cyrus pressed on until he heard voices in the distance. His eyes opened again, and he stared intently at the misty surroundings, waiting for shapes or figures to appear.

"Hello?" he called out.

The voices silenced at once.

Shit.

Cyrus moved forward more urgently, desperate not to lose whoever he'd heard. "Please! You must help me. The queen is wounded!"

No response.

"Dammit!" he growled. He inhaled deeply, registering the sharp smell of demons was still close by.

Were they hiding? Perhaps they were frightened of him. It wouldn't be hard to guess why; the last his subjects had seen of him, he'd murdered someone and nearly torn down the entire palace with his rage.

But that was when Kronos had taken control of him. And, judging by what Prue had told him, Kronos had been devoured by Pandora's magic. He was gone now.

Even so, his people wouldn't know that. According to them, Cyrus was just a dangerous and insane king that they needed to steer clear of.

A heavy sigh dragged him downward, and his steps slowed once more.

"I could really use your optimism right now, Prue," he murmured, his eyes stinging and his heart twisting with grief. A sense of brutal hopelessness flooded his chest, threatening to drown him. With Prue gone, what did he have left? He had turned on his people. He had expended his magic entirely. His realm was destroyed.

A shuddering gasp ripped through him, and he sank to his knees, curling Prue's body to his chest. Broken sobs poured from his mouth. He hung his head, succumbing to the pain and anguish.

It was nothing less than what he deserved. This was his penance for abandoning his people for so long. For ignoring them in his quest for more power.

A low groan burned in his throat, and he unleashed it with his cries, reveling in the agony.

I will own this grief and pain, he thought. *It is mine, and mine alone.*

"My—My lord?" said a hesitant voice.

Cyrus's sobs quieted, and he sniffed loudly before peering over his shoulder.

A familiar figure materialized, stepping out of the fog. He had the body of a man and the head of a bull. His clothes were torn and ragged, and his dark eyes scrutinized Cyrus with part curiosity, part shock.

"Lagos?" Cyrus rasped. He staggered to his feet, then swayed.

Lagos reached out and caught Cyrus by the arm before he fell.

"You're alive," Cyrus choked, laughing with relief. "Gods above, you're *alive.*"

Lagos's gaze dropped to Prue's limp form against Cyrus's chest, and the demon's breath hitched. "Is that— No. I don't..." His voice trembled, his snout quivering as he met Cyrus's gaze again.

"I'm going to save her," Cyrus vowed in a low voice. "What else is left? *Who* else is left?"

Lagos stared at Prue again, his dark eyes swirling with a despair Cyrus understood all too well. If Cyrus watched the demon for too much longer, he would shatter.

"Lagos," Cyrus growled, snapping the demon to his attention once more.

"I'll show you." Lagos jerked his head in the direction he'd come from, then strode into the fog.

Cyrus adjusted his grip on Prue's body, keeping her close, and followed after him. The murky mist swirled in the air, obscuring everything, but he could barely make out Lagos's dark shape ahead of him. And, if anything, he could smell the demon. He wouldn't lose himself in this mist.

The knowledge brought a ridiculous amount of comfort to him. As if all he needed was one semblance of control, of circumstances he could adjust in his favor, and his sanity returned.

One step at a time. He could do this one step at a time.

The first step was following Lagos.

He would map out the other steps later.

So, for now, Cyrus focused on placing one foot in front of the other and keeping Prue close to him, trying to ignore the odor of blood and death that hung around her, shrouding her like a cloak.

Eventually, a dark, massive shape appeared, looming over Cyrus. He stilled for a moment, unease rippling over him, before pushing forward, trusting that Lagos was leading him toward safety.

And if he wasn't? Then Cyrus would be joining Prue in the afterlife.

If there even *was* an afterlife. With the realm in shambles, where did that leave the dying souls? The rivers?

One step at a time, he chastised himself, and he mentally slammed down a wall, blocking out all other concerns and worries.

After a moment, the mist peeled away to reveal the chrome castle. *Cyrus's* castle.

Cyrus stopped in his tracks, his mouth falling open, his neck craning as he drank in the sight of his mighty, shimmering silver palace. It gleamed to perfection, the spires spearing upward, not a scratch or scuff marring the glistening surface.

"What—" he breathed, then shook his head. "Impossible."

Lagos stopped, turning to face him. "Not impossible, with the wards you had us put in place."

Cyrus swallowed hard, then met Lagos's grim stare, his thoughts snagging on the word *us*. Vaguely, Cyrus remembered ordering his subordinates to build this castle, then to ward it against enemies. Specifically, he had been thinking of his brothers trying to take the crown from him by force.

"Lagos," Cyrus said weakly, knowing words were not enough. Even before Kronos possessed him, he had not been a kind ruler, especially to those lesser than him. But no words in this moment would take that away.

Lagos lifted his chin. "You think we only did it for you? Of course we would ensure only the strongest of wards surrounded this place. Our *home*. Because if you were attacked, then so were we."

Cyrus's mouth became dry. Never once had he considered the welfare of his subjects. Gods, what kind of king was he? Prue would be so disappointed in him.

And she *had* been disappointed in him. When she'd learned of the secret village created without Cyrus's knowledge, she had stormed into the throne room to admonish him for abandoning his people.

He might not have left his kingdom to starve and waste away, as she'd accused, but he hadn't been much better.

"I have... much to atone for," Cyrus said softly. "You are decent and good, Lagos. I see now what my wife saw in you."

Cyrus could have sworn the demon's snout twitched as if he were trying to smile. "It's a start," Lagos said, before turning and striding toward the archway that led to the castle entrance.

They crossed the stone bridge, although it felt eerie without the babbling river that ordinarily flowed underneath. Cyrus peered over the edge and saw nothing but darkness. No river. No souls.

The double doors of the entrance hall were already wide open, which felt strange to Cyrus. Then again, what did they have to fear? Everything in this realm was dead. There were no enemies left to keep out.

Unless, of course, Pandora's magic came back.

Cyrus suppressed a shudder and logged the thought away with the rest of his fears. For now, he had to trust that the dark forces believed this realm to be erased from existence.

A crowd of murmuring demons stood in the entrance hall, their voices hushed and frantic. Every voice quieted at Cyrus's approach, and a collective gasp rippled over the crowd. A few demons bowed uncertainly. Some glared at him with hostility. Others covered their mouths, staring openly at Prue's lifeless form.

"I need to get to the lower vaults," Cyrus muttered to Lagos. If the castle had been preserved, then perhaps what he needed was still down there.

Lagos nodded, weaving through the crowd. Cyrus did the same, though only a few demons had the decency to step aside and let him pass. He felt he should say something—offer comforting words, praise the people for their strength, vow to bring Prue back to lead them justly... But he couldn't form the words. His energy was spent. His focus was directed on remaining upright and keeping Prue aloft.

He had nothing left to give them.

So, he averted his gaze and followed Lagos, nudging past the demons who refused to step aside.

As soon as they reached the hallway, the voices broke out again, rising in pitch as the demons discussed Cyrus's dramatic entrance.

But he paid them no heed. They didn't matter right now. Only Prue did.

But I'll be different, he vowed. *If this works and brings her back, I swear to the gods I'll be the leader they deserve.*

He knew the way from here, but he still trailed behind Lagos, grateful for the demon's presence. Right now, Cyrus needed an ally he could trust. And if there was one person in this realm he trusted to be loyal to Prue, it was Lagos. He was Prue's advisor, and the first member of her court when she had taken on the role of queen of the realm.

A chill descended on them as they traveled downward, following the staircase to underneath the castle. The vault was just as Cyrus remembered—filled with boxes and crates, furniture covered in white sheets, and various shelves stocked with items imbued with power.

Cyrus's eyes snagged on the reflection bowl he'd used to search for Kronos. When he was last here, Romanos had been using it to search for a woman he'd met in the mortal realm. He hoped his brother had somehow escaped, though he doubted it. If the castle was the only thing left standing in the Underworld, it most certainly meant everyone—and everything—else was dead.

His father, Aidoneus. Romanos. The rest of his brothers: Marcellus, Leonidas, Evander. Prue's sister, Mona.

Even Prue herself.

"What is it you're looking for, my lord?" Lagos asked, facing Cyrus expectantly.

"Just call me Cyrus. It will make things easier." Cyrus surveyed the darkened chamber, squinting as he searched for what he needed. "It's an ancient spell book my father acquired from a powerful witch eons ago. The Book of Souls."

Lagos went very still, his eyes widening. "The—The Book of *Souls*? But my—Cyrus, I've heard legends of this book. Wasn't it bound to the realm of Elysium?"

Cyrus snorted. "That's what we wanted everyone to believe. If people knew it was here, they would constantly be searching for it."

Lagos's breathing turned sharp. "Such a book is dangerous and deadly. It meddles in the darkest of magic."

"And it's precisely that kind of magic we need right now." Cyrus shot him a meaningful look.

Lagos's gaze dropped to Prue again, and he nodded tersely. "Very well. I will search for it."

"It's bound in black silk," Cyrus told him, unable to sift through anything with Prue in his arms, and he refused to set her down. He inhaled deeply, trying to scent the power that would no doubt emanate from it.

He smelled nothing but dust.

Then again, the silk bindings probably stifled the dark magic. Which was exactly why it was wrapped up.

Objects shuffled around, and glass jars clinked together as Lagos searched the area. Cyrus paced the length of the opposite end of the chamber, glancing along various shelves for that familiar piece of silk. Then again, he hadn't seen the book in years. And if Romanos had found this chamber, perhaps his other brothers had, too.

What if one of them had stolen the book?

"Is this it?"

Heart pounding, Cyrus turned to find Lagos lifting a familiar black bundle, raising it for Cyrus to see. The silk was tied together with brown twine, gathered neatly to seal off every part of the book.

Awareness prickled along Cyrus's skin as he drew closer. Eyes wide, he surveyed the bundle in Lagos's hands.

"Yes," he breathed. "That's it."

Lagos set the book on a dusty table with a loud *thump.* The table rattled, and dust particles filled the air. Lagos pulled at the twine to open the bundle.

"Careful," Cyrus warned. "There are dark powers at play here."

"I survived Tartarus," Lagos muttered darkly. "I've certainly endured worse."

Cyrus nodded as guilt wormed into his stomach. Lagos had spent years as an overseer in the deepest, darkest pits of Tartarus.

Because of him.

Shaking the thought from his mind, he watched from a safe distance—afraid the magic would somehow inflict harm on Prue—as Lagos unraveled the bundle.

Dark energy filled the room, swirling dust together in an eerie funnel cloud. Lagos stepped backward, his head thrown back to gaze at the storm of dust that circled around him, growing taller and taller. A low moan thrummed from within the book.

Cyrus held his breath, his chest tightening with unease. Gods, he hated enchanted books. He'd never had good experiences with them.

But he would do this. For Prue.

Lagos closed his eyes, arms outstretched, as if he thought the wind might carry him away. After a long, tense moment, the storm subsided, and the wind ceased.

Cyrus allowed himself to breathe and looked at Lagos with newfound respect. "You weren't afraid of it?"

"Like I said," Lagos said tersely. "I've endured worse."

Cyrus's eyebrows lifted, and he couldn't help but feel impressed. He knew firsthand the magic of the Book of

Souls feasted on fear. If Lagos had shown any inkling of terror, the magic would have attacked.

The only reason it hadn't was because Lagos had embraced the challenge.

"What spell am I looking for?" Lagos asked, gingerly flipping through pages.

"The book will know."

Lagos's gaze flicked up to Cyrus, then back to the book. He stepped back again, waiting. Wind rustled the pages, and they flipped of their own accord, stopping at a spell about halfway into the book.

Cyrus drew closer, peering at the ancient text. He hadn't read this language in centuries. "Can you translate it?"

"Yes." Lagos lifted his hand, his finger tracing over the words with delicate care. After muttering to himself under his breath, he said clearly, "*To revive a soul in the Underworld, it must be directly infused with the powerful essence of one born of death magic.*"

"Does it say anything about a soul with divine blood?"

Lagos's finger trailed down the page until he stopped, his eyes narrowing in concentration. "*To revive the soul of a god or goddess, soul magic is required.*"

Cyrus nodded, expecting this. Soul magic was born of his god blood. Each time he used it, it required a piece of his own soul. Before Prue, he hadn't used it often because the price was so steep. But when he'd been traveling with her in the mortal realm and she'd fallen down the mountain, he hadn't hesitated; he'd used that magic immediately, just to save her.

And he would do it again. Even at the expense of his own life.

He felt Lagos's questioning eyes on him, but he kept his gaze pinned on the worn parchment of the book. "If I recall correctly, we should be able to find all the ingredients here in the vault."

"Cyrus," Lagos said slowly. "Exactly *how* do you intend to infuse the queen with the essence of one born of death magic?"

"Simple." Cyrus lifted his eyes to meet Lagos's. "I will offer up myself."

MISJUDGED
PANDORA

IF IT WEREN'T FOR THE PLEASANT OCEAN BREEZE wafting in the air, the temperature would have been uncomfortably warm for Pandora, especially with the long sleeves of her black silk gown. Why had she decided to wear black, anyway?

Wishing she'd worn something thin and sleeveless like the courtiers she passed by, Pandora followed Sol down the grand staircase that led to the entrance doors. Sol greeted every single person they passed, except for the servants, of course, whom he ignored completely.

To combat this snobbery, Pandora made an effort to smile or address every servant she came across. She remembered being Prue's lady's maid in the Underworld. Acting as the help truly had made her invisible.

But without the servants, the palace couldn't run at all.

They deserved far better.

The thought nagged at her mind, twisting her thoughts as she realized that *everyone*—including the servants—would perish after her plan was completed.

Doesn't matter, she told herself. *This whole place needs to burn. It can't be helped.*

But she was believing it less and less every time she thought it.

"You know the servants are here, too, don't you?" Pandora snapped as they descended the staircase leading to the courtyard overlooking the beach.

"Of course I do," Sol said over his shoulder.

"So what, you just ignore them?"

Sol paused and turned to face her, a single eyebrow raised and that infuriating half smirk lighting his face. Amusement danced in his eyes. "Do you know what the servants would do if I addressed them every time I saw them? They would shit themselves. I'm doing them a service by ignoring them and allowing them the freedom to accomplish their tasks without the added stress of a deity speaking to them."

Pandora barked out a harsh laugh. "Oh, really? You think that highly of yourself? I'm willing to bet the servants think you're a pompous, arrogant ass. If you spoke to them, they would be startled, yes, but you're no

Apollo, so it really doesn't matter if this *lesser god* whose name they can't remember deigns to speak with them or not."

Sol's eyes narrowed into slits. "Gods, I don't know how you do it."

Pandora blinked. "Do what?"

"Carry around such bitterness and resentment. It sounds exhausting. And you refuse to let others lift you up, so you insist on dragging us all down to where you are. It's a shame, really." He shook his head sadly at her.

Pandora's nostrils flared. "This is not about me."

"Isn't it? Don't you feel like a servant sometimes? Ignored? Undervalued? I'm sure the deities of the Underworld never truly appreciated the work you did."

Pandora rolled her eyes and strode past him, bumping her shoulder into his chest as she did so. "Spare me. What's exhausting is your inability to see anyone's value besides your own. What a relaxing life you must lead, to look upon the world and only see what you want instead of what's really there."

"Thank you." Sol fell into step beside her.

"It wasn't a compliment."

"But I'm taking it as one. Just another example of how *my* way of thinking leads to a much happier life than yours." He flashed a wide grin, revealing gleaming white teeth.

He's getting under your skin, Pandora told herself. *So,*

get under his! You know how he thinks, how his brain works. You can torment him just as easily.

She took a deep breath, then forced a low chuckle.

Sol glanced at her. "What's so funny?"

"I just think it's nice, that's all." She shrugged, feigning nonchalance.

"What's nice?"

"That you're content to simply"—she gestured vaguely at him—"remain as you are. No growth. No progress. You speak as if you're some great high lord, but you're just... Sol the sun god." She grinned at him. "It's nice, really. Not many deities would be pleased with remaining in the same position for as many years as you have, but you refuse to let that drag you down. Admirable indeed." She patted his shoulder, relishing the way the light dimmed in his eyes.

Sol said nothing as they made their way through the entrance doors and down the steps toward the courtyard. The brilliant sun beat down on them from above, and as Pandora was hit with a full blast of its light, she flinched, her body shuddering from an onslaught of memories. Bright light, searing her, scorching her insides, boiling her blood. The light burned and burned and burned until there was nothing left...

Pandora swallowed hard, trying to ground herself, to root herself in this moment. *It's not real. It's not happen-*

ing. You are here. You are safe. She took several shaky breaths and felt Sol's curious gaze on her.

She needed to keep the conversation going before he asked questions she couldn't answer. Before he noticed something peculiar about her that he would undoubtedly report to Apollo.

"I—I should aspire to be more like you," Pandora said as they made their way across the courtyard, the pearly white concrete sparkling under the mid-morning sun. The courtyard steps led to a wide path that disappeared into a copse of beech trees. *Just a few more steps,* she told herself, trying to ignore the relentless heat of the sun above her. Another deep breath. She forced herself to focus on her words, on her desire to bring Sol's smug attitude crashing to the ground.

"I'm too ambitious," she went on. "If I were simply happy with a position like yours, then I wouldn't have to do *anything*, really. I'm already there!" She laughed airily, waving her hand between them. "You and I are the same, you know. Same status. Same position. I was hoping to one day get a title, a task fitting for a goddess, but if I'm to adopt your perspective, I will have to think smaller. It's definitely something I'll be working on."

They entered the cover of the trees, the air much cooler without the sun beating down on them. Pandora loosed a breath of relief, finally able to calm her racing heart and cease her mindless rambling. The shade was a blessed respite from the burning sun.

Sol finally found his voice. "You think I don't know what you're doing?"

Pandora gave him her most convincing look of pure innocence. "Hmm?" Inside her chest, her heart drummed a panicked rhythm as fear crept in. Had he somehow found out who she was? Had he noticed her reaction to the blinding sun?

He sighed. "You're trying to goad me into arguing with you. It won't work."

Pandora snorted, relieved he hadn't noticed anything incriminating. "I'm not goading you into anything. You were speaking of servants and my misguided perspective. Now I'm agreeing with you."

"Right," Sol said doubtfully. "Well, if you *were* trying to goad me, I would tell you it wouldn't work. Because I have no desire to rise above my station."

This time, Pandora halted, her feet scuffing on the path as she gaped at him. "You don't?"

Sol smiled, clearly pleased at catching her off guard. "Not at all. I *am* happy with being a sun god. It's quite nice to know that if I wake up and the sunrise is too perfect to ignore, I can whip out my paints and get to work on a new canvas without risking the destruction of the entire realm due to my negligence. If I don't direct my magic to the skies, there are other sun gods to complete the task. Including Apollo, who cares very much about his public image. He would never sit idly by with so many people watching him."

Sol shrugged, then continued, "But me? You're right. Servants probably don't know my name." He leaned closer to her as if they were sharing a secret, his voice low and sensuous. "And I prefer it that way. Servants talk, you see. And I wouldn't want them spreading gossip about my... private affairs." He lifted his hand and brushed a finger along the exposed skin of her shoulder.

Pleasure sizzled through her at the contact, and she sucked in a breath, so startled and confused by his touch that she had nothing to say.

He strode past her, that cocky grin returning to his mouth, leaving Pandora to stare after him. Who was this person? He certainly wasn't the cruel, ambitious god she remembered from her youth.

And the way he touched her—the way his voice dipped, deep and alluring—made her body tingle with an awareness she had never felt before.

She'd taken lovers, of course. But in the Underworld, there were slim pickings for bedmates.

Pandora shook her head. Sol was *not* an ideal bedmate. He was an ass. An arrogant snob.

But those traits had nothing to do with sharing a bed with him. Pandora had bedded some of the most despicable demons simply because they had attractive bodies.

And Sol's body was *most certainly* attractive.

For a moment, she allowed herself to watch him walk past her, his swaggering steps drawing her eye to the delicious curve of his backside.

Her mouth quirked upward in a smile.

Was she truly thinking about this? As if it were a viable option?

Why not? asked a voice inside her. *This might be your one and only opportunity to experience true, potent pleasure.*

To tangle with a *god.*

And a god with a body like *that...*

Her throat flared with heat, and she forced herself to follow after Sol, utterly bewildered by the turn her thoughts had taken.

More important things, she reminded herself. *More important things.*

But if Sol kept flirting with her like that, she wasn't sure what she would do.

It didn't take them long to reach the village. Once they emerged from the grove of trees, a babble of voices filled the air, growing closer with each step they took. A short bridge spanned a small river, and on the other side was a collection of cream-colored buildings with blue rooftops, separated by a narrow gap that allowed people to traverse between them on foot.

As Sol led Pandora on a winding path between buildings, his steps sure and confident, as if he had taken this route many times, Pandora kept trying to peer around the corner of the buildings to see what caused all the commotion. Several villagers fell into step beside them, hurrying with a sense of urgency.

"What's going on?" Pandora asked, her curiosity getting the better of her.

Sol shrugged. "Probably another market day."

"Market day?"

"Surely you know what a market is." He smirked at her.

She rolled her eyes. "Of course I do. But these people aren't acting like they're going to an ordinary marketplace. They look as if they're running late for an important social gathering."

"Well, that's exactly what market day *is*. Vendors and townsfolk from all over the village come together to show off their wares, haggle, bargain, converse, and fellowship together. It's an excellent opportunity to experience the culture we have to offer here."

Pandora frowned at the word *culture*. "But this is Elysium. None of this is real. All the villagers here are *dead.* Why would they be worried about selling wares or haggling prices?"

Sol turned to face her, eyebrows lifted, a rare look of solemnity on his face. "Just because they're dead doesn't mean there's no economy here. Life doesn't end after leaving the mortal realm. It continues, either in the Underworld, or in Elysium. And from there, a new culture rises."

She had never thought of it that way. To her, death was simply a door opening, leading to another completely different world. But here in Elysium, it seemed as if they were trying to recreate a society similar to the mortal realm.

"It doesn't seem strange to you?" Pandora asked as they continued down the thin walkways between build-ings. "You're a god. You don't need to eat or sleep or toil, and yet that's exactly what this village embodies: a society of humans. Frail, weak humans."

"Why shouldn't they recreate the society they were born into?" Sol asked. "These people *are* humans. We shouldn't expect them to be any different just because they have died."

"And you... like living here? Among humans?"

He snorted. "I live in the castle."

"But you come here often." It wasn't a question. She could tell by his steady pace that he knew the area well.

Sol sighed and stopped, turning to face her. "Do I see

myself as greater than the humans? Yes, of course. I'm immortal and I possess abilities they could only dream of. Does that mean I would never associate with them, never interact, never see what their lives are like? Of course not. How narrow-minded do you believe me to be?"

"Not narrow-minded," Pandora said truthfully. "Just pretentious. You've only ever been concerned with yourself, so of course it would shock me to see you defending the humans."

He shot her a crooked smile, and her heart leapt at the sight. "It seems you don't know me as well as you thought, Trivia."

He turned away, leading her down the path once more, but Pandora wasn't finished.

"Why *do* you interact with the humans, then?" she asked, genuinely curious. She wasn't sure why she was so obsessed with learning the truth behind Sol's smug and arrogant exterior. Ordinarily, she was an excellent judge of character. She wouldn't have been able to keep up her deception for long if she wasn't.

So, it threw her, being wrong about Sol. She needed to delve deeper to see where, exactly, she had misjudged him.

Because mingling with the humans was certainly *not* something the Sol she knew would be doing.

"There is always something to learn," Sol said. "Our

entire existence is tethered to humans. Don't you want to know more about the species that worships you?"

Pandora huffed a dry laugh. "The humans don't give a damn about me." She faltered when she remembered what Prue had said to her: *the witches do.*

Many covens revered Trivia as the goddess of three paths because of her connection to the Triple Goddess. So, her claim wasn't entirely true. There were witches out there who *did* know her name.

"And, how will you change that, if you're busy sulking in your cave in the Underworld instead of getting to know them?" Sol shot a sly grin over his shoulder.

Pandora's eyes narrowed. "You're just looking for acolytes, aren't you? People to serve you. Grovel at your feet."

Sol sighed and waved a hand in her direction. "Stop making assumptions about who I am, Trivia. I'm far too complex for you to draw your own conclusions about me." He half turned to give her a coy smile. "You'll need to get much closer to unravel my true character." His voice took on that low and sensuous tone once more, and Pandora had to drop her gaze before he undid her completely.

Damn this man.

Her face heated as she gritted her teeth, cursing herself for allowing him the upper hand *again.*

What was it about him that vexed her so much? Why couldn't she just keep her distance and ignore him, like she did everyone else?

She had a plan. And she needed to stick to it. It was that simple.

The gaps between buildings opened up to a wide, spacious courtyard with a fountain in the middle. The area was packed with people navigating a maze of tables and booths. A cacophony of voices filled the air. Vendors shouted their prices. Women laughed and twirled their skirts to the rhythm of the music pulsing from a quartet of musicians playing instruments in the corner.

Pandora trailed behind Sol, her mouth open in awe as she drank it all in. Never in her years in the Underworld had she seen anything like this.

Sol whirled to face her, beaming, and spread his arms. "Welcome to market day."

GUIDE

MONA

MONA WENT PERFECTLY STILL, AS IF SHE'D COME across a predator in the woods. Her instincts told her to run, even though it would do no good.

If Prue were here, she would fight, Mona told herself. So, she faced the stranger and lifted her chin, trying to channel as much of Prue's confidence into her voice as she could. "Who are you?"

The woman—the *goddess*—chuckled, a low, melodious sound, as she drew closer, her red eyes narrowing into slits as she took in Mona's appearance. "Don't pretend with me, child. I can smell your blood, and it doesn't belong here." She cocked her head, assessing her, looking every much the predator Mona was envisioning. "Who are *you*?"

Mona's insides quivered, and it took all of her

strength to keep from trembling before the goddess's piercing gaze. Whoever she was, she was powerful.

Think, Mona! she urged herself. *You've read about the gods of Elysium. Who could she be?*

Mona's eyes flicked over the goddess's form once more with a new perspective. She imagined the tomes of books she would pore over that outlined the histories of deities most revered by their witch coven. The woman's muscular stature indicated she was a warrior. Red hair and identical eyes that looked like holy flames...

Mona blinked, staggering back a step. "You're Hestia. The goddess of fire."

Hestia's eyebrows lifted. "I'm impressed. Not many would recognize me so quickly. But that still doesn't explain what a stranger like you is doing in Elysium."

Mona swallowed hard, thinking quickly. Now that she'd activated the clever and bookish side of her mind, the fear was starting to bleed away, making room for more logical thoughts. Hestia hadn't threatened her... yet. Which meant she could be an ally. In addition, as far as Mona knew, fire witches revered Hestia.

Unfortunately, fire witches were hunted all over the Realm of Gaia. So Mona had little to no experience with them. But from the books she'd read, earth witches were viewed as kin to fire witches in some covens. Perhaps that could work in her favor.

Clearing her throat, Mona said hesitantly, "I'm an

earth witch. I *do* possess god blood, but I've never been here before. I'm looking for someone who arrived by accident. I would like to bring him home before anyone finds him."

All truthful words, even if she left out key details. She didn't think mentioning Gaia as her mother would earn her any favors. Gaia had been cast out of Elysium and cursed, so she likely didn't have many allies here. And to mention that Evander was part demon and was slowly dying? That would certainly not benefit her situation.

Hestia inhaled deeply, her eyes closing for a moment. Then she smiled. "Ah, there it is. Faint, but it's certainly potent now that I can identify it. You *do* have god blood, though it is... masked by something else." She frowned, leaning closer, and Mona backed up another step.

Fear must have shone in her eyes, because Hestia withdrew, clasping her hands in front of her. "Apologies. It isn't often I have a delightful mystery to solve."

Mona licked her lips, trying not to fidget. "I—Will you let me pass, my lady?"

Hestia laughed and waved her hand. "There is no need for titles here, little witch. I am not your enemy."

Mona still hesitated. The last time she had trusted a goddess, Trivia had extracted a bargain from her after letting her believe they were friends.

But no friend of hers would abduct Evander and bring him to Elysium to die.

"What is your friend's name?" Hestia prompted. "Perhaps I can tell you where he is."

Mona's tongue felt glued to her throat. She couldn't speak Evander's name... could she? There was no way for Hestia to know he was a death god. Evander had told her he'd never met any gods or goddesses of Elysium.

"Romanos," Mona said hesitantly. If Romanos were here, he would be in far less danger than Evander. At least, she hoped.

And if Hestia didn't recognize Romanos's name, then she wouldn't know Evander's, either.

It was a test to see if she could truly trust the goddess.

Hestia's eyes widened, and her smile grew. "Ah, the death god? He is not here, my child. He is in the mortal realm, alongside one of my chosen vessels. Fret not, for she doesn't yet realize she is the key to undoing his curse. They will help each other. You have nothing to worry about."

Mona's mouth dropped open. Romanos was in the mortal realm? How did that happen? Heart racing, she tried to process this information, while Hestia looked at her expectantly.

Think, Mona, think! Hestia hadn't seemed upset about the idea of a death god possibly wandering around

Elysium. If anything, she seemed to speak of Romanos with fondness.

Perhaps that meant Mona could trust her with more information.

She took another breath and tried again. "I'm... actually looking for someone else, too. Romanos's brother."

Hestia's face turned stony. "You speak of Osiris?" Her tone was icy.

"No, no! I'm looking for Evander."

Hestia's brows knitted together. "I know no one by that name."

Thank the Goddess. Relief filled Mona's chest, boosting her confidence. "His essence is tethered to the magic of the Underworld. He can't be here for long before it tears him apart."

Hestia's face turned solemn. "Then, we have no time to waste. Tell me, which portal did you come from?"

"The one on the beach."

Hestia nodded firmly. "We shall investigate the other. Come, my child, we haven't a moment to lose. If this Evander is in as much peril as you say, then we must find him as soon as possible." She stretched her arm toward Mona, gesturing for her to follow.

Mona hesitated again, biting her lip.

Hestia frowned. "What is it?"

"What—What will I owe you in exchange for your help?"

Hestia blinked, before a slow smile spread across her face. "Ah. You have dealt with deity bargains before, haven't you? Smart girl." She drew herself up to her full height, towering over Mona with a fierce expression on her face. "I only ask that, when you have unlocked the full powers of the Triple Goddess, you will consider me your ally."

Mona felt the blood drain from her face. "Unlocked the... *what*?" She suddenly felt faint. What was Hestia talking about?

Hestia smiled again. "You think I don't know whose blood runs in your veins?"

Terror washed over Mona, making her skin feel prickly. "I—I—"

Hestia leaned in, her eyes now gentle. "I'm your ally, remember? I mean you no harm."

Mona shook her head. "You must be mistaken. I don't know how to unlock any sort of power, let alone the Triple Goddess's."

Hestia's eyes glinted as if she knew something Mona didn't. "Not yet. But you will. Do I have your word?"

Mona was still reeling over this revelation. Unlock the Triple Goddesses's power? How the hell was she supposed to do that?

But Hestia was looking at her, eyebrows raised, as she waited for a response.

"Um, *if* I somehow manage to unlock the power of

the Triple Goddess," Mona said carefully, "then, I swear to you, Hestia the fire goddess, that I will consider you an ally. Unless you seek to harm myself or those I love."

Hestia grinned and bowed her head to Mona. It was a strange thing to see such a gesture performed by someone so powerful. "Well worded, little witch. I humbly accept your offer. Come now, let us find your Evander and send him home."

With a swish of her skirt, Hestia turned and strode down the cobblestone path. Mona lingered for a moment before following after, terrified that she had just made a very grave mistake.

ILLUSION

PANDORA

THE INSTANT SOL AND PANDORA ENTERED THE bustling square, the commotion died, and hushed whispers fell around them. One by one, the townsfolk sank to their knees, uttering Sol's name in reverence.

Pandora stiffened, then glanced over her shoulder at the sun god. He had a gentle, demure smile on his face, a hand pressed to his chest as if the people's praise warmed his heart.

Suddenly, it all made sense. *This* was why he visited the village.

He wanted to be worshiped.

Rage boiled her blood, and before she could stop herself, Pandora spread her hands wide and said loudly, "Don't stop the revelry on our account! We are only two lesser gods on an assignment. Please, continue your merriment and treat us as nothing more than the lackeys that we are." She winked conspiratorially at Sol as if they were sharing a private joke.

To her delight, his jaw was taut, his eyes flaring with irritation.

Several people muttered in confusion to one another, glancing between Sol and Pandora.

With a sigh, Sol said, "My companion speaks the truth. I am not here to converse with you. We are just passing through. Sadly, I cannot hear your concerns or praises today."

Concerns? Pandora had to refrain from rolling her eyes. She doubted Sol would do a damn thing about these people's concerns. He was only here to inflate his ego.

Sol waved his hand. "Please, continue! My companion here has never seen market day before. We must show her all we have to offer here in Amara." He flashed a wide grin, and his words were met with cheers.

And just like that, the music resumed, and the people moved about, continuing with their business. Aside from a few curious glances toward Sol and Pandora, they seemed perfectly at ease.

"Amara?" Pandora asked Sol as she watched a vendor haggle with a woman over the price of beads.

"Villages have names, Trivia," Sol said with a sigh.

"Really," she bit out. "I just assumed you didn't know it. In your mind, this is merely Human Town."

He shrugged but didn't deny it.

Pandora gripped the sleeve of his elbow before hissing, "You come here and make them *worship* you? As if they don't get enough of that from Apollo."

Sol jerked his arm free and raised his palms. "I didn't ask them to do anything. They did it of their own accord."

"Right. You just didn't see fit to stop them, did you?"

That infuriating smirk played at his lips again. "It *is* a bit fun, don't you think? Humans in the Realm of Gaia don't know or care about me, but here? I can be the god I was always meant to be."

"You and I weren't meant to be more than their messengers, their servants, their *slaves*," Pandora seethed. "The sooner you know that, the sooner—"

"The sooner what?" Sol asked, eyebrows raised. "The sooner I can accept my bitter circumstances and be angry all the time? Like you?"

Pandora faltered at that.

He huffed in dry amusement. "Perhaps I am delusional in my beliefs of my own grandeur and power. But at least I am content with it. I'd much prefer that than whatever dark troubles constantly cloud your mind, Trivia." His words were laced with pity, and it only stoked her ire.

Before she could reply, he said, "We are here on assignment, are we not? Let's get on with it."

"Gladly," she snapped, eager to finish this once and for all. She just needed to inspect the wards, infuse the death magic into the weakest section, and then finally be finished with this place.

The sooner the light left Sol's eyes and his severed head rolled on the ground, the better.

Pandora couldn't deny she was indeed curious to see what wares were exchanged at market day. As they strode past the booths, she eyed the villagers as they exchanged clothing, gems, and fresh food with one another. Not a single coin or piece of currency was exchanged. Their wares *were* their currency. A jeweler traded a diamond-studded necklace for a silk cloak. A baker traded freshly baked scones for an elegantly crafted vase.

The sight of it made Pandora's mouth slide into a reluctant smile. She hated to admit it, but Sol was right. There *was* culture here.

Her smile vanished as she realized that she would be destroying it soon.

"For a moment there, I thought you were going mad," Sol said idly at her side.

She scowled at him. "What the hell are you talking about?"

"I thought I saw you *smiling*. But no, she's back. All is well."

Her scowl only deepened. It didn't matter if this village was destroyed. It was built for Apollo's convenience. For the gods of Elysium. If it weren't for them, none of this would even be here.

The world had to be wiped clean. It had to be rid of these vile vermin who called themselves gods.

They had caused her so much pain.

Screams rang in her ears, and Pandora's steps halted, her eyes closing as she tried to block out the trauma of the soul inside her. But, as always, it hammered mercilessly at her mind, forcing entry. She'd hoped that being here in a new place would quiet the voices inside her, but she'd been wrong.

She groaned as pain raked its sharp claws through the fabric of her mind, tearing, tearing, tearing.

"*Trivia!*"

Something shook her violently, and she yelped, jerked from the agony that threatened to consume her.

Her head throbbed as she sat up, dazed and disoriented. She was lying flat on her back on the concrete. When had she fallen? Sol stood over her, his hands on her shoulders and a look of uncharacteristic concern in his eyes. Thankfully, they were tucked in the shadows between buildings, so the hub of villagers didn't notice Pandora's fainting spell.

Gods, had she really *fainted*?

"I'm... fine," Pandora sputtered, hastily climbing to her feet. Sol kept a hand on her shoulder, and as much as she wanted to slap it away, she allowed him to steady her. Black spots swam in her vision, and she wasn't entirely sure she wouldn't lose consciousness again.

"What was that?" Sol asked. His voice was sober, his dark eyes appraising her, glancing over her body as if searching for a hidden injury. She hadn't seen him this serious since she'd told him the Underworld had been destroyed.

"I—Nothing. The heat." Pandora waved a limp hand toward the sun shining in the sky.

"It's an illusion, Trivia," Sol said, his eyebrows lowering. "*What happened?*"

"I don't owe you an explanation," Pandora snapped. "As you said, we have an assignment. Let's get it done so we can be rid of each other."

Sol sighed and dropped his hand. "Fine. But if you fall again, I will *not* be catching you."

He strode forward, but Pandora faltered, her throat tightening. Had he caught her? She raised a hand to the back of her head. If she *had* fallen, there would have been an injury. But aside from the faint, aching pulse in her head, she felt fine.

Knots of emotion cinched in her chest, but she buried them deep and hurried after Sol.

It didn't take long to reach the edge of the city. The buildings became more sparse, and rolling hills with vibrant green grass came into view. The concrete faded into a faint cobbled path that led to a secluded cove where rolling waves lapped and pearly sand glinted in the sunlight. It was a small beach, and not a soul was in sight.

Pandora's mouth fell open at the beauty of it. The lush greenery, the teal and amethyst swirls of water, the...

She frowned. The place looked oddly familiar.

She turned to find Sol gazing wistfully at the scene, and then she figured it out.

"You've painted this before."

He blinked and turned to her, eyebrows lifted. "I— Yes, I have. Beautiful, isn't it?"

"It really is," she found herself saying.

For a moment, the two of them stood there, admiring the view. And it was so shocking and yet... so ordinary, to be standing alongside someone and agreeing with them, that Pandora didn't want to taint the moment. It seemed Sol didn't want to, either.

Pandora inhaled and turned to face him, intent on

asking where the wards ended so they could return to the task at hand. But the words died in her throat as she found him watching her, his eyes gleaming in the sunlight.

"I would paint *you*," he said, his voice low and husky, "if I thought I could capture your light." His hand lifted and caught a lock of her red hair, which burned golden in the light of the sun. He twirled it around his fingers, and her breath caught in her throat.

She didn't know what to say. Not when he looked at her like that. Not when he said such things.

Her mouth went dry.

Sol leaned in, his breath caressing her face. And Pandora's heart skittered, her thoughts scattering as every sensible, logical voice in her head was silenced by his nearness and the warmth of his body. She found her eyelids fluttering shut, her lips parting in anticipation.

His nose brushed hers, and a tingle of awareness skittered across her body like a jolt of lightning, setting her blood on fire.

Sol's lips moved to her ear as he whispered, "Will you join me?"

Pandora's eyes flew open, the breath whooshing out of her almost violently. Gods above, what was she doing? How had her brain simply *shut off* like that?

She took an unsteady step back, swallowing hard.

"Join you for what?" She was relieved to find her voice was level, despite her racing heartbeat.

His eyes took on a sultry edge as he looked at her. "The water is perfect. I'd like to go for a dip. Will you join me?"

Her heart was practically crashing against her ribcage. It was so loud, so thunderous, she thought surely he would hear it.

She forced a laugh. "Hell, no."

He shrugged, clearly unaffected by her dismissal. "Suit yourself."

He ambled down the hill, his feet sliding along the sand as he whipped his tunic off without a second thought. Pandora's stomach hollowed at the sight of his shoulders, the muscles tightening as he loosened his trousers.

Oh gods. Was he about to remove *all* of his clothes? Right here?

For one second, Pandora imagined herself joining him. Perhaps she would remove her clothes as well. The cool water would feel refreshing against her bare skin, and Sol's firm and sculpted body would press along hers and—

"No," she hissed, gritting her teeth against the images that filled her mind. She had more important things to do than dally with an arrogant ass of a god. She'd had a simple lapse of judgment. His nearness and flirting had startled her. That was all.

Stifling the heat burning low in her belly, she made her way down the hill, ignoring naked Sol as he dipped below the waves and flicked his long, wet hair out of his face.

Don't look at him, she told herself. *Don't.*

But even with her eyes fixed firmly ahead, she couldn't stop envisioning his bare torso, and the way the moisture would look as it trickled down his neck and chest...

"Damn him," Pandora muttered, marching along the beach, her steps wobbly in the sand. At long last, she reached the edge of the beach, and the sand faded among the tall grass. Her steps slowed as she enjoyed the tickle of the foliage along her hands. She found herself smiling the farther she got from the water. Soon, the hills swallowed her, and all she saw was the luscious greenery around her. No Sol. No beach.

Nothing but growth and *earth.*

Her home. This, right here, felt like home.

She sank to her knees, allowing her hands to press into the soft ground. She sighed with contentment as the smell of herbs and soil filled her nose. No matter how strong the illusion was in the Underworld, it never fully captured *this.*

A moment of solemnity sparked in her mind as she realized why.

Gaia had lived here. Her mother. She might have even crafted this illusion herself.

The notion spoiled Pandora's thoughts, souring her mood once more. She stood, her arms falling limply by her side as she shook off the dirt and grass from her dress.

Everything—*everything*—in her life was tainted by her past. By memories that didn't even belong to her. The goddess from so long ago was infused into her soul, into her very being. She could never escape it, all because of what Apollo had done to her so many years ago. When she had only been a baby, he had cursed her with the pain, the trauma, the memories of that goddess —her namesake.

It was Gaia's punishment for trying to harness the powers of the Triple Goddess with triplets. And because of Gaia's choices, Pandora was the one to suffer for it.

As much as she yearned for Sol's careless nature, for his ability to see only what he wanted to, it was impossible for her. And it always would be.

Until her revenge was complete.

Only then could she be free.

With a heavy sigh, she made her way up the final hill and stood atop it, gazing at the landscape below her. The grassy plains descended until they reached a cliff overlooking the wide, expansive sea.

And there was nothing more after that. Just the horizon. And, eventually, the end of the illusion.

An illusion was all this place was. It wasn't real. And Pandora had to remember that.

She raised her hands, closing her eyes as she searched for that familiar humming pulse of magic. The energies surrounded her, tingling her skin and making her flesh prickle.

There it was. Something warm brushed against her flat palms, awakening the earth magic inside her.

"No, no," she murmured soothingly. "Not you. Not yet." If she sprouted tree branches right here, Sol would be suspicious.

Instead, she touched the rubies of her necklace, activating the death magic trapped inside. As she coaxed it to life, she pressed it into the wards, feeding it, layering the death magic alongside the magic of Elysium.

The dark magic from her box would be drawn to the scent of death. It would find Elysium in no time.

With the smell of decay and rot on her nostrils, Pandora turned from the wards, confident in her plan.

Nothing would stop her. And soon, this realm would fall.

WAVES
PANDORA

FOR WHAT FELT LIKE AGES, PANDORA STOOD ATOP
the hill overlooking the ocean where Sol swam, her eyes
on the horizon and her mind elsewhere. It wasn't until a
long arm extended in the air, beckoning her forward,
that she realized Sol was shouting something at her.

Rolling her eyes, she descended the hill and made
her way across the sand, her feet resting just in front of
the rolling tide. "What is it?" she called out to him.

"Join me!" he said.

"No!" she barked.

"Come on, Trivia, when will you get another chance
like this? You can't tell me you have such luxuries in the
Underworld."

Pandora opened her mouth to argue, but then realized he was right. She *wouldn't* get an opportunity like this.

Especially if this realm would soon be consumed by death magic.

Why shouldn't she enjoy herself? Her work was done. There was nothing left for her to do but wait.

Her preference would be to swim alone, but that couldn't be helped.

She removed her shoes, and Sol laughed in triumph.

"I knew I could persuade you."

"Shut up!" she snapped, but a smile worked its way across her face. Yes, for this moment, she could be like Sol and pretend nothing else existed. Nothing else mattered but the enjoyment of the moment.

Sol was swimming closer to her, his eyes sparkling. And damn if his wet hair didn't look good, side swept and messy around his face, the water droplets running down his cheeks.

"What else will you take off?" he teased.

Pandora's eyebrows lifted in a challenge. He thought she wouldn't do it. The amusement on his face was plain. She was nothing but a bitter goddess of the Underworld, consumed by her hatred.

Well, she would prove him wrong.

She loosened the ties of her dress and relished the look of surprise on his face as the fabric fell at her feet, leaving her in nothing but her shift.

Yes, shocking Sol was proving to be one of her favorite things.

She grinned as she stepped out of her dress, then let the straps of her shift fall as well. The silk fabric puddled at her feet, leaving her completely bare as she strode into the water. It was indeed cool against her flesh, but not unpleasant. Waves lapped at her skin, the constant motion of the water surrounding her like a rhythmic dance. In and out.

She closed her eyes, enjoying the sensation. Gods, she had never felt anything like this before. She hadn't once been to the mortal realm, and her only exposure to water in the Underworld were the rivers of souls. The roar of ocean waves filled her mind, dulling the rampaging thoughts that always lingered and tormented her.

With a deep breath, she dropped, submerging her head underwater. Light and sound were drowned by the water, and for a moment, she lingered under the surface, reveling in the silence.

When she emerged, she gasped, peeling her wet, sticky hair off her face and grinning widely.

"You are full of surprises, aren't you, Trivia?"

She opened her eyes, finding Sol treading water alongside her, a mischievous smile on his face.

"You don't know me nearly as well as you think you do," she challenged, her gaze roving over him. His chest was bare, but the rolling waters concealed the bottom half of his body. "Are you really *fully* naked under there?"

He laughed. "You think I would wear britches in this, and let them drag me down? You don't know me all that well, either."

So he *was* naked. Just like her.

They were both naked in the water.

Together.

The sheer insanity of it, the ludicrous notion that Pandora would be swimming naked alongside a man she loathed, only made her laugh. She threw her head back and let her laughter echo into the sky, resonating around her.

"Gods," Sol said, his own chuckles joining hers. "I don't think I've ever heard you laugh before. Not like *that.*"

Yes, he had only heard her laugh in derision or incredulity. Nothing else.

"It *is* freeing being out here," she admitted. "I've never done anything like this before, and it's so... unexpected."

"Why do you think I do it?" Sol asked. "Being stuck in that stuffy castle all day can mess with your mind. Sometimes, I need to escape."

"Escape?" Pandora raised an eyebrow. "From the luxuries of the palace?"

Sol flicked water in her face. "From so many eyes and expectations. Being Apollo's apprentice seemed glamorous when I accepted it, but being near him puts me in the public eye far too much for my liking."

"Really? I saw you when we were in Amara. You *love* the public eye."

He rolled his eyes. "Being around humans is far different from being around gods."

"You don't like being around gods?"

He shrugged. "Some of them aren't so bad." He gave her a sultry look under his lashes.

"Oh, like me?" Pandora tilted her head, flashing a smile at him.

He laughed. "Oh no, Trivia, you're the *worst*. I detest you."

"Well, the feeling is mutual." She flicked water at him, too.

He swam closer to her, his leg brushing against hers. "Careful, now. I've heard these waters can be treacherous. Something might pull you under."

"Something? Or someone?"

He gave her a sly smile.

Then, his hands were on her waist, and she yelped in surprise. In one deft movement, he lifted her so she was pulled against his chest, her feet flailing underwater. She clung to his shoulders, worried he would toss her.

"What are you doing?" she shrieked.

Sol only laughed as he released her, but she kept her hold around his neck, wrapping her legs tightly around his middle to keep herself from falling in. She wasn't necessarily scared of being tossed into the water—she just didn't want him to *win.*

Laughter bubbled up her throat as he tried to remove her limbs from his body, but they were severely tangled in each other.

"You can't dispose of me so easily," Pandora said breathlessly, her face close to his.

His chuckles subsided as he gazed at her, and only then did she realize just *how close* their naked bodies were. Her breasts were flush against his chest, her center rubbing directly against him.

And she could feel him. All of him. His arousal pressed along the underside of her leg, making her cheeks heat.

But she didn't loosen her hold on him. The amusement of the moment was gone, but she couldn't bring herself to release him just yet. Something hot and molten churned between them, and she suddenly found it hard to breathe.

"I quite like the way your body fits with mine, Trivia," Sol murmured. Light danced in his eyes, and as she stared at them, she realized they weren't dark brown like she had assumed; they were a deep, midnight blue. The colors of the swirling waves around them brought out the color of his eyes, and she found herself getting lost in them.

"Your eyes," he whispered, as if following her train of thought. "They are like the glowing sun."

She knew her eyes were gold, but no one had ever compared them to the sun before. She'd been told they looked like honey or whiskey, but never the sun.

She was the sun, and he was the sea.

His hand splayed along her back, his fingers running a path up and down her spine. With his other hand, he cupped her ass, bringing her closer against him. Her breath hitched. A riot of heat and yearning bolted through her, and she closed her eyes. How long had it been since someone touched her like this?

Sol's nose brushed against hers, and a shiver of pleasure rippled over her body. Her legs tightened around him, grinding her center directly against him, and he groaned.

"Gods," he rasped. "You're so beautiful." He angled his head closer, lining his mouth with hers, when she jerked back suddenly.

Beautiful.

What was it he'd said? *It's impossible for me to hate a beautiful woman.*

This was lust and nothing more. He was attractive, and she was attractive. They were merely acting on the mutual attraction.

But in reality, they despised each other. Sol was the most pompous and despicable ass she'd ever met, except for maybe Apollo. And he saw her as a filthy urchin from the Underworld.

Clarity slammed into her, removing all heat from her body. She quickly loosened her hold around his neck, dropping her legs and shifting away from him. She couldn't meet his gaze.

"We should get back to the castle," she said quietly. She felt his questioning gaze on her as she turned from him and swam back to shore, overcome with a mixture of shock from what she'd almost done with him, and regret that she hadn't finished what they'd started.

SACRIFICE

CYRUS

"Is everything ready?" Cyrus asked. He had finally rested Prue against a long chaise sofa he had uncovered in the storage vault. His arms ached from holding her for so long, but now, seeing her lying motionless on the sofa, he felt even emptier than before.

He forced himself to look at Lagos, who was busy mixing ingredients into a large cauldron. A bright green substance boiled from within, and Lagos inhaled deeply.

"All the ingredients are assembled," said Lagos. "Cyrus, are you certain this will work? I thought only witches could perform a spell like this."

"Anyone who possesses magic can practice," Cyrus said. "We can perform blood bargains, after all."

Lagos huffed a sigh. "It doesn't need to be *you*. What

do you think she will do if she wakes and finds what you've done?"

Cyrus's heart twisted as he envisioned Prue finally waking up, only to find his lifeless body lying before her. It would destroy her. Just as it had destroyed him.

But she would be a much better ruler for this realm than he ever would. In time, she would realize this. She wouldn't abandon her people like he had.

"It's not like I have any other options," Cyrus said, glancing over the worn and tattered page of the spell book. The power within thrummed at his touch, and he quickly jerked his hand back before it tried to drain his powers.

He needed to save everything he had for the spell. For Prue.

"But your brothers—" Lagos began.

"Are dead," Cyrus said harshly, fixing a lethal stare on Lagos. "And even if they aren't, I don't have the time or the power to fight them into submission. We must act *now*, Lagos. You know this, and I know this. So stop making excuses and finish the damn spell."

Lagos's large nostrils flared, and he growled slightly before bowing his head and stirring the potion ingredients once more.

Cyrus sighed and ran a hand down his face. "Forgive me. You do not deserve to be treated like a servant. I can finish mixing the ingredients, if you like."

Lagos stopped stirring and fixed his dark, emotionless eyes on Cyrus. "You... are offering to do this in my place?"

Cyrus furrowed his brow. "Yes."

Lagos shook his head and resumed stirring, and Cyrus could have sworn he'd heard a snort of amusement. "It is no trouble to perform these tasks if it is in service of my queen." His gaze flicked to Cyrus once more. "She has changed you for the better, Cyrus. I hope you see that."

Cyrus nodded. "I do. I wouldn't be sacrificing myself if that weren't the case."

"It would be a shame to end your life when you are on such a path."

Cyrus closed his eyes, bracing his hands on the table where the book rested. Agony wrestled within him, making his chest constrict. "I know." The words were ripped from him by force. How could Lagos not see there was no other way? How could he not understand that this realm needed Prue far more than it needed him? "If you have any other ideas for bringing my wife back, I would love to hear them."

Lagos said nothing. As Cyrus suspected. The demon used the ladle to pour the vibrant green liquid into an empty chalice, which he brought over to Cyrus.

With a deep breath, Cyrus opened his eyes, his arms

beginning to shake as he read through the spell one last time.

This would be worth it. He knew it, down to his very soul.

And yet, he had spent so long—an eternity, really—fearing weakness and death. His quest for power had been rooted in a desperate desire to survive. To *thrive*. That side of him had been so dominant that it was difficult to stifle the instinct and face his doom.

His voice was steady as he uttered the spell. "*I, Osiris of the Underworld, offer my blood and soul, my god's magic, the very essence of my being, to bring this body back to life. May spirit and soul reunite with flesh. Take this sacrifice, and with it, make her whole once more.*"

He took the chalice from Lagos and brought it to his lips. He downed the elixir in one gulp. It burned against his throat, searing his insides. His blood boiled as the scorching potion worked its way through his body, melting him from the inside out.

Something cracked within him, and he hunched over with a groan. The crack reverberated through his body, snapping bones and breaking him one piece at a time. Darkness flooded his vision. In seconds, he was on the ground, writhing in pain.

Snap. Snap. Snap.

One by one, his limbs failed him. He lost sensation in his fingers, arms, toes, and legs. He could no longer scream, no longer make a sound. Soon, all that was left was the rapid thundering of his heart, thrashing against his ribcage.

After a moment, that stopped, too. And Cyrus was no more.

AWAKE
PRUE

THE SOUND OF THE ROARING OCEAN FILLED Prue's ears. Blissful sleep claimed her, clinging to her even as she returned to full consciousness. She kept her eyes closed, wishing to linger in this state of rest for a bit longer.

She was so tired. So very tired.

A soft hum of contentment filled her throat as she turned her head, relishing the warm sand against her skin. A gentle breeze whispered across her flesh.

She knew in her heart she was in Krenia. Back home. If she opened her eyes, perhaps she would see Mona sitting alongside her. Or her mother.

Awareness crept into her thoughts. Something tugged within her chest—a feeling of bitterness and resentment toward her mother. But why? Why would there be anything but serenity in her heart right now? This was utter perfection.

But the unsettled feeling within her only grew, like drops of light amidst a sea of darkness. As she scrutinized it, clarity burned in her mind, and her eyes flew open.

It was indeed the beach in Krenia. The late afternoon sun hung low in the sky, illuminating the cerulean waves before her.

And next to her in the sand was not Mona, but Gaia.

The goddess of the earth.

She looked like the mother Prue had grown up with. Black curls. Blue eyes. A simple burgundy dress that draped over one shoulder. She hugged her knees against her chest, her eyes fixed on the horizon, and a look of peace on her face.

Was this a hallucination?

Prue grew rigid, her limbs oddly sluggish as she sat up straighter at the sight of her mother.

Gaia sighed and turned to look at Prue with a sad smile on her face. "Hello, daughter."

Prue struggled to control her breathing as reality settled around her. She wore a crimson dress, torn and smeared with dust and dirt. She was *not* in Krenia. The last she remembered, she was...

She jumped to her feet, alarm racing through her. "Cyrus! Where is he? I have to—"

"Relax, Prudence," Gaia said soothingly. "He is well. You are not really in Krenia right now."

Prue's heart wouldn't stop hammering in her chest. She'd been in Tartarus. Pandora's box was opened. And the cavern walls collapsed on her and Cyrus. Was he still alive? Why was she here? This place was so familiar and yet...

"I'm between worlds," Prue realized. She'd been here once before, when she'd tumbled down the mountain and almost died. Cyrus had brought her back with his soul magic.

Mona had been here. And Prue had yearned to stay.

Now, with Gaia here instead, Prue wanted nothing more than to leave.

"How do I get back?" she snapped at Gaia.

"It isn't that simple," Gaia said, her voice still frustratingly calm. "You are here until a powerful magical force can bring you back. The fact that you are awake means it won't be long now."

"Why are you here?" Prue couldn't keep the bite out of her voice. "Where's Mona?"

"You cannot always control who comes to you in this place."

Prue's stomach dropped. "Are you—Are you dead?" Mona had been dead when she'd visited Prue here. Prue hated the dread that filled her at the thought. This woman next to her had lied to her for her entire life.

And yet, no matter how many lies she told, it wouldn't change the fact that Gaia was her mother. As much as Prue wanted to hate her, she would be devastated if Gaia was dead.

Gaia smiled again, but her eyes were grim. "No. But there are dark forces coming for me. Neither you nor I can stop them."

Prue found herself slowly sinking into the sand to sit alongside Gaia once more. As angry as she was with her mother, she still had so many questions. "What dark forces?"

"The magic of Pandora."

Prue stiffened at the name of her second sister—the sister she hadn't known existed until recently. "Why?" Her voice was cautious. She wasn't sure she would like the answer.

Gaia said nothing for a long moment. She inhaled deeply, her eyes still fixed on the horizon. At last, she said, "It is a long story. And I fear it will take too long to tell you here. But I *do* wish for you to know everything, Prudence. Perhaps you will not hate me so much if you understand the full truth. Will you allow me to share my memories with you?"

Prue hesitated. "What does that entail?"

"I will imbue my earth magic into you. With it comes my memories."

"Imbue?"

"Pandora is coming for me, and I refuse to fight her. It will make it easier if I am powerless."

Prue's head reared back. "You want to give all of your magic to me? Mama, you *can't*."

Moisture sparkled in Gaia's eyes, but she continued to smile. "My magic can do nothing for me because of my curse. But I can use it for others. It will only be a fraction of my true power, but hopefully it will help you rebuild the Underworld."

Prue's heart clenched at the reminder. The Underworld had become her home. And with Kronos defeated, she had hoped to live there happily with Cyrus, finally able to celebrate their marriage and rule side by side.

But it had been destroyed by Pandora's magic.

Pandora. The lying, deceitful woman wanted to take everything from Prue. Her home. Her people.

Now, her mother.

Prue's fingers curled into tight fists. "There has to be something we can do to stop her."

Gaia stretched her hand toward Prue. After a moment, Prue took it, squeezing her mother's fingers.

"My memories will give you all the information you need," Gaia said. "Take them, Prudence. Please. Consider it a peace offering. An apology from me for the deception and lies. You deserved better. So did Mona."

A knot formed in Prue's throat. "What about Sybil?"

Gaia's lower lip trembled, and she dropped her gaze.

Tears spilled down her cheeks. "She deserved better, too." Her voice shook.

"Mama," Prue whispered, drawing closer so she could wrap her arms around Gaia. Gaia tucked her arm around her waist and stroked her hair, just as she had when Prue was a child.

"You are fierce and strong," Gaia murmured, her voice soft and gentle. It was the same voice that used to lull Prue to sleep every night. "So much stronger than I ever thought you could be. I wish I had seen it before. You are a queen, Prudence. The Underworld needs you. And with my powers, you can rebuild it. You can create a home for all those lost souls."

Prue's eyes grew hot, and she shut them tightly, trying to ward off the grief that threatened to consume her. Gaia would die. *Her mother* would die.

How could she accept this? She wasn't ready. There were still so many things she needed to say, so many questions she needed to ask.

"Prue," whispered a voice. It was distant, as if echoing across the waves.

"He calls to you," Gaia said, withdrawing to look at the horizon once more.

Prue sniffed and wiped a stray tear from her cheek, following her mother's gaze. A bright light glowed from afar, lightening the sky and reaching toward Prue. It grew closer and closer, practically blinding her.

"There isn't much time now," Gaia said. "Give me your hands, Prudence. This will only work if you accept it."

"But I *don't* accept it!" Prue cried. "Mama, you are giving up! I brought Mona back—surely, I can bring you back, too!"

"It doesn't work like that, and we are out of time," Gaia said, her voice more urgent. "*Please*, Prudence. It will all make sense soon. But you must trust me."

The light burned in the sky, and Prue's ears started ringing. Soon, she couldn't see anything except the outline of her mother's figure in front of her. Everything else was consumed by the glow.

"Prue!" a voice shouted.

It was Cyrus. She knew it was him. No one else had the power to bring her back. No one else called to her soul like he did.

Of course he found a way. Every part of her body yearned to be near him, to hold him, to convince herself he was all right after everything that had happened.

But Gaia...

"Prudence!" Gaia urged.

Panic flooded Prue's mind at the prospect of leaving her mother—of never seeing her again. With a sob, she stretched out her hands, catching her mother's fingers. Power slammed into her, burrowing deep into her mind, tearing through her like sharpened claws. She screamed as the light exploded around her. Her body jerked forward, carried away by the intensity of magic flowing around her.

The last she heard was her mother's echoing promise: "I will always love you."

MEMORIES
PANDORA

PANDORA WAS LYING ON AN ALTAR MADE OF marble, the icy surface chilling her bare skin as she was strapped to it. Her writhing and thrashing made no difference. Apollo's magic held her in place, overpowering her.

"Be still," Apollo ordered. "This will hurt far more if you resist."

But Pandora didn't care how much it hurt. He planned to erase her existence. What did it matter how much pain it caused?

If she merely gave in, it would mean admitting defeat. And she would *never* do that. She wouldn't give the bastard the satisfaction.

"Janus," Aidoneus said in warning. He stood a few paces away from the altar, his long, dark hair falling into his face. His arms were clasped behind his back, and from beneath his goatee, he was frowning.

"Don't call me that," Apollo snapped. "That name belongs to someone else. Someone weak. I am only Apollo now."

"Very well then, *Apollo*. We must do this quickly." Aidoneus's brow creased as he looked at Pandora with a mixture of pity and regret.

"Patience, brother," Apollo said, flexing his fingers and closing his eyes. "Spells like this take time."

"I... will... slaughter... you... both," Pandora growled, still raging against Apollo's magic.

Apollo only smirked at her. "You'll do nothing once we're through with you."

Pandora roared in rage, shoving more forcefully, throwing all of her energy against him.

Apollo grunted, his jaw taut as he fought to control her. "Aidoneus," he warned.

Dark shadows swirled around Pandora, slithering like serpents. They tightened, coiling around her until she could no longer move. A silent scream tore at her throat, but she couldn't even speak.

"I'm sorry," Aidoneus whispered, and the grief in his eyes was so potent that she almost believed him. "But there is no other way. We must contain these dark forces somehow."

Pandora wanted to spit in his face, but she could do nothing more than glare at him.

"Spare your apologies," Apollo said, waving an idle hand. "She isn't worth it. It's her own damn fault this dark magic is wreaking havoc across the realms. It's only fitting she should be sacrificed to put a stop to it."

"But she is a goddess," Aidoneus argued. "She is one of us."

"She rescinded that title when she dabbled with the magic of the Titans," Apollo snarled. "You said it yourself: there is no other way."

Aidoneus fell silent, his lips growing thin and the wrinkle between his brows deepening. Pandora wanted to yell at him, to shake him. His sympathy toward her meant nothing if he was only going to stand by and watch her be sacrificed.

Something hot dripped onto her bare chest. She didn't have to look to know it was Apollo's blood.

Tears burned in her eyes. She couldn't fight this. She couldn't do anything.

Or could she?

Magic burned in her veins, struggling to be freed. Aidoneus and Apollo may have chained her with magic, but she could still wrap her powers around her own soul. Her own essence.

If she couldn't cast magic outward, then she would have to cast it inward.

Blood of my blood, she thought, closing her eyes to channel her energy into her very being. *I summon these dark forces and bind you in a curse. Let them suffer. Let them feel my wrath. Let them be consumed by my fury for all eternity.*

Let my rage never die. As long as they shall live, so, too, will my vengeance.

Power thrummed within her. The ground began to quake, and dust rained from the ceiling.

"Now, Apollo," Aidoneus groaned, no doubt struggling to contain Pandora. He thought she was trying to escape.

But he was wrong. And soon, he would be begging for mercy.

The thought made her want to laugh. She still could not speak, but her laughter echoed in her mind, ringing through her body. It continued to pulse within her, even as Apollo's spell ripped her apart. Her flesh burned. Her bones broke. Sunlight and flame devoured her completely.

And still, she laughed.

With a jolt, Pandora awoke, her throat raw from her screams. Sweat coated her entire body, leaving her hair sticky against her neck. Her shift clung to her body, and her bedsheets were tangled around her legs. Her heart slammed against her rib cage, thundering louder than the storm raging in her mind. She pressed the heels of her hands against her eyes, trying to block out the pain and trauma of those memories.

"They aren't mine," she whispered. "It wasn't me. It didn't happen to me."

But it *did* happen. It happened to the real Pandora ages ago. Long before she was born and absorbed Pandora's vengeful soul.

Before Apollo's magic ripped her apart, Pandora had cursed him to live with her vengeance until he died.

And Apollo's solution had been to imbue that curse into one of Gaia's daughters. He shoved the problem into an innocent child, forcing the broken and damaged remnants of a fallen goddess into a brand new vessel as if he could wipe his hands clean of the mess she had caused.

Pandora covered her face with her hands as violent sobs wracked her body. Her shoulders shook. Her stomach heaved.

She couldn't stay in this stifling room a moment longer.

The moon hung high in the sky, casting an eerie glow on the restless waters below. Somewhere in Elysium, Selene, the moon goddess, was keeping the brilliant white orb aloft in the sky.

Pandora hadn't met Selene, but she respected her. In some religions, Hecate was seen as the goddess of the dark moon, and Selene was revered as her ally. If Pandora hadn't been so consumed with her plan for revenge, she might have become friends with the goddess.

She might have done a lot of things differently, were it not for her revenge.

Just a bit longer, and you'll be free, she told herself. *Soon...*

After wrapping a shawl around herself, Pandora strode toward the doors of her room, then faltered, her gaze turning to the open balcony doors.

No, she wouldn't be using the doors at all. She had a better idea.

A slow smile spread across her face as she discarded her shawl and walked to the edge of the balcony, running her hands along the intricately carved railing. A quick glance at the beach below showed her there was no one else around. With a deep breath, she conjured her earth magic.

It had been dormant for so long that it was difficult for her to summon it at first. But after a moment, she felt long, winding roots spreading from within her, winding around the pillars and beams. Her smile only grew as her branches lengthened, sprouting leaves, twisting and twining as they obediently made their way toward her. A breath of satisfaction loosed in her chest.

This was one thing that was truly and uniquely hers. Her own particular magic. Not the magic of a goddess who lived hundreds of years before. But *hers.*

Sometimes, Pandora didn't know who she was without this aching soul shoved within her. If the soul were removed, would anything remain? Was there anything left besides the trauma and the suffering?

Once she was free, would she cease to exist?

She had spent her whole life believing her essence was tethered to that of the goddess from so long ago. That without that goddess, her entire existence would mean nothing.

But this right here, her tree branches, a mark of her earth magic from Gaia, was proof that she was someone beyond these festering wounds inside her.

"I am more than just a vessel for Apollo to toy with," Pandora whispered to herself. She flexed her fingers, and her branches drew closer until they twisted around her arm, as if welding her to its roots. With a flex of her other arm, her branches did the same on that side. She was one with the roots. A part of the trees.

She closed her eyes, summoning her power, until the branches lifted her above the balcony railing. Then, she was flying, carried by her magic, the strong and sturdy roots clasping her firmly. She knew she would not fall.

This magic, she trusted. More than she trusted herself.

The wind whipped at her hair, rustling her shift, sending cool air against her sweat-slicked skin. It felt glorious, this freeing feeling. Like she could finally breathe after years of suffocating.

The branches brought her to the ground, depositing her gently before they receded into the earth. She couldn't risk anyone catching her using earth magic. Her heart twisted with grief as she watched them vanish, wishing they would linger for a bit longer.

But the risk was too great.

With a heavy sigh, she climbed down the boulders that lined the outer castle wall and made her way toward the courtyard, using the moon to light her way.

When she found a figure sitting on the courtyard steps, she froze. Alarm raced through her. Who was it? Had they seen her earth magic? Why were they here?

After a moment, her heart thundering in her chest, she realized the figure faced away from her and was hardly moving, save for the rise and fall of his shoulders.

It didn't take her long to recognize him. It was Sol.

Frowning, Pandora continued her approach, but Sol did not turn. He sat motionless on the steps, his gaze directed toward the sea.

She wasn't sure why she did it. But she was curious to know why he was out here. So Pandora dropped onto the steps alongside him, watching the ocean as well.

Several silent minutes passed. Sol didn't acknowledge her presence. He didn't even look her way.

But that was fine. Pandora was certain if he opened his mouth, he would say something to irritate her. She preferred the silence.

After a long while, Pandora could keep quiet no more. With amusement in her voice, she said, "What, no midnight swim? This seems like the perfect time to shed your clothes and go for a dip."

It wasn't until after she said it that she realized it sounded like an invitation. Her face heated, but she didn't take it back.

If he offered to swim naked with her once again, she would not refuse. The idea was far too alluring.

Sol huffed a short, quiet laugh but kept his eyes forward. "No. The moon is too sacred for that."

Pandora's brow furrowed at the grim note in his voice. His expression held not even a hint of a smile or a shadow of the usual smirk he wore. His dark eyes were full of sorrow.

She followed his gaze again, only then realizing he was staring at the moon, not the sea.

"You know it's just an illusion, right?" she asked. "It isn't really the moon."

"It is for me." Sol sighed. "Besides, someone has to raise it, don't they? After all, that's my job with the sun."

Pandora stared at him. "You raise the sun in Elysium?" She'd always assumed the sun and moon gods only worked in the mortal realm. Then she remembered Sol had never been to the mortal realm.

"Yes. But Apollo wants to train me in the mortal realm. He detests it there and has yearned to find someone to take his place."

Ah. It all made sense now. That was why Apollo wanted Sol to take his place as the sun god. The bastard didn't want to associate with mortals any longer.

"Is that why you're out here sulking?" Pandora asked.

Sol finally turned to look at her. The heaviness in his eyes seemed to drag her down along with him. Gods above, the pure devastation on his face was almost too much to bear. Her smile vanished, and regret took its place.

She shouldn't be teasing him. She wasn't sure why, but he was out here grieving.

"Sol," she whispered, feeling the insane urge to reach for him.

"It doesn't matter if I'm here or in the mortal realm," Sol said quietly. "It follows me wherever I go."

Pandora's lips parted, and her throat went dry. She desperately wanted to know what pain he suffered from, but at the same time, a sense of foreboding filled her. Perhaps she *didn't* want to know. If she did, it would make her sympathize with him more.

And she couldn't afford that.

Even so, she couldn't stop herself from asking, "What follows you?"

He offered a sad smile. It was so different from the usual smug satisfaction she witnessed from him that she couldn't help but stare. The corners of his mouth curved upward slightly. His dark eyes were full of potent emotion and anguish. The lines of his face were gentle but weary.

He looked like a completely different person.

"Good night, Trivia." Sol rose to his feet and walked away, his slow and soft steps retreating as Pandora watched him leave.

When she was alone, she faced the sea once more. The moon hung so low it almost brushed the waves. Even if she didn't know exactly what Sol had been referring to, she felt a sense of familiarity with his words.

It follows me wherever I go.

Yes, she understood this concept intimately. Her thirst for vengeance. Her memories of another time and another being.

It all followed her, too. Relentless and unforgiving.

Was Sol suffering from something similar? Was it

possible his arrogance and casual pleasure-seeking persona were only masks he wore for the world to see?

Pandora could understand that, too.

She turned, looking over her shoulder for Sol's retreating form, tempted to call him back.

But he had vanished.

CLUES
MONA

MONA STILL WASN'T SURE WHAT TO MAKE OF Hestia. For now, she would follow her, knowing there were no other options.

But that didn't mean she trusted her.

"Where is the second portal?" Mona asked as they weaved through the cream-colored buildings.

"The gates," Hestia said without glancing back at her. "At the edge of the village."

Mona frowned, hurrying to keep up with Hestia's brisk pace. The goddess's legs were much longer than her own. "Do you think it's possible Evander is still there?"

"Not at all. Being so close to the village, this portal is far more public. If he *did* come this way, he likely hid immediately, or was captured by the royal guard. Either way, we will find remnants of his magic, and that will give us a clue as to where he went."

Panic and terror tightened in Mona's chest at the thought of Evander arriving in a foreign place, surrounded by strangers and possibly enemies.

All while fighting for his life as his dark curse consumed him.

"This Evander," Hestia said. "What is he to you?"

"As I said," Mona said carefully, "he is my friend."

Hestia gave her a sly smile over her shoulder. "I gather he is more than that, little witch. I scent his demon magic all over you. You are his mate."

Mona tried to hide her wince, but Hestia chuckled.

"Fear not, child. I will not share your secrets."

"You keep saying I should trust you, but it isn't that simple," Mona said. "I know you are powerful. I know you are revered by witches. But that doesn't mean I believe you."

To her surprise, Hestia nodded. "I would consider you a fool if you did. That is why I am proving my loyalty by guiding you to the portal. But I won't lie to you, Mona. It is very likely he's been captured. Or worse."

Or worse.

Mona swallowed hard, unwilling to consider the worst. Instead, she focused on that word: *mate.*

It sounded so animalistic. Like a basic need to fulfill. So simple compared to what she truly felt for Evander.

He was more than her mate. He was her soul. The melody of her song.

It took all of her restraint not to scream, to pound her fist into the earth and summon her magic, to track down Trivia and wring her throat for what she had done.

Why? Why had she taken Evander? To kill him? Or was there something else Mona wasn't seeing?

She wracked her brain, remembering the events leading up to her passage through the portal.

Evander had vanished. At first, Mona believed Trivia had abducted him. But Evander was more powerful than that. He would have fought.

No... He must have followed her.

He had figured something out. Something Trivia wanted to keep quiet. *That* was why she had taken him through the portal. Not to kill him.

But to silence him.

"You are awfully quiet," Hestia commented. The statement wasn't accusatory, but observant.

"I worry for him," Mona admitted. There was no use in denying it. Hestia could already sense that much.

"I am surprised you care for him so. Magic like yours does not mingle well with the magic of a death god."

"Ours does," Mona said. "He was the guardian of my

soul in the spirit world. My soul remains anchored to his even now."

Hestia stopped in her tracks, her spine going rigid. Slowly, she turned to face Mona, her eyes flaring wide. "The guardian of your soul?" Her voice was deadly quiet.

Alarm raced through Mona's chest, and her pulse quickened. "Yes."

"Are you saying you died? That you went to the Underworld as a spirit?"

Mona's thoughts spun as she tried to reach whatever conclusion Hestia had come to. "Yes."

Hestia approached her and placed her warm hands on Mona's shoulders, bending low to meet her gaze. "Mona, this is very important. When you came back from the dead, was your magic different?"

Mona's mouth turned dry as she reflected back to her resurrection. She hadn't done much with her magic until she'd returned to the Underworld, and even then, things had been hazy because she had lost her memories. It was the price she had paid to return.

But one memory burned bright within her—a memory she would cling to until her dying breath.

It was the moment her memories returned to her. The moment she had rescued Evander from Kronos's clutches, her magic burning to life and allowing her to heal him.

The ground had cracked, and her earth magic sprang to life, not in the form of roses as it had once been, but thorny brambles.

"Yes," Mona repeated. "Why is this important to you?"

Hestia glanced left, then right, as if searching for eavesdroppers. She grasped Mona's elbow and pulled her into the shadow of an alley and leaned close, her murmured whispers rushed and intense. "There is an ancient tale of three earth witches whose magic is rooted in both the Underworld and Elysium. Only once their mortal skins have been shed can they unlock the full powers of the Triple Goddess."

Mona shook her head in confusion. "I don't understand. What does that have to do with me? And why are you speaking as if this is something to fear?"

"Because if you have died and returned and your magic has changed, it is quite possible you are one of the three witches. It is possible this prophecy will soon be fulfilled." Hestia leaned closer, her words barely more than a whisper. "And it means Apollo will hunt you down and destroy you."

Mona's head reared back. "*What?*" she hissed. "Why?"

"He wishes to keep his throne," Hestia said, her words coming out in a rush. "All who challenge him have failed or died, the last being Gaia herself. She was cast out of Elysium as punishment. He is desperate to hold the crown of Elysium, and he will stop at nothing to keep that power. There are rumors that he was behind the demise of his predecessors. Nothing can be proven, but the clues are there, Mona. Be very, very cautious. It will take little to no effort for him to wipe you from existence and sever this prophecy before it is completed."

Mona's heart lurched at every word, her breaths turning sharp and ragged. "But surely this doesn't apply to me. Surely there are other earth witches out there who are more fit for this?"

"It doesn't matter. Whether you are one of the three or not, it is irrelevant. If Apollo catches wind that there is even a *chance* you might be related to the prophecy, he will end you without question. The throne means that much to him."

Mona licked her lips, thinking fast. Fear clenched a tight fist around her heart, but she clung to her own knowledge of Elysium and the history of gods and goddesses to keep her mind from succumbing to terror.

"Jupiter," she recalled. "He was defeated centuries ago."

Hestia nodded. "He was not the only one. Athena. Demeter. Several others. Some challenged his claim to the throne, but others did not. There were always whispers that those who vanished had either plotted against Apollo or held information about how to defeat him."

Mona's eyes snapped to Hestia. "And where do you stand in all of this? Do you support Apollo? And if you do not, then how are you still here? How has he not killed you as well?"

Hestia's mouth curved in a satisfied smile. "You are wise to ask these questions of me. Fear not, I do not support Apollo. Gaia was one of my dearest friends."

Mona's stomach tumbled at those words. This woman—this *goddess*—had been friends with her mother?

Did Hestia realize Mona was Gaia's daughter? Was that why she was helping her?

"But, unfortunately, I have not escaped Apollo's punishment, either. I, too, am cursed."

Mona took an unconscious step back from Hestia, her skin tingling with unease.

Hestia laughed. "Fear not. It will not affect you. It only affects how I interact with my acolytes. I am unable to assist them in the mortal realm. I am... cut off from my people." Sorrow filled her eyes.

Mona's heart twisted. Hestia was revered among fire witches, and yet she could not help them. She could do *nothing* for them.

Gaia had mentioned that she, too, was cursed. She could only access a fraction of her power, and she was stranded in the mortal realm.

Oh yes, Apollo certainly knew what he was doing. It

seemed as if he had cursed both goddesses so they could not interact with one another again. They could no longer plot his downfall.

Mona wasn't sure what she believed. She didn't even know Apollo. Perhaps he was a good ruler. Perhaps the people of Elysium were protected under his care. It was entirely possible that both Hestia and Gaia were wrong to oppose him.

But a feeling deep within Mona's chest ached with the knowledge that people were suffering and dying under Apollo's watch. Gods and goddesses were mysteriously vanishing.

Her own mother had been cursed and ripped away from her magic. The very essence of her being. Mona didn't think very highly of Gaia, particularly because she had lied to her daughters their entire lives, but she still didn't wish such a fate on her.

"I am sorry you have suffered because of him," Mona said softly. "I vow to do what I can to help."

Hestia's smile grew. "I knew you would. I admit I have selfish intentions in helping you. If you *are* a part of this prophecy, then you are the key to bringing down Apollo."

Mona quickly shook her head. "I make no such promise. That isn't why I'm here."

"I know. But still, I hope. Besides, if we do find this Evander of yours, then he may be able to help as well. A death god is powerful and will not be tied down by the magic of Elysium."

"He has other forces that tie him down," Mona said darkly.

Hestia's expression sobered. "Yes, I know. Come. We are almost there."

She tugged Mona out of the shadows, and they continued winding between buildings. Gradually, the path widened and the buildings grew more scarce, making way for neatly trimmed bushes and lush gardens. They reached a wide courtyard flanked by mighty pillars with ornate carvings sculpted into them. A wrought-iron gate spanned the length between the outer walls of the courtyard, and Mona's chest fluttered with fear at what she saw.

The gate doors were crushed, the metal bent at unnatural angles. One door had been torn clean off, as if a feral creature had ripped it free.

Evander.

Hestia sucked in a sharp breath, her red eyes darting around the scene. But they were completely alone.

"I believe this is our first clue," Hestia murmured.

Mona nodded numbly, too shocked to reply.

Hestia inhaled, her eyes closing for a moment. "I only smell death magic. Nothing else. It's likely the guards have not found him yet." She grasped Mona's arm again. "This is good, Mona."

Mona tried to focus on breathing, but her heart continued to flutter wildly within her chest, making each inhale a strain on her lungs. She remembered how uncontrollable and savage Evander had been when he'd succumbed to Typhon. It had been ages since she'd seen that particular side of him—now that he and Typhon had merged, he had seemed in complete control of the beast.

But if he was dying, she had no idea what he was capable of becoming.

"You don't understand," Mona whispered in a shaky voice. "If he is like *this*"—she gestured to the misshapen gate—"then I fear what he will do." She turned to Hestia, her eyes hot with tears. "Hestia, I worry he will kill someone." She closed her eyes, struggling to breathe evenly. A million thoughts and fears raced through her mind.

What if I can't find him in time?

What if he hurts someone?

What if someone hurts him?

And, louder than all the rest, one particular thought screamed in her head, over and over: *How do I find him?*

"Breathe, little witch." Hestia's warm hands pressed into her shoulders, grounding her. Only then did Mona realize she was wheezing, struggling to inhale, to keep herself afloat.

"You have a quick mind," Hestia said, her voice low

and soothing. "Use it. Do not fall prey to this fear. You are stronger than this."

Prue's reminder coursed through her: *You are not a coward, Mona. You are brave.*

"Use my mind," Mona whispered. Gradually, clarity broke through her panicked thoughts, and her breathing slowed.

Her eyes flared wide with realization. In the Underworld, Evander had always managed to find her when he needed to. They were linked that way.

Perhaps she could do the same to locate him.

"I know what to do," she said as a plan began to take form. "I know how to find him."

RAGE

PANDORA

NOT SURPRISINGLY, PANDORA AWOKE THE NEXT morning with a splitting headache, the echoes of nightmares still haunting her thoughts. Every time she closed her eyes, she saw Apollo's steely glare or Aidoneus's dark eyes full of pity. She heard her own screams of anguish and rage.

She felt the power of her final spell—her curse—thrumming in her veins.

Pandora had spent her entire life despising Apollo and Aidoenus for what they had done.

But deep down, she harbored a more potent hatred for the goddess who had cast the curse in the first place. The goddess whose thoughts and memories she now bore.

If it weren't for that curse, Pandora would have been free.

But how could she exact revenge on a person who no longer existed? All that remained were her memories.

So Pandora focused on those she *could* punish. She had successfully destroyed Aidoneus's home—and the god himself. He had already become a shell of the man he once was. His demise was easy. Pandora only needed to push, and he had fallen.

Aidoneus had been ready to die. That much she knew.

But Apollo? This revenge would be so much sweeter. He had plans. Ambition. Pride.

And she would tear it all away from him, piece by piece.

Pandora remained in her bed for as long as time would allow, twisted up in the sheets with fluffy pillows covering her face to block out the blinding light of the sun streaming in through the window. Every time she glimpsed the brilliant light, she felt Apollo's magic ripping her body apart. She heard those screams once again.

She couldn't bear it.

So, she kept herself buried under pillows and blankets, not wanting to rise ever again.

Hours of fitful sleep later, a servant burst into her

rooms. She didn't move, hoping they would leave, until a gentle hand jostled her.

"Wake, my lady," said a timid voice. "I must get you dressed."

Pandora groaned and threw the pillows off her face. "I am perfectly capable of dressing myself."

"Yes, my lady. But I also must get you fitted for your gown."

Pandora blinked sleepily as the pale, rosy-cheeked face of the servant came into focus. "My gown?"

The woman bit her lip and nodded, as if worried Pandora would thrash her.

"A gown for what?" Pandora couldn't keep the dread out of her voice.

"For the solstice ball."

Pandora sat up, her head throbbing from the movement. The servant staggered back a few steps, clearly alarmed at the look on her face.

"This realm is on the brink of destruction by means of dark magic, and they are throwing a *ball*?" Pandora asked incredulously, her voice rising.

The servant wrung her hands together and dropped her gaze. "Yes, my lady. It is an annual tradition. The realm has always celebrated the summer solstice. Not once has it been missed."

Ah. Summer solstice. The longest day of the year. Of

course Apollo wouldn't miss an opportunity to celebrate the day of the most sunlight.

Clarity burned in Pandora's mind as she remembered what Sol had told her the night before. He would be replacing Apollo and leaving for the mortal realm soon.

What better time to announce this appointment than the solstice ball?

Pandora threw the blankets off the bed and rose to her feet. The servant skittered backward again. Only then did Pandora realize she held a bundle of red satin fabric in her hands.

"My—My lady?" she asked uncertainly.

"I have to go," Pandora said, striding to the wardrobe and throwing open the doors, searching for the simplest dress to wear. She had to find Sol.

"B-but your gown..." the servant protested.

Pandora whirled to face her, noting the panic and fear in the girl's face. Gods, this poor thing was downright terrified.

No doubt she was under orders to dress Pandora appropriately for this godsforsaken ball. And she would likely be punished if Pandora gave her any trouble.

Pandora threw her head back with another groan, resisting the urge to scream, as she was certain it would only frighten the servant even more.

"What's your name?" she asked with a heavy sigh.

"Mera," the woman said, bobbing a quick curtsy.

Pandora nodded once. "All right, Mera. I will let you take my measurements and dress me for the day, if you can do one thing for me in return."

Mera's face twisted with unease. "Yes, my lady?"

Pandora was already at the desk in the corner, hastily scribbling a message on a sheet of parchment. When she was finished, she folded it and handed it to Mera. "Get this to Lord Sol as soon as you can."

Mera visibly relaxed, as if she had been expecting far worse. Perhaps Pandora already had a reputation for being a troublemaker. The servant set the fabric down on the edge of the bed and took the parchment. "Of course, my lady." She closed her eyes, and a humming sound filled the room. The parchment glowed a brilliant white before vanishing, leaving a tiny puff of smoke in its wake.

Pandora's eyes widened. "What was that?"

Mera smiled. "The magic of Hermes lives in my bloodline, my lady."

Hermes—the messenger of the gods. Technically a deity himself, but because of his responsibility to the other gods, he was seen as inferior. Just like Pandora. While Hermes himself had perished hundreds of years ago, she wasn't at all surprised that the gods of Elysium had found a way to preserve his magic. After all, it was far too convenient.

"Damn," Pandora muttered with a soft chuckle.

"That's awfully helpful." She turned to Mera, determined to make the servant feel at ease in her presence. It was the least she could do. "Come now, Mera. Show me that fabric you've got."

Two hours later, Pandora paced the length of the library, fisting her violet skirts in her hands as she waited for Sol to arrive. She had been nothing but patient as Mera tended to her, and then she had flown down the staircase to meet Sol.

Only to find he wasn't here yet.

Perhaps he hadn't seen her message yet? Or perhaps he was with Apollo.

It didn't matter. Pandora would wait.

Another half hour passed, and Pandora had stopped pacing and was now sitting by the window, her eyes following the motion of the waves in the sea. Up and down. Rough, then calm once more.

It was strangely soothing to her. Despite the depth of each wave, the ocean always became smooth once more. Even if only for a moment.

Loud footsteps echoed nearby, and she heaved a sigh of relief, rising to her feet.

"About damn time," she snapped, turning to see Sol

marching toward her. She froze at the look of darkness and rage on his face.

"Who the hell do you think you are?" he barked. He wore his usual tunic of royal blue, his long blond hair neat and combed back.

But his eyes were full of venom and hatred.

Pandora's head reared back. "Excuse me?"

"You think you can just summon me like I am your lackey? Like I have nothing better to do than cater to your needs?"

Her eyes narrowed. "I wasn't summoning you. I asked you to meet me in the library. Or did you forget we have a task to accomplish?"

"Did *you* forget that Apollo has reassigned me?" Sol bit out. "Our work together is finished. We have no need to associate with one another any longer."

Pandora's eyes grew wide. Was he serious? Just like that, they were done working together?

She should have felt relief. How many times had she yearned to be finished with this arrogant asshole?

And yet, her stomach dropped, and an icy coldness crept through her body.

Sol continued to glare at her, and his expression of bitterness and anger only made her own defiance rise up to meet it.

"What's the matter with you?" she demanded. "The

last time I asked you to meet in the library, you simply ignored me and painted in your room."

Sol's nostrils flared, his lips growing thin. A muscle feathered in his jaw.

Pandora's eyebrows lifted. "Ah, I understand. You weren't in your room this time, were you?" She crossed her arms and gave him a smug smile. "Where were you, Sol? Were you in another woman's chambers? Were you embarrassed to have such a *lesser* god as me requesting your presence?" She paused, scrutinizing him, the rigid set to his shoulders, the stiff fists at his side.

No, if Sol had been with another woman, he wouldn't have been this furious. He would have merely laughed it off.

What would have gotten him so angry?

Cold realization settled along Pandora's skin. "You were with Apollo."

"Yes," Sol seethed. "And do you know what he told me? He felt the presence of dark magic—*Pandora's* magic—against the wards early this morning. He strengthened the wards in time to deflect it, but without Hestia here, he can't fully reinforce them. Dammit, Trivia, he is furious with us. Furious with *me*! What the hell were you doing yesterday? I thought you intended to strengthen the wards so this wouldn't happen!"

Pandora's eyes widened as she struggled to process this information.

Her spell had worked. Pandora's magic had tried to get through.

But Apollo had been alerted. And he'd stopped it.

Now he was suspicious of her.

Shit, shit, shit...

"This is the one thing you're good for, Trivia," Sol spat, his face contorted with rage. "The *only* reason we allowed you to stay here. If you aren't able to do this one simple task, then maybe you should leave the realm."

Pandora's mind finally caught up, and she stared hard at Sol. "You really are a child, aren't you? Poor little Sol got reprimanded by Papa, so he's taking it out on me. Understand this: it isn't *my* fault Apollo has no faith in you. It isn't *my* fault he already believes you to be incompetent, and this incident is only further proof of that. I *was* doing my job yesterday. And what were you doing? Swimming in the godsdamned sea! Did you tell Apollo that? When you should have been assisting me, you neglected your duties to play instead."

Sol stepped closer to her. Though he stood taller than her, she still glared up at him, refusing to back down. "Understand this, little goddess: I don't give a shit about you or your magic. I don't give a shit where you live. You can crawl into Tartarus and rot for all I care. You are *nothing*. And you always will be."

Pandora offered him a cruel smile. "You can't hurt me, Sol. But it's cute that you think your words mean anything to me." She scoffed and shook her head. "And to think I was actually worried about you."

His brows knitted together. "What?"

Damn. She hadn't meant to say that aloud.

Half Sol's mouth quirked upward in that infuriating smirk. But coupled with the rage in his eyes, the expression was downright terrifying, like a predator closing in on its prey. "You were worried about me? Ah, Trivia. Perhaps I should have warned you about the effect I have on women. I can't say I'm sorry you fell victim to my charms."

Pandora rolled her eyes. "Get over yourself, Sol. I was only worried you wouldn't survive when you leave for the mortal realm tomorrow. But now?" She shrugged. "I hope the humans destroy you. And when they do, I will only laugh."

Sol's smirk faded, and the bright fury in his eyes dimmed. "Ah. Yes. No doubt you heard Apollo will be announcing my appointment at the ball tonight." He tilted his head at her, looking her over. "And that made you *worried*?"

Pandora threw her hands in the air. "After last night? Yes."

"Last night?"

"Do you not remember? You were... not yourself."

"I was taking a midnight stroll."

"You were staring at the ocean as if you wanted to drown yourself."

Sol's mouth curved upward again. "Well damn, Pandora. You *do* have a heart." He pressed a hand to his chest and gave her a look of mock sympathy. "Did you pity the poor god? Did you fall for my act last night?" He snorted and shook his head. "You are as shallow as the other goddesses I lure to my bed."

Pandora stepped back. "That was an *act*?"

Sol barked out a laugh. "Of course it was! Do you really think I would be sitting out there *reflecting on my feelings* of my own accord? You think it was mere coincidence I ran into you? No. I heard you climb down from your balcony, so I positioned myself in your path, hoping to snare you." He sighed. "I truly thought it would work. But perhaps it was for the best. If I'd shared my bed with you, you only would have come begging for more."

Pandora shoved his shoulders hard, and he stumbled backward. "You asshole! I hope the humans tear you to pieces. Gods, I *hate* you."

"The feeling is quite mutual, little goddess."

She shoved him again, but this time he caught her wrists, pinning them against his chest. "Call me that again, and I'll—"

"You'll what?" He smiled, his eyes darkening as they bore into hers.

She tried to remove her wrists, but he only pulled her

closer. His chest heaved with heavy breaths, and her skittering pulse matched it. Rage boiled in her blood, flaming and burning inside her. She wanted to slap him. She wanted to impale him with her tree branches.

She wanted to...

Desire seized hold of her, and she gripped his collar tightly, pulled his face to hers, and kissed him.

RIVALS

PANDORA

PANDORA WASN'T SURE WHAT HAPPENED. ONE moment, she wanted to snap Sol's neck.

The next, she was kissing him.

And even stranger—*he was kissing her back.*

For several moments, nothing but raw, carnal need took over. Their mouths crashed, their tongues collided, and their bodies aligned, as if both were trying to push harder against the other. Even in kissing, they were still rivals.

But gods above, his lips were hot and dangerous against hers, his tongue smooth and delicious. He grasped her hips, pulling her flush against him. Then his hands slid lower, cupping her ass and pressing hard. She writhed, grinding directly against his arousal, and he groaned into her mouth. Her teeth captured his bottom lip, and she tugged, this time eliciting a growl from him.

In this moment, they were animals. And it was a power struggle to determine who was the more dominant species.

Pandora couldn't deny it. She wanted to win.

But another, more desperate side of her wanted to lose. Because gods, the way he was ravishing her, made her bones melt into a puddle of pleasure.

He broke their kiss, only for his mouth to find her neck. He nibbled there, his teeth grazing lower until he bit the space where her neck met her shoulder. She gasped, throwing her head back, her eyes closing as she let desire fully take over.

No, she told herself. *Stay alert. You can still win this. You will* not *give him this control over you.*

You will not be controlled.

She pushed aside the bursting stars in her vision, the need to spiral away into her lustful fantasies. Grasping hold of what little clarity she still had, she gripped his belt, tugging him closer, and plunged her hands into his trousers.

He made a startled sound against her throat as her fingers wrapped around his hard length, clenching tightly.

Another sound escaped him, something between a roar and a groan. The outburst made her toes curl, but it also brought smug satisfaction. It was the sound of a man in the throes of passion.

She had him.

He backed her against the wall, slamming her so hard that a handful of books fell from the nearby shelves. The sconce on the wall rattled from the impact, and the back of Pandora's head throbbed. He hitched up her legs, spreading them on either side of him while his hands worked at bunching the violet fabric of her skirts.

Oh gods, oh gods, oh gods...

Would he take her right here in the library?

And would she let him?

She kept her fingers wrapped around him even as he hiked her dress higher and higher, clearly looking to retaliate. His mouth was no longer on her neck. Instead, he looked at her, his eyes dark with desire and fiery need. His breath was hot against her skin, his chest rising and falling with hers. She could feel his heartbeat drumming even through his tunic.

He was just as manic as she was.

But, like her, he would never admit it.

She stared back at him, lips parted as her own ragged breaths swept through her.

She'd had lovers before, of course. In past experiences, this would be the moment they would utter things like, *Gods, I want you,* or *You are so beautiful,* or *Tell me how you like it.*

Sol would do none of those things.

These were not the touches of an affectionate and doting lover. These were the touches of someone who wanted to claim her thoroughly.

His fingers trailed up her leg, tightening around the bare skin of her thigh. And damn, it felt so good to have his warm skin pressing against hers.

But if he thought he'd won, he was sorely mistaken.

Pandora let her legs fall, startling him. Her skirts dropped, and a triumphant smile lit Sol's face.

He thought he'd won.

Pandora knelt before him, keeping her eyes trained on his, savoring the look of surprise as she unfastened his belt buckle and unbuttoned his trousers.

"Trivia," he said, his voice a low rasp.

She smirked, delighting in the alarmed intensity of his gaze.

When his trousers were fully open, she stroked him once more, and he went rigid, his limbs tense. "Oh *gods*," he moaned.

Then she took him in her mouth.

His hands slammed into the wall above her, and he cried out, the sound wrenched from him, tearing from his throat. Her mouth opened wider, taking his full length inside her, and he trembled as her tongue caressed him.

Come on, she silently urged him. *Give in to me. You are mine, Sol.*

Strangled moans poured from his mouth, and he thrust against her, pushing deeper until he was so fully inside her that he tickled the back of her throat. She swept her tongue over him again, feeling him twitch in her mouth.

"I can't—*I can't*—Trivia, I—" He broke off with another moan, pumping faster and harder.

Oh yes, she had him.

She closed her lips around him and ran her teeth along his length. He plunged deeper into her, so deep she wasn't sure she could take any more without retching. His hands fisted in her hair, tugging forcefully, but the sensation only aroused her further. She *wanted* the pain. The rough, vicious intensity that made her gasp and cry out for more.

"Oh gods," Sol said again, his fingers digging into her scalp. "Yes. *Yes.* I need you, Pandora. I *need* you."

Pandora was so swept up in the need to make him come that she almost didn't notice at first. She almost continued to suck on him, to inhale him until he came in her mouth. A part of her yearned for it. Just to see what he would taste like.

And then, awareness crept into her mind like a bitterly cold mist. It drained all the heat from her body, making her insides chill with apprehension and horror.

She released him, practically spitting him out of her as she drew her head back to look up at him. She could still feel that smooth skin along her tongue, and her mouth felt emptier without it, left unsatisfied.

But she couldn't think on that now. How... *How*...

"What did you call me?" she whispered hoarsely.

Sol's face had drained of color, as if he hadn't realized what he'd said. His eyes were no longer dark with lust, but flared wide with terror.

Sol was *frightened*.

Pandora rose to her feet, her eyes never leaving his. "Sol. *What did you call me?*"

It was imperative that he answer her. She needed to know why he called her that.

Did he know who she was? That could be the only explanation.

She was in danger. If Sol knew...

Oh, shit. What if *Apollo* knew?

Sol seemed incapable of speaking. His mouth hung open as he stared at her as if he had never seen her before.

Several tense moments passed. Neither of them looked away, but neither of them spoke, either. Pandora could barely breathe as she waited for him to respond.

Then, his movements swift and panicked, Sol pulled his trousers back up and fastened his belt, then began backing away from her.

No, no, no.

"Sol," Pandora pleaded, drawing closer to him.

He was shaking his head, his face still ghostly pale. "No. I can't."

"*Sol!*" Pandora shouted, grabbing his shoulder. She would *not* let him leave this room without answering her.

"Ah, there you are," said a loud voice.

Pandora and Sol both jumped. Pandora's hands went to her hair, quickly patting it down and smoothing it as she looked to the entrance doors of the library.

It was Apollo, looking as regal as ever in robes of luminous gold that swished with every step. "I must speak with you at once."

Sol turned from Pandora and bowed low to Apollo. "Of course, my lord."

Apollo waved an impatient hand. "Not you. Hecate."

Pandora stiffened, her spine tingling with alarm. "Me? I—Well, surely your apprentice must also remain."

"Not at all. He has been reassigned. It is I who will continue to work with you to strengthen this realm against the attack of Pandora's magic."

Pandora's gaze shot to Sol's. He was watching her, his eyes wide with warning.

As if he wanted her to keep quiet.

What the hell did that mean? Why would he wish her to keep his outburst quiet from Apollo?

Her hands were itching to grab him, to snatch his collar and demand answers until he shared everything.

She realized Apollo was expecting a reply. Curtsying, she dipped her head in submission and stammered, "I-I am at His Majesty's disposal."

Apollo nodded with a smile. "Very good. Leave us, Sol. You are dismissed. For now." His eyes flashed with fury as he glared at his apprentice, and Pandora remembered Sol had just been reprimanded.

Because of her.

A riot of emotions crashed through her. She was not ready for this. She was unprepared to face Apollo. This was happening too quickly. She needed time. She needed a *plan*.

Sol turned on his heel and strode away from them.

Before Pandora could stop herself, she blurted, "Sol, wait!"

Apollo straightened, eyes narrowing at the shrill note in her voice. Sol turned warily, his shoulders tense as he turned to face her.

Pandora's face was on fire as she met his gaze. She had never seen him look so lost and helpless before. This was *Sol*, the arrogant bastard who treated her like dirt, who gloated over his grandness and finery, who cared nothing for serious matters like the safety of the realm.

And yet, that was not the man who met her gaze. This man was someone completely foreign. A stranger.

"I will see you at the ball?" Pandora asked hesitantly.

Sol's gaze flicked to Apollo, who was frowning in confusion. After a moment, he nodded once. "Yes, Trivia. I will see you then."

Without another word, he left the library, his quick strides implying he couldn't leave fast enough.

POWER
PRUE

PRUE LAY IN A CHASM OF DARKNESS. FOR ONE horrifying moment, she thought she had returned to Tartarus. She tried to sit up, to scream, her body tense with terror and dread... only to find she couldn't move.

"Peace, my child," whispered a soothingly familiar voice. "You are safe. You are still between worlds. But you are now traveling through my memories."

"Mama?" Prue tried to reach for Gaia, but she still couldn't move. Only darkness surrounded her, swallowing her whole. If not for her mother's voice, Prue would believe herself to be dead.

"You cannot interact with any part of my memories," Gaia went on. "I will be here with you through it all, but only in spirit. Remember, Prudence, you cannot change anything. This is only to give you the answers I do not have time to divulge myself. Please know that I will always regret lying to you, my darling. But I hope this will help you understand why I did."

Prue tried to protest, but her voice was drowned out by a rushing noise that filled her ears. It reminded her of the lapping waves on the beaches of Krenia, and for a moment, she allowed herself to be consumed by it.

Lightness bled through the void, burning and scorching. Prue flinched against it, raising a hand to her eyes—only to find she now had a body. She wore the same ripped red dress as before, when she'd been in Tartarus with Cyrus. She wiggled her fingers in front of her, just to convince herself she was truly alive and here.

Wherever *here* was.

She blinked against the burning sun, waiting for her eyes to adjust.

But it wasn't the sun at all. The brilliant display of light was coming from a person.

A *god*.

"You have enough, Janus," crooned a voice. The voice was familiar and foreign all at once. There was a lilt to it that Prue recognized, but it was younger, more coy and drawling than she was accustomed to.

"There is never too much power, love," said another voice. This one was deeper, one Prue had never heard before. It was smooth and sultry and confident.

A pair of figures came into view. They stood on a

beach similar to Krenia, but Prue knew instantly this place was different. There were rocks and boulders surrounding a cliff's edge, and the waters were more green than back at home. A tall, muscular man stood at the cliff's edge, arms raised high as he speared his magic toward the sun in the sky.

No, he wasn't feeding magic into the sun. He was siphoning magic *from* the sun. Jets of white light curled in the air, slithering toward him like serpents. The more he took, the brighter his form became, until an ethereal glow surrounded him.

Behind him, Gaia lay stretched out on a blanket, her head propped up on one arm as she munched on a piece of toasted bread. Her blue eyes lazily appraised Janus with mild interest.

"Janus," she said again.

With a sigh, Janus dropped his arms, panting. His dark eyes roiled with intensity, coils of light drifting in and out as if his vision had taken the sun's energy as well.

"Incredible," he murmured, staring at his hands and turning them over slowly. "I never knew the mortal realm held such power."

"I still think it's rather dreary compared to home." Gaia wrinkled her nose.

Janus scoffed. "Dreary? *You* created it, love."

Gaia waved a hand. "I could have done so much

better. If I had waited until my powers had grown, this place would be as magnificent as Elysium."

"The mortals do not *need* anything grand like Elysium. They will be content with this."

"Perhaps." Gaia took another bite of bread as Janus sauntered over to her and sprawled on the blanket alongside her.

"What shall we do once we return home?" Janus mused, fiddling with a strand of Gaia's black hair.

"You know what I want." Gaia's voice had turned solemn.

Janus groaned, dropping her hair and throwing his head back in exasperation. "Dearest, I have told you before. We cannot be married until I take the throne."

"And how long will that take?" Gaia whirled toward him, eyes flashing. "Jupiter is still alive and well, and his brother Neptune is in line after him. I will not wait an eternity for you, Janus."

"It won't be an eternity," Janus promised, taking her hand and bringing it to his lips. "I promise." His eyes glinted.

Gaia hesitated, drawing away from him. "What does that mean?"

"Let's just say I believe Jupiter's reign will come to a rather... abrupt end." Janus's mouth stretched into a wide grin.

Gaia's eyes flared wide. "You—"

Janus pressed a finger to her lips and shook his head. "There are ears everywhere, love. Do not speak it. Just know I have a plan, and you will not have to wait much longer."

He inched closer and brought his mouth to hers. After a moment, Gaia returned the kiss, her hands twining in his brown hair.

"I will do anything for you," Janus murmured.

Gaia laughed. "You will do anything for *power*."

"Well, that is also true. But you must always remember that nothing—*nothing*—will ever stand between us. Nothing can keep me from you, nor you from me. We are destined to be together, you and I. And I always fight for what is mine."

"This was when I knew," said a voice in Prue's ear.

She yelped, whirling around in search of the voice, only to find herself alone on the cliff. The lovers on the blanket had vanished.

"Knew what?" Prue asked her mother, knowing Gaia was with her even if she couldn't see her.

"Knew what he was capable of. He meant what he said, even long after I had left him. Nothing could keep him from me. And nothing would stand between him and his thirst for power."

The memory shifted, and then Prue stood underneath a dome-shaped ceiling with glistening marble floors and magnificent pillars. A twin pair of thrones sat atop a dais on one end of the room. Before her stood Janus, his hands wrapped around the neck of an unfamiliar man with pale skin and auburn hair. Sitting on the throne behind them was Gaia, looking on with apathy in her eyes.

When light burned from Janus's hands, the man went rigid, his spine jerking and his neck snapping as he fell over, lifeless. Behind Janus, Gaia flinched.

"Was that truly necessary, my love?" she asked.

"He knew too much." Janus wiped his hands on his tunic, then snapped his fingers toward a pair of guards in the corner. They hurried forward, hoisting the dead body up and dragging it from the room. "And he was growing too powerful for my liking."

"You killed him because he was powerful?" Gaia arched an eyebrow.

Janus offered an amused smile. "Do not worry, beloved. I would never do such a thing to *you*. I trust you completely."

"I was not worried for myself," came Gaia's voice in Prue's ear once more. "He did not know then that I was pregnant. And I had just discovered there were three souls inside me. The power of three is a dangerous entity. I feared if he knew, he would destroy our children."

Prue's blood ran cold. *Our children.* "Are you saying..." She swallowed, her mouth turning dry. "Mama, are you saying that Janus, the god of two faces, is my..."

"Yes." Gaia's voice was sad. "Janus is your father. But now, he goes by a different name: Apollo."

RISK
PANDORA

STILL REELING FROM THE CONFUSING ENCOUNTER with Sol, Pandora wrung her hands together before smoothing them along her dress as the library doors closed with Sol's departure.

Why did Apollo want to speak with her alone? Did he want to yell at her, too, because of the attack on the wards?

Pandora's skin felt hot and cold all at once. She could still taste Sol in her mouth, still hear the sultry groans pouring from him.

And yet, *he had called her Pandora.*

What the hell did that mean?

Her chest burned and ached with the need for answers... but also a different need. Something she didn't think she was capable of feeling.

She wanted Sol.

Desperately.

She wanted to take him in her mouth again and finish what they had started. She wanted to feel his warm hands on her naked flesh, pleasuring her in ways she'd never felt before.

She wanted that battle between them once more, where they each tried to get the other to break.

She wanted him to *break* her. Ever so slowly. Ever so fully.

Her mouth went dry as these thoughts consumed her, but when Apollo cleared his throat, she straightened, forcing her mind to clear.

Whatever Apollo had planned, she needed to be prepared.

The death magic from her necklace had failed. She needed an alternative plan. *Now.*

Think, think, think...

"I have no doubt you already know what I wish to speak to you about," Apollo said, approaching the fireplace, where flames crackled merrily. He braced his hands on the mantle and stared into the fire as if it could provide him all the answers he needed.

"I have a guess, Your Majesty," Pandora hedged.

Apollo turned to look at her with a knowing smirk that reminded her so much of Sol that her chest began to ache anew.

Don't think about Sol. Focus on your plan.

The wards were too strong. The only way to proceed would be to have them removed completely. But she wasn't powerful enough to do that.

Only Apollo was.

How could she convince him to take down the wards when he was already paranoid from the attack on them?

"There was a breach on the wards earlier," Apollo went on, pacing in front of the fireplace. "Suspiciously, right after you and Sol worked to strengthen them. Can you explain that?"

"Begging your pardon, Your Majesty, but I don't think it's suspicious at all," Pandora said carefully, a plan beginning to form in her mind.

"Excuse me?"

"This is exactly why I came here—to warn you. Pandora's magic has already destroyed the Underworld. It will look for something else to devour next, and there is a whole arsenal of power here, far more than we had in the Underworld."

A satisfied glint shone in Apollo's eyes. *Yes, that's right. Let me flatter you,* Pandora thought savagely.

"That power will draw the dark magic," Pandora went on. "And quickly. The magic will be hungry after having been trapped for so long. I'm surprised it's taken this long for it to come after Elysium."

"So, you're saying it was no coincidence, then? That

the darkness attacked right after you inspected the wards?"

"That's exactly what I'm saying. In fact, I believe the dark magic is drawn here *because* of the wards."

Apollo frowned, stroking his beard. "What do you mean?"

Pandora's heart raced. She would be taking an enormous risk with this next step. Either Apollo would agree, and her plan could continue... or he would only suspect her *more*.

If this backfired, he would cast her out. Or worse, kill her.

But she had no other choice. *It has to be done,* she reminded herself.

Swallowing hard, she summoned all her resolve and took a deep breath before continuing, "Your wards are strong. Even my death magic could not get through, so I commend you on crafting such a powerful defensive magic."

Another smirk tugged at the corners of his lips. Oh yes, he certainly loved the flattery.

"I'm assuming it took quite a bit of power from you to create them?" Pandora asked.

Apollo laughed. "Yes, my dear. Quite a lot. Hestia and I worked tirelessly to create them. I was spent for half the day afterwards, and that never happens."

Pandora nodded. "Well, that explains it, then."

"Explains what? Speak plainly, Hecate."

Pandora had to refrain from flinching at the degrading way he said *Hecate*. As if it were a foul curse. "The wards are the most powerful magic in this realm, aside from the gods themselves. No other enchantment holds as much magical energy as they do. And with the Underworld destroyed, all that's left for Pandora's magic to attack is Elysium and the mortal realm. There isn't nearly as much magic in the mortal realm as there is here. What I'm suggesting is that your wards are a beacon alerting Pandora's magic to your presence. I would be surprised if we made it through the night before another attack."

Apollo's expression had gone rigid, his dark eyes calculating as he considered her words. She held her breath, not moving, not daring to hope that he would believe her.

But he had to. This had to work.

She tucked her hands behind her back, fisting them, preparing to lash out with her earth magic if she needed to. It wouldn't be powerful enough to defeat him if he attacked her, but perhaps it would be enough to buy her time so she could escape.

After a long moment, during which Pandora's palms began to sweat, Apollo nodded slowly. "Yes, I have accrued much magic over the years. It would make sense that Pandora's magic would be drawn to it."

"Yes. You are extraordinarily powerful, Your Majesty. Even an ordinary attacker would thirst for such power. But this is no ordinary attacker. It is much, much worse."

Apollo waved his hand. "I have dealt with Pandora before."

Pandora's fists began to tremble, and screams echoed in her ears. "Not like this. It has been a long time since that box was crafted. The darkness within has only grown. I've seen it for myself. It devoured an entire realm. Aidoneus's realm."

Apollo's eyes flicked to hers, something unreadable stirring in his gaze. "He is dead, then?"

"Almost certainly. I saw for myself. There were no survivors."

Not a complete truth, but he didn't need to know that.

Apollo exhaled slowly and shook his head. "Gods above. This is a disaster. And with the solstice ball, too!" He ran his hands through his hair as if that damned ball was the most important thing on his mind.

"May I offer a suggestion, Your Highness?"

He waved a hand impatiently toward her. "That is why you're here, Hecate."

"We must take down the wards and infuse them with death magic."

A grave silence filled the air, her words echoing in

the space between them. Apollo's eyes narrowed slightly. "I beg your pardon?" His voice was low and dangerous.

Come on, Pandora, she told herself. *Convince him! You can do this.* Her trembling fingers fisted the fabric of her dress, twisting it back and forth to soothe her agitated nerves. "The dark magic is lured by the power behind your wards because it is *foreign.* It is new. That's what attracts it. But if we infuse *my* magic into the wards, the darkness will see it as familiar. Something born of the Underworld. Something it already has. It will lose interest, believing this is ordinary magic it already possesses, and it will move on to something else."

Apollo's eyes narrowed further, becoming tiny slits. "That is quite a hunch, Hecate. But I'm not sure I'm willing to wager the entire safety of my realm on it."

"It is *not* a hunch," Pandora said sharply. When Apollo's eyes widened, she quickly added, "Your Majesty." She stepped toward him, lifting her chin and projecting an air of confidence. "I saw the magic for myself. When it devoured the magic of the Underworld, it roared with satisfaction... but also greed. The more it feeds, the more it wants. And it wants something more. Something stronger." She paused before she layered more flattery into her argument. "Your magic is *far* stronger than any magic of the Underworld, Your Majesty. But if we disguise it with death magic, something lesser, something inferior, then the darkness of

Pandora will look for something else. It doesn't want to feast on a lesser magic. Not anymore. It will only keep looking until it has found something to satisfy its appetite, which has grown significantly.

"Your Majesty, I *know* this will work. We can use my magic as camouflage. We can mask the power of Elysium with something unassuming. Something worthless and weak. If a predator is stalking through the forest, its prey would do well to pretend it was already dying. That it was weak and sickly and there was nothing to harvest from it. The predator will move on to something stronger and healthier."

Apollo was stroking his beard again, his gaze distant as he mulled over her words. She waited with bated breath, giving him a moment to consider.

Please, please, please...

This had to work. It *had to.* The screams in her head demanded it.

Avenge me! the voices inside her roared. *Destroy them all!*

"Let me think on it," Apollo said at last. "I will discuss with my council. If they agree, we will move forward with this after the solstice ball." He turned to leave.

"No!" Pandora blurted, surging toward him.

Apollo faced her again, arching an eyebrow.

Pandora's mouth clamped shut, and she curtsied

quickly. "Forgive me, Your Majesty. I only mean... the wards have already been attacked. Pandora's magic *will* try again, and it will be stronger. We must act *now.*"

Apollo offered a patronizing smile. "Dear child, these things take time. And the wards are there for a reason. It did not succeed before. I am confident we have enough time to consider our options before we take action. Thank you for your suggestion, Hecate. Your presence here is much appreciated."

With that, he turned on his heel and strode from the library. Pandora watched, her resolve faltering with his departure.

It had worked... and yet, it hadn't. If he took this idea to his council, she knew what they would say. They would laugh that the suggestion of a lesser goddess like Hecate would even be considered.

She needed something more. Something drastic to force Apollo's hand.

If the dark magic from her box could not be lured into Elysium, then Pandora would have to attack it herself from the inside.

MELODY
MONA

Mona told Hestia of her plan, and to her credit, the fire goddess did not hesitate.

"We need to get you to the fulcrum," was all she'd said before striding purposefully away from the broken gate.

"What's the fulcrum?" Mona hurried after, struggling to keep up with her long, graceful strides.

"The midpoint of the realm," Hestia answered over her shoulder. "The place where our power is most potent. It amplifies our abilities." She stopped, turning to face Mona with a grim expression. "And, unfortunately, this means there will be witnesses for what you are about to do."

Mona shook her head. "I don't care. There will be witnesses either way. He can't stay hidden for long."

Hestia nodded once before turning again, leading Mona back through the village, winding between buildings with ease. Mona recognized the path until Hestia took a sharp turn to the left. They climbed up a steep incline, the buildings rising around them. Mona panted, her legs straining, sweat pouring down her face as she hiked after Hestia.

When they reached the top, Hestia gestured to the space in front of them. "This is the fulcrum."

Mona's mouth fell open as she took it all in. The fulcrum was a vast courtyard with a pedestal in the center surrounded by pillars and braziers. A small circle of trees ensconced the courtyard, and the fulcrum overlooked a cliff facing the ocean. As Mona turned her head to take it all in, she could see the entire village behind her, stretching for miles. Miles away, a mighty palace stood on the cliff along the opposite side of the village, gleaming in the sunlight.

Up here, the realm seemed as vast as the Realm of Gaia. It was endless and breathtaking.

"We are lucky," Hestia murmured next to her. "Normally, there are many deities here. With the solstice ball, most of them are likely preoccupied."

Only two people stood in the courtyard—a pair of women chatting a few paces away. One of them, tall and dark-haired, was idly twisting her fingers in the air and conjuring icicles. She stopped when she noticed Mona and Hestia, her gaze flicking between them.

"Hestia," she said cautiously. "I didn't expect to see you roaming about."

"No, I'm sure you didn't," Hestia said coldly, her frame rigid.

Mona's eyebrows lifted. This woman was certainly no ally of Hestia's. Her presence might complicate things. Would she stand in the way of what Mona needed to do?

"I only came to show young Mona what the fulcrum can do." Hestia waved a hand toward Mona, who offered a weak smile, trying to play along. "Go on, child."

Mona hesitated. The two women were watching Hestia with wary apprehension, and they clearly didn't seem too bothered by Mona. For a brief moment, Hestia widened her eyes at Mona with a warning. *Hurry,* she seemed to say.

Hestia's eyes never left the dark-haired woman as Mona rushed to the pedestal. She sensed the two women watching her with curiosity, but she paid them no heed.

She was here for one purpose: to find Evander.

And she wouldn't let the blatant stares of these strangers deter her.

As soon as she set foot on the steps leading to the dais, she felt power surge through her, wild and volatile.

She yelped and staggered backward, nearly falling to the ground from the intensity of it. Her magic sprang to life, and vines crept along her feet, achingly reminding her of Prue. Thorns and brambles followed after, and, to her surprise, roses blossomed from the foliage as well.

One of the women gasped behind her. "It's earth magic!" she shouted. "Gaia has returned!"

Mona's palms began to sweat as she climbed the final step until she stood in the center of the fulcrum. Energy crackled along her fingertips, and the vines slithered toward her obediently. Her magic flowed like a churning river she couldn't control. In no time at all, a lush garden surrounded her, sprouting flowers and thickets and herbs so potent they made her nose itch. The plants grew taller and taller until Hestia and the others were completely shrouded from view.

She tried to rein in her powers, but it was too much. She couldn't stop it. A startled cry poured from her throat, and the vines only grew faster. It wouldn't be long before her own plants suffocated her.

She had to act *now* before her magic swallowed her.

Blinking back tears from the strain of remaining upright, Mona took a deep breath and started singing.

Her voice was shaky at first, wobbling from the emotions coursing through her. But when she closed her eyes, she saw Cocytus, the river where she'd first met

Evander. She saw the forest behind him, and the soothing sound of the river washed over her. In her mind, Evander stood with his hand outstretched, his silver eyes beckoning as he urged her to take his hand.

The melody flowed through her, her voice stronger as confidence filled her. She sang the song of her soul, the song she knew Evander would recognize. He would hear her call. He would come for her.

A pair of hands closed around her wrists, cutting off her song. Mona jerked, but whoever held her was much stronger. They grasped her arms tightly, dragging her from the dais. As they descended the steps, Mona's earth magic flickered and vanished, leaving only cold fear in its wake.

Mona thrashed against whoever restrained her, whipping her head around to see who it was. A tall, burly man with curly brown hair and a navy blue uniform gripped her tightly. Another, with an identical uniform, stood behind him with a sword drawn. On the other side of the fulcrum, Hestia was shouting something, her hands pinned behind her by the dark-haired woman while the other held a magical white dome that encased the fire goddess.

Oh, Goddess, Mona thought, panic gripping her as forcefully as the hands that held her. She tried to summon her magic again, hoping that just being close to the dais would be enough. But something blocked her. It felt as if an invisible wall stood between her and her powers. She slammed against it over and over until the man holding her chuckled.

"It's no use, I'm afraid. I'm a shield. You won't be able to use your magic as long as I'm holding you."

The other uniformed man approached, his dark eyes pinned on her and his face twisting into a sneer. "She isn't Gaia. But she wields her magic. Apollo will want to question her."

Mona continued jerking her arms, but it was no use. The man was much stronger. "You don't understand!" she pleaded. "The realm is in danger. I'm trying to help!"

The man laughed again. "I'm sure you are. And, if what you say is true, then His Majesty will want to know about it. Either way, I'm taking you to him."

Mona shook her head in disbelief. No, this couldn't happen. Apollo was the one who had banished her mother. If he discovered Gaia's daughter was here...

Her gaze slid to Hestia, who watched her with eyes wide and full of terror.

Mona unleashed a piercing scream, her voice ringing around her. The soldier elbowed her in the gut, and she fell to her knees, one wrist still in his grasp. But still she screamed.

"*Evander!*" she shrieked. "*Evander, where are you?*"

Her voice continued to fill the air, echoing in the vast space. Surely, he could hear her. Surely, he would come, or this would all be for nothing.

Something heavy slammed into her skull, and then everything went dark.

FORGIVEN

PRUE

STILL REELING FROM THE REVELATION OF WHO her father was, Prue wasn't prepared for Gaia to thrust her into the next memory. The world shifted around her, and when her surroundings settled, she found herself in a wintry mountain village that reminded her of when she'd crossed the Emdale Mountains with Cyrus. That felt like an eternity ago.

Curled up by a crackling fire, Gaia held a newborn baby in each arm as she sat in a rocking chair, humming to herself as she coaxed the babies to sleep. In a tiny cradle opposite her chair was the third sister, and she had the faintest sheen of red in her hair.

Pandora.

Which must mean the babies in her arms were Prue and Mona.

Prue's throat tightened at the sight of Gaia like this, her face the picture of relaxation as she sang to her babies. She was alone, and the cozy cottage gave Prue the impression that no one else lived here.

It was only Gaia and her three daughters.

"What is this?" Prue asked, her voice strained. She couldn't tear her gaze away from Gaia, who smiled down at one of the babies, shushing her when she began to fuss in her arms.

"This was the life I was hoping to create for myself," came Gaia's voice. "For *us*."

Prue blinked, her eyes hot with tears as she watched Gaia press a gentle kiss to the baby's forehead. For just a moment, she allowed herself to envision what life would have been like if the memory ended here—if the three daughters had been raised together in these wintry mountains. Somehow, she couldn't imagine herself growing up in such a climate. Krenia was always home for her.

Who would she have become if she had grown up like this? With two sisters instead of only one?

"Were you ever trying to harness the power of the Triple Goddess?" Prue asked, her voice a whisper. She'd been told Gaia had been punished for trying to recreate such powers. That Prue and Mona had been the product of her experimentation.

Gaia didn't answer for a long moment. "Yes," she

finally said. "At first, I was looking to protect myself with the power of three. To protect Elysium from Apollo's reign. But..." She paused, and when she spoke again, her voice cracked. "But then you three were born. And I found I loved something far more. More than Apollo. More than myself. More than Elysium. And I changed my plans."

Tears spilled freely down Prue's cheeks. She knew Gaia could be lying. But as she watched the warmth in her mother's eyes, the way the light shone in them as she gazed upon her infant children, Prue found she believed her.

The door crashed open, swinging on its hinges and bringing a swirl of snow flurries with it. Gaia was on her feet in an instant, clutching the babies tightly against her chest and wrapping a blanket securely around them. Her eyes were fierce as she glared at the intruder.

Dressed in furs and boots, Apollo stepped over the threshold, his expression murderous. His lip curled with a sneer, his eyes surveying the cramped cottage. "*This* is where you've been hiding? How disappointing. I really expected more from you, Gaia."

"You are not welcome here," Gaia seethed, withdrawing a step away from him. "Leave now. I don't want to fight you, Apollo."

"Then, don't." He strode closer to her, his boots

tracking snow on the wood floors. "Just hand over my children, and I will be on my way."

"Never," Gaia spat.

Apollo's eyes narrowed into thin slits. He glanced over his shoulder and jerked his chin. Only then did Prue realize a dark figure lurked behind him. Heavy footsteps thunked, and a man appeared alongside Apollo.

Prue's gasp stuck in her throat, and she covered her mouth with her hand. It was Aidoneus—Cyrus's father. The former king of the Underworld.

Gaia stiffened, drawing her children closer to her as she glanced between Apollo and Aidoneus. "What is this?" Her voice sharpened.

"You have no one to blame but yourself for this, Gaia," Apollo said. "If you had handed them over to me, they would have been spared."

"Spared from what?"

"It just so happens that there is a curse afflicting Elysium, thanks to the dreaded Pandora." Apollo spat her name like a foul curse. "Just before dying, she left her magic with us, doomed to haunt us for all eternity."

Gaia's brows knitted together. "I lived in Elysium for years and never caught a whiff of such a curse."

Apollo's mouth stretched into a cruel smile. "Yes, well, it appears the curse has only affected us." He gestured between himself and Aidoneus. "For years, we've searched for a way to break it. But the magic is too strong."

Gaia barked out a laugh. "Well, I can't say I'm surprised. You brought this on yourself, Apollo."

Apollo's gaze darkened. "Perhaps I did. But recently, we discovered a solution. You see, if the curse is transferred to another, then we can be free. So now, one of my children will carry the weight of that curse *for* me."

Gaia's face drained of color. "What? No—"

Before she could react, the two gods stepped toward her. Aidoneus blocked Gaia's path, his bulky frame a barrier between her and the cradle as Apollo scooped up the third daughter in his arms.

Gaia glanced down at the two babies nestled against her chest, as if only just realizing the third child was not with her. "Apollo, *no!*" she screamed. The ground rumbled, and she tried shoving past Aidoneus, but the death god raised his hands, conjuring black smoke to obscure Apollo from view.

But Apollo's words still echoed in the cottage.

"I leave my own curse upon you, Gaia," Apollo murmured. "May you be doomed to a life among the mortals for the rest of your days. May you never access your full abilities until your earth magic chooses to free you. For all eternity, you may *never* use your powers for yourself again."

Gaia unleashed a violent sob, falling to her knees as

she clutched the babies closer to her, weeping against their tiny heads. She screamed, and power burst from her, making the walls tremble. Roots and vines burst from the floorboards, snaking toward Apollo. But Aidoneus's shadows smothered them, turning them to ash. Magic flooded from Gaia's figure, exploding outward, but Apollo countered it with an idle wave of his arm, summoning a shield of pure light that protected him from Gaia's wrath.

From within her arms, the two infants began fussing and squirming in Gaia's grip. The goddess shushed them, her face conflicted between sorrow and rage, and Prue had no doubt that if she hadn't been holding her children, she could have bested Apollo.

Defeat and resignation shone in her eyes, and she slumped, her frame sagging as she surrendered. She knew there was nothing she could do. Not if she wanted to protect her two remaining children.

Apollo smirked with triumph, knowing he'd won. With a soft chuckle, he tucked Pandora more securely in his arms and strode out the door.

Aidoneus, however, lingered, staring down at Gaia's weeping form with a look of pity. She glared up at him, her eyes blazing with fury. With a shout, her vines snaked forward, wrapping around his ankles and pinning him in place.

"Foul demon," she spat. "You will *pay* for this."

Aidoneus's expression was somber, and although it did not hold a fraction of the venom Apollo had shown earlier, it was still set with grim determination. "What did you think would happen when you defied him, Gaia? Did you think he would simply give up? If you did, you're an even bigger fool than I thought."

Gaia bared her teeth at him, and for a moment, Prue expected her to unleash the raw power of her magic on him. But a shuddering gasp ripped from her, and she hunched over. The arms holding her babies started shaking.

"Apollo's curse is taking effect," Aidoneus said sadly. "I am truly sorry for this, Gaia."

And he turned and followed after Apollo, leaving Gaia to sob in her cottage.

In a flash, the cottage vanished from view, and Prue found herself standing on the beach in Krenia once more, with Gaia sitting beside her. The earth goddess was weeping openly, just as she had all those years ago. Misery filled her eyes as she gazed at the ocean.

"From that moment on, I vowed to never share my past with you and Mona," Gaia whispered. "I was terrified he would come back and claim one of you. It's why I fled to Krenia, where I thought we would be safe. I sought out a witch coven that could protect me and hide my true identity. And with you two raised to believe you were earth witches, you would never attract the attention of the gods." She closed her eyes, and more tears fell. "I do regret lying to you, Prue. But if it kept you safe from Apollo all these years, then it was worth it."

Prue brushed tears from her own face. "And you never tried to break his curse? I heard what he said—your earth magic can free you."

Gaia offered a watery smile. "That's the tragic part. I'm not allowed to use my magic to help myself. But only *my* earth magic can free me. It's the cruelest part of all; there is a way out, but the curse Apollo left me with prevents me from ever accessing it."

"And now Pandora is coming for you because she believes you abandoned her."

Gaia nodded. "Apollo left her in the Underworld under the care of Aidoneus. And I was never allowed to leave this realm to find her. Of course, Aidoneus would tell her lies about how I had been unwilling to raise her myself. He let that resentment fester all these years. And with the soul of Pandora raging inside her, it was only a matter of time before she sought her revenge against me."

"But you had nothing to do with Pandora's death."

"That's not entirely true. I knew what Apollo was doing to her. And... I stood by and did nothing." Gaia shook her head, regret filling her eyes. "All those years, I did *nothing* to stop him. It wasn't until I had children that I was finally forced to see the monster that he was.

To see that there *was* another way to live. And by the time I realized this, it was too late."

Prue reached forward and clasped her mother's hand. "Can't you explain all this to Pandora?"

"Do you think she will listen?"

Prue pressed her lips together. She had been angry before. She hadn't *wanted* to listen. But her only grievance with Gaia was how many lies she'd told.

Pandora had far more reasons to despise her.

And Prue highly doubted her sister would sit and listen to Gaia's explanations. The only reason Prue had was because Gaia was her mother and, despite everything, she still loved her.

"Now you know," Gaia said with a sniff, facing the horizon once more. "You can share what you've learned with Mona. I wish I could tell her myself, but I sense Pandora's dark magic growing stronger. It will not wait much longer."

"Mama," Prue sobbed, grabbing her mother's shoulders and wrapping her in a tight embrace. Gaia wept into Prue's shoulder, clutching her close, just as she'd done so long ago when Prue had only been a baby. "I was angry with you before, and I'm sorry. But I understand now. And I forgive you."

Gaia squeezed her as another sob broke free. "You will be just fine, Prudence. You have a fierce husband who has the power to bring you back. I doubted it before, but I now understand the lengths you two will go for each other. And I know he will protect you."

"How?" Prue asked, withdrawing to look at her mother quizzically. "How can Cyrus bring me back? He has death magic, not the magic of life."

Gaia brushed a few stray curls out of Prue's face. "I'm not entirely sure. The magic of death gods is not as familiar to me. I know with our magic, the magic of the earth, we are able to breathe life into beings. But the god of the Underworld?" She frowned. "I'm not so sure."

Dark clouds swirled in the sky, and strong winds whipped at Prue's face, tousling her hair and clothes. She squinted toward the sky, surveying the darkness that drew closer.

"You have to leave now," Gaia said, following Prue's gaze. "You can't be between worlds when Pandora comes for me. You could be trapped here permanently."

"Mama, I can't leave you."

"You can and you must." Gaia's voice was urgent as she hauled Prue to her feet. "Find Mona. Protect each other. And trust your magic, my darling." She pressed a kiss to Prue's forehead.

"Mama—" Prue protested, but as soon as Gaia stepped away from her, she vanished.

"*Mama!*" Prue screamed as the darkness swallowed her completely.

SOLSTICE

PANDORA

"You look radiant, my lady," Mera said, standing back to admire Pandora with awe.

Pandora surveyed herself in the mirror. She wore a gown of crimson silk that matched her hair perfectly. The dress hugged her waist, then flared wide over her legs. Gold embroidery lined the bodice and sleeves, along with the bottom of the skirt. The neckline plunged low, revealing the swell of her breasts. Her hair was pinned up into an elaborate knot with a single braid crowning the top. Gold-studded pins secured her hair in place, adorned with a matching gold tiara. Kohl rimmed her eyes and her lips were stained a deep red.

She couldn't deny it. She *did* look like a goddess. Someone far grander than she actually was.

"You are very talented, Mera," Pandora said,

smoothing her palms along her skirts. Ever since her conversation with Apollo—no, ever since her confrontation with *Sol*—she found it difficult to breathe, to form a coherent thought.

Sol knew her name. Somehow, he did. And the thought made Pandora nauseous.

Did he think she was the *real* Pandora? The one from all those years ago who had dabbled in dark magic?

Was that why he had looked so horrified when he'd left the library?

Her mind was scrambled. She had a plan: orchestrate an explosive attack on Elysium to urge Apollo to take down the wards. Then, the magic from her box would swoop in and do the rest.

And yet... for the first time, her heart twisted with uncertainty.

Was this the right plan?

Yes, screamed the voice inside her. *Yes! The pain. The torment. The agony. I must be avenged.*

It must be done.

Yes, these were the words Pandora often reminded herself.

But why must it be done?

This was the first time she considered that perhaps there was another way to be free. Perhaps destruction wasn't the only course of action for her to take.

She didn't want to be a monster. She didn't want Sol

to look at her that way, as if she were a terrifying creature intent on slaughtering everyone.

In truth, that's what the soul within her *wanted* her to be. A creature of vengeance and death.

She didn't know why she suddenly cared what Sol thought. But the idea that someone like him—so self-centered and loathsome—would look at her as if she were even *more* despicable than he was... It made her insides tremble.

The memories within her raged at her uncertainty, thrashing against the restraints of her mind. But she forced them down, turning her attention to Mera.

The servant was beaming, clearly taking pride in what she had accomplished with Pandora's appearance. Mera wouldn't even be attending the ball because she was lowborn, and yet here she was, glowing like a princess herself.

Pandora's heart twisted further, like a knife digging deeper into her ribs.

Mera would die. Along with all the other servants.

They were only following orders. They weren't responsible for what had happened all those years ago. Hell, they probably didn't even *know* what Apollo and Aidoneus had done.

Rattling gasps tore through her, and she braced her hands on the vanity to keep herself upright.

"My lady?" Mera was by her side, hands wrapping

around her to guide her toward the edge of the bed, where she sat, her hands shaking.

"You are unwell," Mera observed. "Let me fetch a healer."

"No." Pandora swallowed hard, closing her eyes as she slowly found her breaths. "Forgive me. I am well. I can—It was just... a trying day. I will be glad to distract myself with merriment tonight."

Mera smiled, but her eyes still shone with concern.

This servant, this *stranger*, was genuinely concerned for Pandora.

"Shall I send for someone to escort you downstairs?" Mera asked.

Pandora cleared her throat and stood, finding her resolve. "Thank you, Mera. I am fine." She paused, eyeing the servant, her gaze sweeping over the drab brown dress she wore. "You should come."

Mera blanched. "To... the *ball*?" When Pandora nodded, Mera's cheeks flamed red. "Oh no, my lady. I couldn't possibly."

"It's clear you know how to dress someone for it." Pandora gestured to her own gown. "Have your pick of the dresses in my wardrobe. I may be a bit taller than you, but I think you can make it work. Shall I help you dress?"

"My—My *lady*," Mera objected breathlessly as Pandora strode to the wardrobe and threw open the doors. She sifted through several bundles of silk before she came across a stunning peach one that complimented Mera's complexion perfectly.

"Here." Pandora thrust the gown into the stunned servant's hands. "It's fairly easy to do up, and if I recall correctly, it came a little short on me. It should be perfect for you."

"I—I cannot!" Mera sputtered, her eyes wild with fear.

"And why not?" Pandora placed her hands on her hips. "Do you think anyone will notice? None of these bastards ever look at a servant's face. Live a little, Mera. You may not get another opportunity." When Mera said nothing, Pandora sighed and dropped her arms. "The choice is yours. I won't force you. But if I see you in the ballroom, it will give me such delight to know you are enjoying yourself." She smiled broadly before striding from the room, hoping and praying Mera would take her advice.

If Pandora went through with her plans, Mera would die, and she would never get the chance to dance at an extravagant ball.

Her heart felt significantly lighter as she left the room and made her way down the hall. Only then did she realize she hadn't felt this free in...

Gods. She didn't know when she had last felt this

way. And all because she urged a servant to sneak into a ball?

Pandora stopped at the end of the hall, her fingers gripping the banister and tracing the elaborate carvings etched on it. *This* was what she wanted—to bring joy to those who could not find it themselves. To help those who were overlooked and ignored.

She didn't want to destroy people. She didn't want to erase the realms from existence.

The soul within her did. The goddess from before, whose memories she shared. That was what *she* wanted.

But Pandora was not that woman. She was different. She was her own unique individual.

And for once, *she* wanted to choose her path. Not because of revenge or trauma or the memories inside her, but because it was something she wanted on her own.

Her chin lifted as she descended the stairs. She would proceed with one step, one choice at a time. And right now, her choice was to enjoy herself at this ball.

So that was exactly what she would do.

The ballroom was crowded with people dressed in extravagant finery. Thick, powerful magic churned in the air, a result of so many deities filling one space. Pandora took a flute of champagne as a servant ambled past her and downed it in one gulp, letting it burn down her throat and fill her with courage and confidence.

These were the people she despised. The people who had tormented her.

No. The people who had tormented someone else so very long ago. True, Pandora did not like these people at all. They were like Sol—arrogant and oblivious to the needs of others. Utterly infuriating.

But that didn't mean she wanted them dead.

Her thoughts turned to Sol, and something fresh and hot lanced through her. He'd said he would be here. She had to see him again. Not only to press him about how he'd said her name, but...

But what?

To finish what they had started in the library?

Her stomach churned at the reminder.

No. That wasn't important. The most important thing was to determine what he knew. If he knew her true identity, then...

Kill him, urged the voice inside her. *You must erase him from existence. There is far too much at stake.*

Pandora shuddered and closed her eyes, bracing her hand on the wall for support as she gathered her thoughts.

No. She could not kill Sol. As much as she hated him,

as much as she longed to make him pay for his igno-rance, she could not bring herself to kill him. She had never actively taken a life before. The closest she had come was with Evander.

All she had done so far was unleash death itself and stand by while it did its work. Her hands certainly weren't clean; she had still let it happen. But it would be so different if she took the life with her own powers. Could she really stand in front of her victim and choke the life out of him? Watch the life leave his eyes as her branches strangled him? If Mona hadn't turned up at that portal, would she have really ended Evander's life right there?

"My, my, you do look unwell," said a smooth voice beside her. "Perhaps the sight of so many people enjoying themselves only makes you more bitter."

Pandora's eyes snapped open. She straightened, finding Sol standing next to her, sipping from his own flute of champagne. He was dressed in a luminous gold uniform with gleaming buttons and embroidery on the sleeves and collar. The glow from his attire brought out the honey tones of his hair and the warm hue of his tan skin. Overall, he looked luminous. More radiant than the sun.

It took her breath away, and all she could do was stare.

Sol smirked over the rim of his glass. "I've rendered

you speechless, I see. Yes, this uniform *does* have that effect on women. It's why I only wear it on special occasions. If I wore it too often, women would be fainting at my feet constantly. It would be such a bother."

Irritation flared, igniting her blood, and she finally found her voice. "It's a relief to see you're still an arrogant prick. I worried after our encounter in the library that I'd permanently damaged you." She relished the way his hand tightened around his glass. It was almost an imperceptible motion, but she noticed it.

Her words had struck him.

"I am far more resilient than that," Sol said, his tone still smug. But Pandora caught the way his eyes darkened slightly.

"Are you?" Pandora leaned closer, a smile quirking her lips. "Because it really felt like I was on the verge of... breaking you." She flicked her tongue along her lower lip, and Sol's breath hitched.

Oh, yes, she certainly had him.

Music rang in the ballroom, a sweeping, flowing melody. All around them, couples peeled away from the crowd to fill the dance floor. Pandora placed her flute on a nearby tray and gathered her skirts, hoping to escape before she was coerced into dancing.

Before she could flee, however, Sol caught her arm.

"Ah, you didn't think you could get away from me so

easily, did you?" His eyes glinted as he tugged her arm, bringing her into his chest.

Her hands came out, pressing against the firm muscles of his torso before she smacked right into him. Their faces were inches apart, and her breathing turned sharp.

"Come, Trivia. Dance with me."

Pandora couldn't protest, even if she wanted to. Sol steered her to the dance floor, his steps smooth and graceful, his eyes never leaving hers. When he stretched his arm out, his fingers lacing with hers, her body went rigid.

"Don't fret," Sol said, his smile widening. "Just follow my lead."

Pandora snorted. "Follow *your* lead?"

He arched an eyebrow. "Do you know the steps, dear Trivia?"

Pandora fell silent, her mouth clamping shut as she scowled at him.

"That's what I thought."

The dance began, and Pandora scrambled to keep up with his steps. They turned and twisted, his arm guiding hers. At first, she fought to maintain control, but after a moment, she relaxed, finally giving in. She let him steer her, controlling their movements. Her feet followed his. She turned when he turned. And gradually, she slid into the flow of the music. She even felt a smile tugging at her lips.

"There we go," Sol said, smug as ever. "That wasn't so hard, was it?"

"Only because I kept expecting you to let me fall flat on my face."

He clicked his tongue at her, pausing as he twirled her. She spun, her skirts swishing, and returned to his chest, a bit closer than she'd been before. "You really think I would disgrace myself with a clumsy dance partner?"

"Ah, of course. It's only to protect your image. How could I forget?"

His eyes warmed. "I suppose that's how it is between us, isn't it?"

"What?"

"This dance between us. I lead, you lead. I push, you pull. One step forward, one step back."

Pandora raised her eyebrows. "You see it as a dance? I see it as more of a battle. An exchange of blows."

His hand tightened around her waist, bringing her closer until her breasts were flush against him. Each breath had her chest rising, pushing on his. She could feel his pulse hammering, keeping rhythm with hers. "Yes," he said, his voice a low murmur. "If I recall correctly, I had you pinned against a wall. Powerless and desperate."

Her eyes narrowed. "And if *I* recall correctly, I had you disarmed and helpless, begging me for mercy." She leaned in, her lips brushing his ear. "Begging *her* for mercy."

He stiffened and fumbled his next step. To his credit, he recovered quickly, sweeping her in another turn as they followed the other couples around the dance floor.

"I don't know what you're talking about," Sol said stiffly, his eyes fixed on a point above her head.

Her smile widened. "I think you do."

His hand curled around hers, tightening in warning. "Trivia, *don't.*"

"Don't what? You called me Pandora. Am I supposed to forget that happened?"

"Yes," he said between his teeth.

"Why?"

He growled something unintelligible, his eyes sweeping over the room as if worried someone would be eavesdropping. Then, quite suddenly, he tugged on her hand, pulling her off the dance floor and through the open doors that led to a wide balcony. The setting sun was low in the sky, reflecting a glistening array of amber and fuchsia in the roiling ocean. It was much quieter out here, and Pandora relished the open air, which finally allowed her to breathe after being surrounded by so many people.

"What's going on, Sol?" she demanded. She was

through with his games. Clearly, something had him frightened. And now, she was beginning to think it *wasn't* her, but some other secret he was hiding.

Sol didn't answer for a long moment. Carefully, he shut the balcony doors, sealing out the music and chatter from the ball. "I am leaving tonight," he said, his face uncharacteristically sober.

Her mouth fell open. "What?"

"Apollo has already activated the portal for me. I'm to leave for the mortal realm immediately following the ball."

Pandora was silent as she registered this information. She wasn't sure what to say. She *wanted* to feel relief. After all, wasn't this what she wanted—to be rid of him forever?

And yet, something tightened in her chest at the thought of parting from him so suddenly.

"Why are you telling me this?" Pandora asked, crossing her arms and frowning at him.

For the briefest of seconds, his eyes dipped to her breasts, and she realized that folding her arms had pressed them together, drawing his eye to her cleavage. She hastily dropped her arms, but Sol's gaze had darkened with a hunger that made her toes curl.

"I'm telling you this to warn you. Whatever you think you heard in the library, you're wrong. Do not ask questions. Do not dig further into this."

She glared at him. "Is that a threat?"

His eyes widened. "What? No. It's a warning. I'm trying to protect you."

She snorted. "Protect *me*? Since when have you ever been concerned with someone other than yourself?"

He gritted his teeth, a muscle feathering in his jaw. "Fine. You're right. See, *this* is why I never concern myself with others. If you want to get yourself killed, go right ahead. Forget I said anything."

He strode past her toward the ballroom, but Pandora grabbed his arm to stop him.

"Sol."

He paused, giving her a stony look over his shoulder.

"Please explain." She tried to make her voice as tender as possible. This was not a time to goad him. If she wanted answers, she would need to play nice. She released his arm and looked at him with earnest curiosity. "I'm listening."

He sighed and ran a hand through his hair. It had been slicked back, but with the motion, it became tousled and alluringly handsome. Pandora couldn't help but let her eyes rove over the strands of hair that fell loosely around his face.

"I did know Pandora," Sol said, his eyes fixed on the ocean below them.

Pandora stiffened, her blood running cold. The screams, the memories, threatened to overtake her once more. She stepped forward, gripping the railing of the balcony and forcing her thoughts to remain intact. She needed to be lucid for this discussion.

"That was hundreds of years ago, Sol," she said weakly.

He nodded. "Yes. I am *that* old." Amusement touched his voice.

Pandora shook her head, turning to look at him in shock. "So, you know what happened to her?"

"Yes. She dabbled with the magic of the Titans, and it devoured her. She became a cautionary tale to the deities, an example. A reminder of why we should never defy the powers we've been granted."

Pandora's eyes narrowed as she scrutinized him. His words were solemn, his eyes haunted. "Is that all?" she probed.

He frowned. "What do you mean? Yes, that's what happened to her."

Gods above. He didn't know. He didn't know that his master, his *king*, had been the one to tear Pandora apart.

Of course he didn't. Apollo was so concerned with protecting his image and keeping up appearances that Pandora was almost certain he would have kept this quiet, even from his own apprentice.

What if no one else knew?

If that were true, then this realm was full of innocents.

Just like the Underworld.

Pandora thought of her sisters, who were likely dead because of her. So many demons. So many innocents.

Dead at her hands. Because of her actions.

"That doesn't explain why you said her name in the library," Pandora said, struggling to keep her voice even. She kept her eyes trained on the horizon, determined not to succumb to the anguish coursing through her.

Screaming. So much screaming. Apollo's blinding white light, ripping her to pieces.

Her eyes closed, and her hands shook as she gripped the railing.

Sol inhaled deeply, and Pandora looked at him. He, too, was bracing his hands on the railing, hunching over as if he were in physical pain.

Just like her.

She remembered what he had said to her that one night she'd found him staring at the sea: *It doesn't matter if I'm here or in the mortal realm. It follows me wherever I go.*

Only then did she realize he'd been lying in the library. He had claimed he'd only been awake that night to seduce her, to lure her into his bed. He claimed he'd seen her climb down her balcony and followed her.

But it hadn't been true. If he *had* seen her, he would have identified her magic as Gaia's. He would have seen the earth magic and known who she truly was.

Pandora had been so furious with his words that she hadn't stopped to think about it. He was deflecting the attention away from his insecurities.

"What role did you play in her demise?" Pandora asked softly.

"Nothing. I played no role." The words were hollow.

She pressed her hand against his arm, squeezing gently. "Sol."

His eyes met hers, and they were filled with such agony that her heart cinched in her chest. Only one time had she seen such sorrow in his eyes: that night on the steps, facing the ocean.

"She was my lover," he said.

SURRENDER

EVANDER

When Evander first arrived at Elysium, a splitting pain rocketed through his body, snapping his bones and scorching his blood. It felt as if his very soul was being ripped from him by force. From within, he felt the wrath of Typhon, the demon presence inside him, as the energy in the air ate at him, too.

They were both dying.

He had hoped it would be quick. Perhaps the magic of Elysium would be so powerful that it would overcome him instantly. Perhaps death would be swift.

Unfortunately, that was not the case.

He faded in and out of consciousness, just as he had when Typhon had taken over his body. But this was different. He felt Typhon's confusion mirror his own. When Trivia—no, *Pandora*—had dragged him through the portal, he'd watched her stride up to the gates without a second glance at him.

Then, darkness had claimed him.

He thought that was it. He was dead. He would never see Mona again.

When he'd woken, the gates had been torn off their hinges, the metal bent at an odd angle. He was panting, covered in sweat, with dirt staining his hands and clothes.

He had no memory of what he'd done. But the evidence surrounding him indicated *he'd* ripped the gate doors off.

He'd run off, clinging to the small semblance of sanity while it lasted, trying to find help, to find a safe place to hide.

He managed to duck into an alley before the darkness had claimed him once again.

It went on like this for days. Sometimes his blackouts only lasted a few minutes, leaving him in the same spot he'd been before, with only minor changes. Other times, a longer stretch of time passed, and he would wake to find it was the middle of the night, or he was miles from where he'd started.

The most terrifying part of it all was the utter lack of control. At least when he'd shared his consciousness with Typhon, he had *known* who was in control. But this was maddening. Who was taking over his body?

And what were they doing?

Why wasn't he dead yet?

He tried to be optimistic. Perhaps this was a way of prolonging his life, to allow him to find a way out of his predicament. A way back home and back to Mona.

But a dark dread seeped its way into his chest, making his very bones tremble.

He knew in his soul that something was very, very wrong. And it was only a matter of time before he awoke to find he'd killed someone.

During his wakeful moments, he had tried to go back through the portal. But he never made it. He was so far from the gate that he only made it a few minutes, a few steps, perhaps even an hour before he blacked out again. And when he woke, he was even farther from the gate than before. It was as if whatever possessed him knew he was trying to leave the realm and wanted him to stay.

That frightened him even more.

What darkness had claimed him? What did it want with him?

And what was it trying to accomplish by keeping him here?

Death would be better, he thought bitterly. There was no hope in this. He was a puppet being controlled by another.

His thoughts often turned to Mona. He clung to his memories of her, cherishing them, relishing them, preserving them for as long as he could. They gave him clarity and focus, allowing him to stay awake for longer.

The only thing that kept him sane was her melody pulsing through him. The song of her soul. It grounded him. He kept the tune in his head constantly, humming it, singing it to himself.

Somehow, just like in the Underworld, his connection to Mona gave him power and strength.

So, he held on to it. Everything about her—her scent, her voice, her laugh—flooded his mind. It was torture, remembering her, thinking of every beautiful piece of her he would never see again.

Yes, death would have been more merciful. So much better than dwelling on the love he could never have.

Even so, he pushed on, forcing his mind toward Mona.

One day, he managed to stay awake for three full hours. His feet were raw and throbbing, the soles of his shoes torn and tattered from his constant aimless walking. Sweat poured down his face and neck, and he was so filthy that he could barely see his pale skin beneath the layer of dirt coating his flesh.

In spite of all this—and the fact that he had gotten lost several times—he had found his way back to the broken gate that led to the portal.

Victory coursed through him, but it was short-lived.

The portal was closed. It was nothing more than a

darkened archway. No magic emanated from it. No energy surrounded it.

His knowledge of the Underworld told him a portal needed to be fueled with a powerful source of magic in order to be activated.

But he couldn't use his magic here. The one time he'd tried, he had blacked out again. Conjuring his death magic was the surest way to bring the darkness back.

And he couldn't risk it.

Despair crashed through him, and he sank to his knees in utter hopelessness. He slammed his fists against the ground once, twice, three times, not caring when his skin split and blood trickled down his palms.

It was no use. Even if he *could* find a source of magic powerful enough to open the portal back up, the darkness would take him before he could go through. This was the longest stretch of time he'd been awake, and he knew it wouldn't last much longer.

Sobs wracked through him, and he hung his head and wept.

He would be like this for the rest of eternity. He would succumb to the darkness again and again until it took him fully. Until he was nothing more than an empty shell being controlled by someone else.

He inhaled as tears streamed down his face.

Then it hit him. A whiff of something so fragrant

and familiar that for a moment, he thought he'd imagined it.

Mona.

Roses and parchment and the sea...

Gods, it felt like she was right next to him.

He blinked tears from his eyes, looking up, not daring to hope that she could be here, that she had somehow followed him to Elysium.

"Mona?" he rasped. His tongue felt like lead in his mouth, his voice crackly from dehydration and disuse.

He sniffed again, and he sensed Typhon stirring within him, called forth by the primal nature of his senses. Typhon was the better tracker, but he had been dormant for days now. He was much harder to awaken than Evander himself because the powers of Elysium kept smothering his demonic nature.

But Mona... Mona had always been able to reach Typhon, even when Evander couldn't.

Mona, Typhon rumbled within him.

"Yes," Evander said hoarsely, rising to his feet. "She's here, Typhon. We must find her."

And then a familiar, haunting melody flowed in the air.

Evander went perfectly still as the song surrounded him like an embrace, reminding him of a sparkling river, a lush forest, and a pair of emerald green eyes.

His mouth turned dry, and his heart slammed

against his ribcage. Every ounce of his awareness homed in on the sound of that melody.

"Mona," Evander whispered.

He stepped forward, intent on following the melody like a bloodhound would track a scent....

Until Mona's scream cut through the air.

Evander's blood ran cold, his spine rigid as horror washed over him.

"*Evander!*" she shrieked. "*Evander, where are you?*" Her voice was full of panic and terror and desperation.

"*Mona!*" Evander roared, breaking into a run. Renewed energy burned through him, laced with urgency and pure terror.

She was in trouble. He had to get to her. He had to save her.

Mona! Typhon cried out.

Only then did Evander recognize the crazed hysteria in Typhon's voice. It intensified, growing and morphing into something else, something foreign and dark and powerful.

Typhon's rage and power coursed through him, rising and surging like a tidal wave. It knocked Evander over until he fell on his rear, his head rocking backward and slamming into the concrete. Stars burst in his vision, and he trembled from the intensity racing through his body.

No, no, *no*...

Claws raked through him, slashing at flesh and bone as the darkness claimed him, clutching him so tightly he couldn't breathe.

The darkness was *Typhon*. And Mona's scream had ignited some feral side of the demon that Evander could not reach. They had bonded in the Underworld, but this place, this realm, had altered Typhon.

He was now something unrecognizable.

And this time, Evander was too weak to fight it. Typhon was stronger, and that power kept rising and rising with a primal need to protect Mona, to find her. He was no match for Typhon now. Even with Mona's melody still lingering within him, he couldn't hold on any longer. He had no strength left.

He surrendered fully to the demon inside him.

REKINDLED

PANDORA

EVERY NERVE IN PANDORA'S BODY WENT STILL AT
the sound of Sol's admission.

Pandora was my lover.

But it couldn't be true. Surely, this was Sol trying to
mock her or play one of his games with her.

But the torment in his gaze was so potent, so raw and
wounded, that she knew he was telling the truth.

"I don't understand," she said, her voice weak. And it
was the truth. She didn't understand *any* of this.

Is this true? she asked the voice inside her. But the
soul of the goddess within her made no response. Even
the echoing screams from the past had been silenced.

There was nothing but emptiness. And she wasn't
sure what that meant.

Had the goddess felt nothing for Sol? Or did she not remember him?

Sol shrugged as if brushing off the notion that he had been the lover of a woman who had quite literally been ripped apart by Apollo and Aidoneus, whose darkness now roamed the realms in search of something to devour.

Whose darkness was now a part of Pandora.

"I was young and naive," Sol said, gazing over the balcony toward the setting sun. "And she was beautiful and alluring. I couldn't resist her. For a year, we were inseparable, our very souls connected to one another. And then..." He trailed off, his eyes dimming and his jaw going rigid. "And then, she made a choice that separated us forever."

"That's not true," Pandora seethed.

Sol blinked and looked at her in confusion. "What are you talking about?"

Pandora clamped her mouth shut, but she couldn't take the words back. Sol was staring at her in shock and wariness, and she needed a distraction *now* before he asked too many questions.

"Why did you think I was her?" Pandora asked. "In the library."

His expression smoothed into that familiar look of apathy and boredom. He shrugged again, returning his gaze to the horizon.

"Answer the damn question, Sol," Pandora said with a sigh, tired of having to pull the truth out of him.

He rolled his eyes and braced his arms along the balcony railing. "I've had plenty of lovers over the years."

Pandora made a retching sound, and Sol laughed.

"What I mean to say is, I've tried to forget her," Sol said, the ghost of a smile still on his face. "But I've been careful not to get too wrapped up in someone. Not like I was with her."

"Ah. You've kept your distance."

He nodded. "Until you."

Pandora's heart jolted within her, and she straightened in surprise. "What?"

"At first, it was merely a game with you. I wanted you in my bed, and that was all. But then, in the library..." He trailed off again, his nostrils flaring. "I had never wanted *anyone* as much as I wanted you. Not since her."

Pandora's throat tightened at the admission. Her insides warmed, and a blush heated her cheeks.

He had *wanted* her.

Desperately.

But she couldn't find it in her to be pleased by this. Not when she knew he'd been thinking of *her*. The very goddess who constantly invaded her thoughts and dreams.

"I can't have been the only woman to taste your cock," Pandora said, trying to lighten the mood.

Sol cut an exasperated look at her. "Of course not. But this was different. You knew exactly what to do to drive me mad. You knew how to push me, how to send me over the edge. As much as I hate to admit it, Trivia, you owned me in that moment."

Pandora crossed her arms, and a satisfied smirk spread along her mouth. "I knew it. I beat you." She flicked his nose, and he chuckled.

"You rekindled something I'd lost," Sol said, straightening and turning to face her. "Something I thought had died long ago. With her."

Pandora's smile vanished, and something cold slithered into her chest. "Don't compare me to her."

He winced. "Sorry. Not the most exemplary of goddesses, was she?"

Pandora shook her head. "It's not that. I am not her. You know that, right? I refuse to be preserved in the shadow of your former lover. And I'll be damned if I just stand by while you hold me to her standards."

He huffed a dry laugh, raising his hand to catch a stray curl that had fallen against her cheek. "I wouldn't dream of caging you like that. Besides, it doesn't matter, does it? I'm leaving for the mortal realm in a matter of hours."

"Right." That twisting sensation returned to her

chest. "And don't expect me to come with you. I could never live in that realm."

"I would never. I myself can scarcely believe I'm to live there." He wrinkled his nose. "Among *humans*, of all things."

Pandora clasped her hands in front of her, trying to ignore the way his hand lingered against her cheek, his knuckles creating a path of fire on her skin. "So, we'll part ways then. You, a changed man, rekindled anew thanks to my delicious tongue, and I remaining the stunning goddess that I am."

He threw his head back and laughed, the sound raucous and vibrant and so damn alluring that Pandora couldn't help herself. When his laughs subsided, she pressed her palms to his cheeks and brought his mouth to hers. His lips opened for her as if he'd been waiting all evening for this. His tongue swept along hers, and his hands came around her waist, sliding lower until they cupped her ass and brought her body closer. Their hips aligned, and he ground against her, his tongue running along her teeth and fully tasting her. Ravishing her. Devouring her.

She moaned into his mouth, sliding her hands along his neck until they tangled in his hair. His mouth left hers and moved to her throat, her collarbone, and the swell of her breast. She gasped, throwing her head back as he licked the hollow of her throat, then slid his tongue between her breasts.

"Sol," she breathed, closing her eyes and relishing the feel of that wicked tongue, of the hot moisture pooling between her legs.

Much to her dismay, he withdrew from her bosom to bring his lips to her ear. "It's my turn," he whispered, then caught her lobe between his teeth.

"For what?" she rasped, hardly able to think straight.

He brushed his lips along her throat again, the motion feather-light and sending shivers of pleasure through her body. "It's my turn... to own you." His breath tickled her skin, and she arched her back at the sensual promise in his voice.

"I still hate you," Pandora whispered, her hips writhing against his. "You're an arrogant asshole. This doesn't change anything."

"Mmm," he purred against her neck. "I know. You are a *loathsome* creature, Trivia, and that won't change, either."

She chuckled, but the sound was breathless and airy as he dragged his nose up the column of her throat. His fingers at her waist teased the fabric of her dress, caressing the exposed flesh of her back and sliding under the silk. They traveled lower and lower until they grazed the curve of her ass, and she shivered again from the feel of his warm hands against her bare skin.

When he removed his hands, she almost whimpered in protest.

Until she found him lifting her skirts from the front, a wicked grin on his face.

"This dress is stunning, but it's covering up far too much of you for my liking," he murmured.

She tugged on his collar, trying to undo the elaborate buttons of his tunic, but he shook his head. "Oh, no, Trivia. You don't get to ravish me tonight. Right now, it's *your* turn to be laid bare before me."

Pandora huffed in exasperation. "Really? You won't let me undress you at all? That's hardly fair."

"You had me begging for mercy in the library. It's only fair I return the favor."

She rolled her eyes. So it was another competition between them, then.

That was fine. She would prove she had more restraint than he did.

Sol's grin widened as if he could see the stubborn resolve in her eyes. "I will unravel you, Trivia," he promised, his voice low and sultry. "Piece by piece."

Her insides trembled from his words, but she lifted her chin, challenging him. "I doubt that. But you can certainly try." Her skin still tingled from his touches earlier, and she secretly yearned for his tongue to explore more of her body.

But she would never admit this.

He clicked his tongue at her. "Such an obstinate thing you are."

She was about to snap a retort at him, but the words died in her throat as her skirts rose up to her thighs and his hands moved beneath the fabric, brushing between her legs. He swiped a finger at her center, and she groaned in spite of her conviction to remain unaffected by him.

"So wet already," Sol taunted, lifting his fingers to his mouth and sucking on them. Pandora followed the motion with her eyes as heat pooled in her stomach. "I think this will be quicker than I thought."

"Prick."

He laughed. "You taste divine, though. Almost as if you were a *true* goddess."

"Gods, you really know how to flatter a lady," Pandora said sarcastically. "Truly. It's a miracle I haven't melted into a puddle at your feet."

His grin turned feral as his hand dipped beneath her skirts again, his fingers tracing circles along her center. She bucked her hips in silent demand, her head thrown back once more as fire coursed through her veins. She wanted him deeper. Harder.

But he was teasing her, his fingers only brushing the lightest of touches against her.

"Bastard," she breathed.

He chuckled. "If you wanted a benevolent lover, you would have sought someone else." He dragged his lips along her cheekbone, her jaw, then to her ear. "But I don't think that's what you want."

No, it certainly wasn't. She'd had affectionate and tender lovers in the past, and while they had been pleasant encounters, they hadn't been as intoxicating as this. Never before had she been with a man who had challenged her, who had infuriated and aggravated her, who had elicited such hateful venom but also such uncontrollable lust from her.

It was arousing. All of it.

"No, you're right," Pandora quipped. "What I want is someone whose touches are so slow and light that it takes *hours* to make me come. That's much more satisfying."

He plunged a finger inside of her, and she gasped.

"Trust the process, darling," Sol crooned in her ear.

Her eyes closed as he inserted another finger, pumping them in and out, his movements ever so slow. She clenched around him, tightening and demanding more. He curled his fingers inward, brushing her inner walls and making her inhale sharply. She pressed against him, riding his hand, urging him onward.

He pushed into her, guiding her backward until she was pressed against the cool marble wall. He pinned her to it, then lifted her until her legs were draped over his shoulders. She cried out in alarm, her arms flailing as she searched for purchase, but Sol only laughed.

"I've got you."

"Forgive me if I don't take your word for it," Pandora said, her voice shaking.

Then, his tongue was on her, and she forgot everything. Her skirts lifted higher, and his fingers were still inside her as he licked her inner thigh. His tongue swept over her center, and her legs cinched around him. Her insides quivered, and she moaned.

"That's it," he said, his voice tickling her flesh.

His fingers withdrew to make way for his tongue, which slid deeper inside her, fully tasting her. It was smooth and hot against her skin. She arched against the wall, eyes closing as he licked her again and again. Her legs tightened as she ground against him, the friction of his mouth and tongue driving her to the brink.

"You want me," he teased. Gods, the way his breath felt against her...

"No," she rasped, even as her body thrashed against him, demanding more.

"Say it."

"Never."

His teeth grazed her, and she cried out. His tongue worked her, in and out, bringing her closer to the edge.

"You're mine, Trivia. Say it."

"I can't—I *can't*—" She didn't even know how to form words anymore. The fire pulsing through her, pounding relentlessly against her restraints, was driving her mad.

She couldn't think. Her mind emptied of all thoughts except for that singular focus of his tongue burrowing deeper into her.

"Sol," she gasped, her hands fisting his hair, tugging hard, pulling him more firmly against her. He obliged, his tongue plunging farther into her, another finger joining the other as he pumped and thrust. Each motion had her panting, moaning, rasping...

"I can go harder," he said. "All you need to do is ask." He continued driving into her, and white stars danced in her vision as release drew nearer.

Oh gods, she wanted more. She wanted it hard.

But she couldn't. She couldn't give in

All reason fled her mind as his teeth clamped down on her, and she shoved her fist into her mouth to keep from screaming.

She didn't care anymore. She didn't even know why she was resisting. "Please, Sol," she begged. "*Please.*"

"There it is." Triumph tainted his voice, but he obliged. His fingers dug deeper, claiming her fully. His tongue seemed to burn her skin. Each stroke became more aggressive, more violent. His fingers pushed,

pushed, *pushed,* until they were so deep inside her she couldn't see straight.

"Come for me," he demanded, then bit down hard on her.

She screamed, unable to contain it any longer as release barreled through her, bringing sparks of white light flashing across her vision. Pleasure spiraled within her, cascading in a raging river that couldn't be stopped. Oh gods, *oh gods,* she had never felt like this before. She continued writhing against him as she came, her breathing ragged and desperate.

He removed his hands and gripped her thighs, steadying her. He was panting, too, but she took small satisfaction in this. In the end, she knew he'd won. He'd claimed her fully, just as he'd promised.

Slowly, he lowered her, keeping her back against the wall. She looked at him, still dazed from her release, as he smirked at her in triumph.

"Ass," she whispered.

He only grinned. "Consider that a parting gift."

Her eyes widened. "What, that's it?"

He arched an eyebrow. "You want more?"

Heat filled her face. She did. She wanted him fully inside her, his clothes shed and his skin flush against hers.

She wanted *all* of him.

His eyes glinted. "Another time, perhaps."

"You're leaving for the mortal realm."

"Yes, we established that. But we also established I'm an arrogant prick, didn't we?" He grinned again before retreating toward the ballroom.

"Sol—" Pandora surged forward, then realized her dress was still bunched around her waist, and her hair was likely a wild mess around her. She was in no state to return to the ball.

But at her outburst, he stopped and glanced over his shoulder at her. So many words left unsaid between them, and for the briefest of seconds, his expression sobered into something thoughtful and yearning and full of regret.

He had bared secrets to her. And she understood him now. The lazy, apathetic mask he wore was only a ruse to protect him from caring too much. Because the last time he had, his love had been taken from him.

But tonight, she had seen all of him. And in the heat of the moment, Pandora hadn't cared that he'd known the goddess who inhabited her body. She had pushed aside any thoughts of that connection, ignoring the possibility that this might be the only reason they were drawn to each other.

But now, that truth hung heavy between them. In the end, he was haunted by the ghost of a woman long gone. And she was bound by the fate of that same woman, destined to destroy this realm and all its inhabitants.

A large part of her felt relief in knowing Sol would be safely in the mortal realm, away from all this destruction.

But once he knew what she'd done, he would never want to see her again.

Perhaps it was for the best that they took this no further. This would be the last they would ever see of each other.

So, she nodded in understanding. And he turned and left her there alone on the balcony, her skin still thrumming from what he'd done to her.

She would have remained out there for hours, processing her emotions and thoughts. But the excited babble of the guests behind her turned piercing and shrill.

Then several people screamed.

Pandora adjusted her skirts and impatiently pulled the largest pins free of her hair, letting it fall around her shoulders as she hurried into the ballroom. She almost ran into Sol, who stood rigid as he stared at the creature prowling forward.

It was a demon with large, leathery wings and gleaming red eyes that surveyed the guests with hungry delight. Elongated claws extended from his hands, and small horns protruded from his temples. Though his appearance was much more wild and animalistic than when she'd last seen him, she still recognized him.

It was Evander. And he was fully in his demon form.

A roar poured from his mouth as he pounced, diving straight for the crowd.

LIES
MONA

FOR THE HUNDREDTH TIME, MONA TRIED summoning her magic, spreading her arms and calling upon the earth beneath her. But nothing happened. Her attempts at removing her restraints were no use. The shackles were clamped tightly around her wrists as she waited in the dank dungeon cell for someone to retrieve her. Her bones rattled with fear, and she paced the small space.

"Hello!" she cried out, shaking the bars of her cell. "Let me out!" The metal rattled from her frantic motions, and she let out a growl of frustration.

She was trapped down here, helpless, as she waited for Apollo to interrogate her.

She had no idea where Evander was. Or Hestia. She

hoped the fire goddess wasn't punished too severely for assisting her.

"Hestia, are you in here?" she called.

No answer. For all she knew, she was alone down here.

She crossed her arms over her chest, shivering from the chill that swept in. Terror gripped her chest in a tight vise, and she found it difficult to breathe. Her inhales turned into ragged gasps, and she doubled over, clutching her stomach.

"Goddess," she moaned. "Can't. Breathe. Can't. Do this." She wheezed, struggling to get air into her lungs.

More than anything, she wished Prue was here with her.

If my sister was here, what would she say?

That was easy. She would yell at Mona to get a grip and stop being a coward. She would say, *You are brave, Mona. And you can do this.*

Mona remembered what Hestia had told her: *You have a quick mind. Use it. Do not fall prey to this fear. You are stronger than this.*

"I am stronger than this," she whispered, inhaling deeply through her nose and counting to ten with each breath.

Gradually, her pulse slowed and she could think straight.

"Trust your mind," she told herself. "See through the fear." She swallowed and gave herself a sure nod.

Fear wasn't helpful. She had to see past it to reach her mind.

"What do I know of Elysium?" she thought aloud.

Home of the gods, yes. A powerful source of magic, yes. But what use was her magic if she couldn't access it?

Her eyes suddenly grew wide. She was a witch, wasn't she? While she couldn't access Gaia's earth magic, perhaps she could cast something with her blood. She recalled helping Prue do something similar when she was in a prison cell in the mortal realm. Runic magic was accessible to anyone, even those with very little magical blood.

She could do this.

She glanced down at her wrists, which were rubbed raw from her fruitless attempts to loosen her restraints. Raising a hand to her mouth, she dug her teeth deeper into one of the wounds until she drew blood. With a hiss of pain, she withdrew her hand to allow the blood to drop onto the stony ground.

"*Excito*," she murmured.

A plume of smoke drifted from where her blood lay on the ground. That was a good sign. It meant *some* modicum of power was available down here, even if it wasn't her full reserve of magic.

She dug her fingernails into the wound on her wrist,

drawing more blood, and painted the bars of her cell with it. Angling her hands, she trickled blood on her chains as well.

"*Aperta*," she whispered, gathering every ounce of energy within her. Though her wrists throbbed and her throat ached and her stomach growled, she inhaled deeply and drew from that well of power she knew so well. It was there, even if it was stifled. She had no doubt some anti-magic enchantments were built into these cells.

But Mona was more than just a prisoner. She was a powerful earth witch. The daughter of a goddess.

And she would not be contained.

With a *snap,* the chains on her wrists split open and clattered loudly as they fell at her feet. A louder sound cut through the air as the bars of her cell broke, and she staggered back in surprise. Another *crack*, and the bars clanged to the ground, leaving a small gap just wide enough for her to step through if she stooped.

With an excited gasp, Mona hurried through the gap before someone came to investigate the loud noises. She crept down the dark, narrow hallway until she found a set of stairs.

She was almost at the top when she heard the screams.

Oh, Goddess...

Her steps quickened, and she reached another long

hallway. Following the screams, she raced down it, climbing another smaller flight of stairs that opened to a wide foyer. The gleaming windows built into the walls reflected the light of the setting sun. Several figures raced past her, muttering about demons and dark magic.

Evander.

Ignoring the strange looks cast her way, Mona elbowed her way through the crowd, fighting to get toward the chaos, toward whatever they were running from.

She reached the magnificent ballroom, still filled with people dressed in their finest attire. And in the center, hunched on all fours with his great wings spread wide behind him, was Evander.

But this wasn't the Evander she knew. She had seen him when Typhon was in control—wings, horns, flashing red eyes. But this was more monstrous than that. His skin was like gray leather, and he was completely bald. He wore no clothes, but the wrinkles on his skin made him look more animal than human.

He was in a complete demon form right now. And Mona didn't know if she could reach him.

But she had to try. Already, several gods and goddesses approached Evander with magic sparkling from their fingertips.

They would hurt him. Or kill him. She had to do something.

Without hesitating, her mouth opened, and the song of her soul poured from her lips, echoing in the vast space. Around her, people whipped their heads around to determine where the noise was coming from, but she didn't acknowledge them. She kept her eyes pinned on Evander as she edged closer to him, her voice rising in volume as she sang. The shouts around her quieted in shock as the crowd gaped at her. But still, she sang.

And then, miraculously, a low voice joined in with hers. It wasn't quite the singing she'd heard from Evander before—more like a low, gruff humming—but it was the harmony that matched her melody perfectly. Tears burned in her eyes as she continued to sing, slowly closing the distance between herself and Evander. He had turned to face her now, his red eyes drilling into hers. She did not flinch. She did not back away.

This was the man she loved. And she loved every part of him. The good and the bad. The beautiful and the ugly.

He was *hers*.

She raised her palm and found him lifting his hand to meet hers, his claws stretching for her.

"*Enough!*" bellowed a voice.

Mona jumped, and Evander stiffened with a low growl. Together, they turned to face the tall figure emerging from the crowd, stomping furiously toward them. He had a powerful, muscular form, with sleek brown hair and a neatly trimmed beard. His dark black eyes seemed to boil with his fury.

He raised his hands, summoning light that speared straight toward Evander's chest.

"No!" Mona shrieked, stepping in front of him. The man's magic struck her instead, and she screamed, falling to her knees.

With a roar, Evander lunged, ignoring Mona's protests. His wings flapped and he swiped his claws, but the man was faster. More sunlight poured from his fingertips, assaulting Evander. Evander screeched, trying to use his wings to shield himself from the onslaught of power, but it was no use. The magic was too strong.

"Stop it!" Mona cried. "*Stop it!*"

"Go back to the pits of Tartarus where you belong!" the man bellowed, the light in the room intensifying.

Fury churned in Mona's chest, raw and powerful. She spread her hands, her fingers coiling with her rage, and summoned roots from the ground. The elegant marble floors cracked as brambles shot forward, winding around the man's ankles and wrists, pinning him in place.

Shock filled the man's face as he gazed at Mona with horror.

"Release him," she hissed, tightening her hold on him. His arms jerked from the movement.

"Gaia?" he whispered, his face paling.

"No. I am her daughter. And you have ensnared a prince of Hell. Unless you wish to wage war against the death gods, *you will release him.*"

To her surprise, the man laughed. She kept him chained by her magic, but her resolve faltered.

"Do not speak of that which you do not understand, child," the man scoffed. "There are no more death gods. The Underworld has been destroyed."

"He is the son of Aidoneus!" Mona cried, gesturing to Evander.

"And Aidoneus was my brother," the man spat. "I don't give a shit who he is. He is invading my realm, and he is a demon! He must be destroyed."

Mona felt her heart drop to her stomach. She should have known. She should have realized when he'd used the power of the sun to attack Evander.

This was Apollo.

The king of Elysium.

"I was benevolent when I cursed Gaia," the man went on. "I let her children live. A mistake I will not repeat tonight."

Vines snapped, and the brambles surrounding him fell to the floor, turning to ash at his feet. He gathered a ball of light between his palms and flung it toward Mona. She shrieked, but Evander shot forward, spreading his wings and absorbing the impact.

"*Evander!*" she cried as he roared in pain, his great

wings riddled with charred holes and burn marks. He slumped to the floor, shuddering violently. Mona crouched beside him, pressing her hands to his face. He blinked blearily, his red eyes burning with regret.

Apollo summoned more power, but another figure stepped between them, her hands blazing with fire.

Hestia.

"*Do not touch her,*" Hestia commanded, her voice ringing with authority.

Apollo's face slackened in surprise before his eyes narrowed. "Don't be a fool, Hestia."

"I stood by when you banished Gaia. I will not stand by while you obliterate her daughter as well." Hestia's form was rigid as she faced off Apollo.

"Step aside," Apollo ground out.

"No."

"Then I will curse you as I cursed her!" Apollo bellowed, gathering light in his palms once more.

"Apollo, *stop!*" cried a voice.

A new figure stepped forward, his face pale and his eyes darting between Apollo and Hestia. He had shoulder-length blond hair and wore a gleaming gold uniform. His eyes were full of betrayal as he looked at Apollo.

"Stay out of this, Sol," Apollo ground out, keeping his eyes trained on Hestia.

"I will not let you banish my mother," Sol said.

Mona stiffened, her eyes darting from Sol to Hestia, and then to Apollo. Goddess above… Hestia was his *mother*?

"She is openly defying me," Apollo growled. "She has been an ally of Gaia's from the beginning. This is her punishment." He turned his furious black eyes on Sol. "Would you prefer I kill her instead?"

"She is defending Gaia's daughter!" Sol argued, gesturing to Mona. "What harm has this woman done to our realm?"

"She is protecting the demon!"

Sol's eyes drifted to where Evander lay sprawled on the floor with Mona protectively hovering over him. Slowly, Sol's eyes narrowed, his expression calculating as he looked at Apollo with sudden realization.

"You said their kind were toxic," he said softly.

Apollo's brows knitted together. "What?" he said, his tone sharp and impatient.

"You said the demons of the Underworld were *toxic*," Sol repeated, striding closer to Apollo. "You told us all it was unsafe to go there, lest we be poisoned by the death magic that saturated the air. Yet here stands a daughter of Gaia, unaffected by this demon she clearly cares for!" His voice rose in pitch with each word until he was red in the face as he spat at Apollo. "None of us are affected by his presence, Apollo, so I ask you—why did you lie? Or were you simply mistaken?"

Apollo's face had drained of color, his eyes shifting to the crowd now murmuring around him. Mona held perfectly still, clutching Evander's clawed hand in hers as she surveyed the argument. She didn't know who this Sol person was, but if he exposed Apollo for the liar that he was, then he was on her side.

"The Underworld is not toxic," Mona said loudly. "I dwelled there for a time, as did my sister, Prue. We possess the blood of Gaia and were unaffected."

The murmurs grew louder. Apollo fixed his lethal gaze on her and bit out, "*Be quiet,* daughter of Gaia."

"I refuse to be silenced like you silenced my mother!" Mona shouted, rising to her feet. "She cannot speak for herself, so *I* will speak for her! I committed no crime against you or your realm. I should be welcome here, just like any other god or goddess. As should Evander, your nephew."

"Demons are not welcome here!" Apollo bellowed.

"He is not a demon. He possesses god blood just like the rest of us!"

"*Silence!*" Apollo roared.

Mona spread her arms, prepared to impale him with her thorns, when he slashed his arms through the air, hitting her with a burst of white light. Mona screamed, shielding her face with her hands. Evander shrieked a shrill, feeble cry, unable to save her this time. Brambles shot forward to protect Mona, but they were singed away by Apollo's fury.

A wall of flame appeared between Mona and Apollo's strike, disintegrating the magic of his attack. Hestia stood there, wielding a sword of flames as she deflected another blow.

"This is not your fight, Hestia," Apollo seethed.

Hestia only leveled her sword at him, her eyes bright with rage. "It is now. I have taken my stand."

"Guards!" Apollo shouted. "Seize the fire goddess and escort her out of my sight. She is not worth the energy it would take to end her life. Instead, she can rot away in a prison cell."

No one moved.

"*Guards!*" Apollo said, his voice rising.

A few navy-clad soldiers shifted amongst the crowd, but they made no move to follow orders.

"You've lost their support, Apollo," said Sol. "You lied about the Underworld. What else have you lied about?" He cocked his head, considering. "Why did you banish Gaia?"

"I do not owe *any* of you an explanation!" Apollo said, his nostrils flaring and his eyes wild.

"You do if you wish to maintain the throne!" shouted a woman from the crowd.

"Jupiter *never* would have lied to us like that," said another.

Apollo threw back his head and screamed, his body quivering with fury. Light poured from his hands, and he struck, his magic slicing through the air. The ground rumbled as his power shook the very walls. A dome of fire encased Mona and Evander, and she gasped, flinching as Apollo's magic hammered against it. But the shield held in place, protecting her.

Relief filled her chest, but it was short-lived. In front of her—outside the shield—a familiar figure crumpled to the floor, her body taking the full impact of Apollo's rage.

"Hestia!" Mona screamed.

The shield of fire dissipated, and she hurried to Hestia's side. Sol joined her, his face ashen and his eyes wide. Shouts erupted from the crowd, and Apollo staggered back in shock, as if he hadn't intended to strike her at all.

Smoke furled from a charred gash in the center of Hestia's chest. Her face was pale, her hands cold and trembling as Mona clasped them in hers.

"Oh, Goddess, *Hestia*," Mona whispered, tears filling her eyes. "What have you done?"

"Tell your mother," Hestia choked, silver blood bubbling from her mouth, "that I am sorry I did nothing. I—I hope... this c-can atone for that."

"Someone fetch a healer!" Sol shouted into the crowd, but Hestia placed a hand on his arm.

"My son," she whispered. "Y-You can still do good. You have seen him for what he truly is. *Do... something...* about it. Rebuild this realm."

Sol shook his head. "I—I cannot! We need you. We need your *magic*. This place cannot function without your fire to fuel it!"

A sad smile spread across Hestia's lips. Her eyelids fluttered. "That is my one regret with you, Sol. I taught you... that power... was more important... than love. And for that, I am s-sorry. Please forgive me. I know you l-loved her, but I hope you can find love again... and see... for yourself... what truly matters."

Her head slumped backward, and Sol shook her. "Mother. *Mother.* You must wake! We need you!"

But Hestia didn't move.

Tears streamed down Mona's face as she shut her eyes, saying a prayer to the Triple Goddess.

Hestia had died. For *her*.

A knot formed in her throat, and she couldn't breathe. Sobs tore from her chest as if her body were ripping in two.

Then, the ground began to quake. Dust trickled from the ceiling. And a burst of energy exploded in the room, knocking everyone to the ground. Mona slid backward but caught herself before her head crashed into the marble floor. A collective cry rose from the crowd as people staggered to their feet. Mona glanced around, confusion and fear gripping her chest. What was happening?

"Trivia!" Apollo shouted, his gaze fixed on a figure in the crowd. "The wards are down. I need your death magic to craft them anew before Pandora's magic destroys us all."

Mona's blood ran cold as a woman stepped forward, her dark red hair shimmering and her hard gaze fixed on Apollo.

It was her. Trivia—the one responsible for all this. The one who had dragged Evander through the portal.

Mona shot to her feet, fury boiling within her. And Trivia's gold eyes fixed on her.

"Hello, sister," she murmured.

Mona went rigid at that word. *Sister.*

What was she talking about?

She opened her mouth to speak, but Trivia said, "I invoke the terms of our bargain, Pomona. You will do nothing. You will say nothing. I call in my favor and order you to stand by and *watch*. When the sun rises, consider our bargain fulfilled."

Mona stiffened, and it took her thoughts a moment to catch up. Only then did she remember—when she had come back to the Underworld, intent on finding Prue, Trivia had met her first. She had asked for one favor in exchange for revealing Prue's location.

And she was calling in that favor.

Fire surged through Mona's veins as the magic between them solidified. She opened her mouth to scream, to rage at Trivia for what she'd done, but no words came out. She could not speak. She could not *move.*

A slow smirk spread on Trivia's face as she brushed past Mona and faced Apollo.

"Are you ready, my king?" she asked, her voice low.

"Yes," Apollo said, nodding vigorously. It seemed he believed if Trivia could rebuild the wards with him, then he could save face. But the glares from the crowd proved he had shattered the trust of his people. "Give me your death magic." He stretched out his hand to Trivia, but she did not move. She looked at him with a mixture of loathing and triumph.

"I hope you burn, Apollo," she said, her voice full of malice.

Apollo stilled, his eyes flaring wide.

Then Trivia turned to Sol, who remained crouched by Hestia's body. He gazed up at Trivia with shock and disbelief, his eyes full of betrayal.

"I am sorry, Sol," she whispered. Her eyes were so earnest that if Mona didn't know better, she would think Trivia meant the words. "But there is no stopping this. I wish—I wish you had left for the mortal realm."

Sol only gaped at her, his head shaking slightly, as if he was in denial.

Trivia stretched her arms wide, and a deafening *boom* quaked from beneath the ground. Black smoke poured in from the windows, filling the air with a churning storm that Mona had seen once before. Fear tightened in her chest, and she tried to scream, but Trivia's bargain prevented her from doing so.

It was the dark magic from Pandora's box. And it had come to destroy them all.

INEVITABLE

PANDORA

P ANDORA HAD KNOWN AS SOON AS A POLLO struck Hestia. She had known when Evander appeared in his full demon form.

She had known when Sol rushed to his dying mother's side.

It was happening. And she couldn't stop it, even if she wanted to.

She had forgotten Hestia was Sol's mother. That was an unfortunate turn of events.

But the instant the chaos of Evander and Mona's appearance broke through the crowd, she'd known it was too late to turn back.

The events were set in motion.

With Hestia's death, the wards she helped create had fallen. And it was only a matter of time before the dark powers from the box came surging in, beckoned by the death magic Pandora had brought here.

She would never forget the look of anger and betrayal in Sol's eyes when he looked at her. He had stared up at her with accusation and disbelief. Like he didn't even know her.

And the truth was... he didn't.

Pandora didn't know why she'd tried to believe otherwise. Whatever feelings she had for him were doomed from the start.

She never wanted to care for him. She was perfectly content with loathing him for the rest of eternity.

But she *did* care for him. And the look he'd given her sliced far deeper than any magic.

Darkness swirled around her as the shadows from her box gathered and encircled her. She kept her arms outstretched, welcoming that magic home. Urging it onward.

Because it had to be done. She couldn't go back now. She had to embrace the inevitable destruction of this world.

Apollo stumbled back a step, his mouth falling open in horror. He pointed a shaking finger at her. "You're— You're—"

"Yes," Pandora said, her mouth stretching wide in a cruel smile. "You thought you could be rid of me so easily? But her thirst for vengeance runs deep. And she cursed you, Apollo, so that you would suffer from her wrath. Now, she has returned to exact vengeance."

"Who?" Sol barked, but his eyes weren't on Pandora —they were fixed on Apollo. "Who is she talking about?"

Apollo's mouth opened and closed. He seemed incapable of speech.

So Pandora answered for him.

"The soul of Pandora, the goddess, rests in my body," she said loudly. "All thanks to Apollo. It was part of Gaia's punishment, to imbue her third child with the soul and memories of the goddess." She jabbed a finger toward Apollo. "*You* did this. You sentenced this realm to death when you ripped her apart! These people have no one to blame but you!"

Sol had shot to his feet, his hands curled into tight fists. He fixed his enraged eyes on Apollo. "You—You killed her? It was *you* who killed Pandora?"

But Apollo ignored Sol. He was staring wide-eyed at Pandora as if she was a ghost. Slowly, he backed away from her, but she only laughed.

"It's too late, Your Majesty," she spat. "The darkness will devour you first."

A scream filled the air, and at first, Pandora thought it was her own imagination—that the goddess's memories had overtaken her once more. But several people cried out in alarm, covering their ears, and she realized the screams came from the dark magic. Coils of smoke speared toward Apollo, who yelped, trying to run from them before they strangled him.

Pandora lost sight of him as darkness flooded the room, crashing into walls and pillars. Screams pierced the air. Debris rained around them. And all the while, Pandora stood there with her arms outstretched, waiting to be freed of the memories and turmoil that had claimed her for so long.

This is it, she thought. *Now, I can be free.*

No, hissed a low voice inside her. *Gaia is next.*

Pandora stiffened. She had forgotten there was more to her revenge. But killing Gaia would be simple. Easy, even. Much easier than destroying an entire realm.

No, the voice said again. *We will not stop there. We will claim the mortal realm. We will claim all the souls for our own!*

Pandora shook her head, her arms trembling. "You cannot," she said aloud. "That was not part of the plan."

We changed the plan, cackled the voice. *We want more, young goddess. And we will take it.*

Pandora gritted her teeth, fighting against the bloodthirsty rage boiling inside her. For the first time in her life, she actively opposed the forces within her. And she hadn't realized until now how *strong* they were.

"I... don't... want... this," she bit out, every word ripped from her by force. Her fists trembled. Her bones rattled. The endless churning of the soul inside her only intensified, roaring in indignation.

Avenge me!

It couldn't be stopped. No amount of destruction would be enough for it. It would constantly yearn for blood, for death, for endless suffering. The goddess's soul was a yawning chasm that would never be filled.

Pandora had thought she would be free of this. But she was a prisoner of these memories and emotions for all eternity.

She would *never* be free.

This had all been for nothing.

"Stop," she commanded.

But the voices inside her only laughed.

"*Stop!*" she screamed, stretching her arms wide and summoning her earth magic. Her voice broke on an enraged cry as she sank to her knees, digging deep within her reserve of magic, unleashing *everything*.

Cracks split the ground, and her tree branches sprang forth obediently, surrounding her in a protective dome that shielded her from the darkness.

"No!" she shouted, frantically waving her hands. Around her, screams filled the air as the dark magic feasted. "Help them! Save them!"

She was finished being a pawn in a dead goddess's game for revenge. She was finished bowing to the whims of the lost memories trapped inside her.

Even if it killed her, she would resist them.

They had used her. She thought they were her allies, that they only wanted to be free. Just like her.

But in the end, the goddess's soul and memories had just been another prison for her.

Everything in her life was born of pain. There was nothing left for her. No one she could trust or turn to. No one, not even herself, could save her.

Sobs poured from her throat. She let the tears fall, covering her face with her hands as the misery drowned her. She felt her magic expanding with her grief, widening the dome of tree branches to span the entire ballroom.

But it wasn't enough. Beyond the palace, the screams of the villagers echoed. Out there, people were dying. And her magic wasn't strong enough to stop it.

A familiar voice bled through the chaos around her. It was shouting orders, and it rang with authority and strength.

Sol.

Pandora had never heard him speak like that. He sounded like a leader. A *king,* even.

Her eyes snapped open, and with the shade of her trees as cover, she could make out the dark figures flitting around the ballroom.

Only a few paces away was Sol, gesturing frantically as he gave orders. One man—a servant, from the looks of it—nodded obediently and darted away, climbing through the brush of Pandora's magic to fulfill some task Sol had given him.

Just behind Sol rested his mother's dead body.

Emotions tightened in Pandora's chest, and she wanted to collapse and sob some more. But here was Sol, who had never accepted any responsibility, who hid himself away from the public eye, who avoided hard labor at all costs... Now, he was taking up the mantle Apollo had left behind.

Where was the great king? Had he died? Or fled?

In this moment, Pandora didn't care. Her feet were moving before she realized it. In an instant, she stood before Sol.

He stiffened at her approach, his eyes blazing with fury.

"I can help you," she said, her voice thick with tears.

A blast of white light slammed into her chest, sending her crashing to the floor. Pain exploded through her skull, ricocheting off her body. She groaned, struggling to rise, but Sol struck her again.

"Everything you said when you came here was a lie," Sol seethed, his face contorted with rage, making him unrecognizable. "You deceived us all. This whole time, you were harboring this darkness. *Her* darkness." His voice cracked on the last word. "You attacked my home.

Thousands will die because of you." He raised his arm again, light burning from his fingertips.

But Pandora forced herself to hold his gaze. Even though her instincts demanded she flinch away from another blow of his magic, she held steady, knowing full well she deserved it.

Sol hesitated, going still at the resolve in her eyes. Slowly, he lowered his arm, his nostrils flaring. Mingled with the anger on his face were wounds she recognized far too well.

Hurt.

Grief.

Betrayal.

Sorrow.

They shone plainly on his features now. There was no mask in place to hide them.

"I should destroy you," he growled. "Perhaps if I did, this darkness would stop."

"Then do it," Pandora rasped, her voice weak and pathetic. Never before had she sounded so feeble. But she had nothing left. No strength. No conviction. She was too exhausted to don her Hecate mask, or even her Trivia mask.

Right now, she was only Pandora. But she didn't even know who that was.

Was she the embodiment of the goddess who

perished long ago? Or was she Gaia's daughter, blessed with earth magic?

Was she anyone at all? Or was she merely a pawn in this grand scheme?

"*Do it*, Sol," Pandora begged. "Please, end this. She— She won't leave me be! Her memories, her screams, haunt me daily and I just want it to stop. I—I thought it would be finished after this. That I would finally be free. But she'll never release me. I am caged for eternity. So I am *begging* you to end this. For me. For Elysium. I don't want to be her weapon for revenge anymore."

Sol's face hardened into an expression of unyielding steel. There was no sympathy on his face. Only pure hatred.

"Ending you would be a mercy I am not willing to give," he spat. "You deserve this, Trivia. And if you wanted to be free of her, you would have stopped this before it destroyed my home."

Pandora's mouth trembled. Tears poured down her face, and her chest constricted with more sobs.

"Lord Sol." The servant from before hurried to his side, and Sol turned his fiery gaze away from Pandora. She strained to listen and barely heard the man's words: "The portal is open."

Sol nodded. "We need to get everyone we can to that portal."

But the servant shook his head. "There isn't enough power."

"Then we will find something to fuel it!" Sol barked. "But we have to try."

"I will do it."

The two men turned to look at Pandora. The servant's eyes grew wide, but Sol's face twisted into another sneer.

"Like hell you will, Trivia. I'm not letting you anywhere near that portal."

"Look around you." Pandora spread her arms. "*My magic* is protecting us. It's Gaia's magic, and it's the only thing strong enough to counter Pandora's darkness."

"No," Sol ground out.

The servant lifted a finger. "If I may..."

Sol whirled to him, enraged, and the servant flinched under his glare. "What?" Sol snapped.

"If she uses her magic, her *essence*, to fuel the portal, then she cannot travel through it. She must remain here."

Slowly, the two men turned to face her once more. The servant wore an expression of anxiety mingled with curiosity. Sol's was full of loathing, his eyes narrowed.

Pandora nodded at them. "Then, so be it."

LIFE
PRUE

PRUE'S EYES FLEW OPEN AS A RATTLING GASP escaped her, grating against her throat as if she hadn't spoken or eaten for days. Her tongue felt dry and scratchy. Her limbs ached and throbbed. She tried to sit up, but her body was stiff. She choked on a panicked cry.

"My queen!" Shuffled footsteps hurried closer.

Prue's eyes opened to find a darkened room surrounding her, with shelves and various dusty pieces of furniture. The walls were made of a chrome-like silver that she knew quite well.

She was in the castle. *Cyrus's* castle.

Hands were on her, and she almost fell forward with relief. Thank the Goddess Cyrus was here.

But she stilled immediately. The fingers grasping her were cool and unfamiliar.

"I've got you." She recognized the voice, and it wasn't Cyrus.

Realization dawned on her. "Lagos." His name was breathless on her lips, and she was both relieved and disappointed. "You're alive."

He'd gotten out of Tartarus. He'd protected the castle, just like she'd asked.

But where was Cyrus?

"The book said it was natural to feel quite weak when awakened," Lagos said gently. "Do not overexert yourself."

Prue's head whipped to him. "What book? What do you mean by *awakened*?" As her vision came into focus, she made out a huge, boiling cauldron standing behind Lagos. A book sat open on a table next to it, and the pages thrummed with energy.

"Lagos," she said, her voice low and full of warning. "What have you done?"

"It wasn't me, Your Majesty. It was Cyrus."

Her body went cold at that. She remembered what her mother had told her: *You have a fierce husband who has the power to bring you back.*

Her throat swelled with emotion, and her next words came out strained. "Where is he? Where—Where is my husband?" She scanned the dark room as if expecting him to be hiding behind a pillar.

"He is here, my queen." Lagos kept her hand in his as

he guided her toward the cauldron.

Immediate relief filled her. He was *here*, he was still alive, he—

She faltered as Lagos led her to the other side of the cauldron, where a body lay sprawled on the stone floor. A broken sob tore from Prue's throat as she lurched forward, ignoring the pain in her limbs and the pulsing agony in her skull from her sudden movements. Her knees scraped along the floor as she dropped beside Cyrus, tears pouring from her eyes at the sight of him.

"Oh Goddess, Cyrus... *Cyrus!*" she wailed, clutching his face in her hands. His eyes were closed, and... She sucked in a breath, her hands trembling as she held him.

He was different. He didn't smell the same.

And his tattoos were gone.

Not only that, but his hair had lost its silver luster. It was now inky black.

"He still breathes, my queen," said Lagos.

Prue's head snapped up, her eyes flaring wide as she looked at him. "He's alive?"

The demon nodded, the motion slow and hesitant. His dark eyes were filled with a wary apprehension that made Prue's stomach coil with dread.

"Lagos, tell me," she demanded. "Tell me what happened." Her voice was deadly calm, but only a thread of sanity held her intact. She was so close to breaking, to shattering completely.

Lagos quickly explained everything to her—how Cyrus had emerged from the rubble with her body, how he had sought help from Lagos, how he had unearthed the book and discovered the awakening spell.

With each passing second, Prue's breathing became more ragged. By the end, her eyes shut against the dizzying pain in her head, and she thought she might faint. It was too much.

What had Cyrus done?

"He was desperate, my queen," Lagos said softly. "He would have done anything to bring you back, even sacrifice his own life."

"No. He couldn't—He shouldn't—" She broke off with another shaky breath, glancing down at Cyrus and brushing strands of black hair out of his face. She leaned closer, detecting the faint, slow breaths coming from his mouth.

"If he's alive, then why won't he wake?" she asked Lagos.

The demon took a long, slow breath before responding. "He is different. I sensed it as soon as the spell was complete. The magic of the Underworld no longer lives in him."

"What does that mean?" Prue asked in a hollow voice.

"You remember how the magic of the Underworld

granted you power? You commanded me to speak to you when you first arrived in this realm."

Prue nodded absently, recalling the time when Kronos had possessed Cyrus and he'd chained her up in a cave. Lagos had come to bring her food, and she'd unknowingly invoked her power as his queen to force him to speak to her.

"We demons can sense the power of this realm," Lagos went on. "I could always sense it within Cyrus and you. But I don't feel it anymore. Not from him."

Prue's heart dropped like a stone as she looked down at Cyrus once more. "He has no magic?"

"None that I can discern."

"Is that why he won't wake?" Prue pressed a hand to Cyrus's chest. His skin was cold, but a faint heartbeat thrummed against her palm.

"I don't know." Lagos's voice was solemn. As if he expected the worst.

As if he, too, feared Cyrus wouldn't wake at all.

Prue found it hard to breathe; each inhale was a ragged gasp tearing through her over and over. "I can't— I can't—" Prue's voice broke on the words. *She* broke.

She was broken from this. And she would not recover.

Cyrus had given his entire soul for her.

She had known, in the Realm of Gaia, the lengths he would go to to save her. She'd fallen down the mountain, and he had used the soul magic inside him to save her. "How could he have done this?" she moaned.

"Wouldn't you have done the same?" Lagos prompted.

"Of course I would have," Prue said at once, her voice strained. And she froze.

She already had. This was the same sacrifice she had made for Mona. She would have done *anything* to bring back her sister. Even give up her own magic, her own soul.

And if it had been Cyrus instead of her who lay dead from the destruction of Pandora's magic, then Prue would have done it all over again to save him.

Her thoughts turned to Gaia, and the pride and sorrow shining in her eyes. She, too, had sacrificed everything to save her daughters. She'd had a glamorous life in Elysium. A throne. A husband.

But she'd given it all up to keep Prue, Mona, and Pandora safe.

Now that third daughter was coming for her because of a price she had never meant to pay.

Tears stung her eyes, falling freely once more. She pressed a kiss to Cyrus's temple, cradling his head in her lap. She sat there, holding him as if she could breathe his magic and power back into him.

Her head snapped up as Gaia's words returned to her once more: *I know with our magic, the magic of the earth, we are able to breathe life into beings.*

"Holy shit," she whispered, her eyes snapping to Lagos, who cocked his head at her in question. Still watching him, Prue lifted her hand and summoned her earth magic.

The ground cracked beneath her feet, and vines, roots, and brambles burst from the fissure, springing to life beneath her.

Lagos stumbled back a step, grunting in surprise.

Prue huffed a breath that was half relief, half shock. Her magic was here, and it was more powerful than ever. She wiggled her fingers, and white sparks danced between them, lighting the dark space around her. The power came effortlessly; she only had to will it to life, and it was there.

Her gasp melted into a laugh. "How is this possible?"

"You died," Lagos said slowly. "Magic changes with death."

Prue stared at him. Had Mona experienced the same thing when she had returned? They hadn't been together for long enough for Prue to notice.

"It's still earth magic," Prue said. "The magic of life. I can bring his magic back."

A grunt mingled with an animal-like growl as Lagos strode toward her. "Are you sure that's wise, my queen? Tampering with this kind of magic has untold consequences, as we've already seen."

"If this works, do you know what this means?" Prue's tone sharpened as she looked up at Lagos. "This means I can rebuild the Underworld. Just as Gaia created the mortal realm."

Lagos stilled at her words. "Are you sure?"

"No. That's why I need to try it with Cyrus first."

Lagos lifted a hand and scratched the top of his head, another snort puffing from his snout. "Yes. I'm beginning to see you and Cyrus are much the same in that respect. I cannot honestly say I'm surprised."

Prue laughed weakly and sat up straighter, still holding Cyrus's head in her lap. "All right. How do I do this? Goddess, Mona was always the better one with spells…"

"I don't think it's Mona you need," Lagos said slowly. "She has never restored a person's magic before, has she?"

Prue's eyes darted to his. "No," she said. "But my mother has."

"Gaia cannot come here," Lagos said at once. "The magic—*her* magic—forbids it."

"Then I will use *her magic* to allow it," Prue said through gritted teeth. She sucked in a deep breath and spread her arms wide around her. With all her energy, she focused on that space between worlds, where she had last seen Gaia. She remembered the light in her mother's eyes, the despair in her voice as she told her tale, and the hope in her smile when she spoke of Prue and Mona.

In her soul, she knew the words she needed to speak. After all, Gaia's earth magic flowed through her veins. The very magic that was the key to breaking the curse. Perhaps Gaia could not free herself... but Prue could.

"Gods above and below, hear my words," Prue said, her voice an ethereal rhythm that was foreign to her ears. *"With the earth magic coursing through my veins, I hereby break the curse placed upon Gaia, the mother of realms. Let her magic be freed. Let her chains be broken. With the magic of life do I grant her freedom."*

Lightning crackled, causing the castle walls to quiver. An echoing boom resounded in the room, and Lagos shot out a hand to steady himself against a pillar. Prue clutched Cyrus tighter against her, bringing her forehead to his as the earth continued to shake.

A burst of white light exploded, illuminating the room and momentarily blinding Prue. She shielded her eyes, flinching from the intensity of its power.

Then, a stunned cry filled the air, following by heaving breaths. Prue's head snapped up to find her mother on all fours, retching.

"Mama?" she asked hesitantly.

Gaia looked up, her blue eyes wild and full of fury, before they settled on Prue. Something new stirred in her gaze, and she slowly rose to her knees to take in the scene around her. "This place..." she said slowly. "Prudence, what have you done?"

"You must help me bring him back," Prue pleaded, weeping freely as she begged her mother for help. "*Please*, Mama. I know your magic can do it."

Gaia stiffened, glancing around the room. Her eyes shifted to Lagos, and suspicion crept into her expression.

"He's a friend," Prue said at once. "He helped to bring me back. Please, Mama. I—I need this." She closed her eyes as more tears fell, splashing against Cyrus's face. "I need my husband."

Gaia dropped her gaze as she took in the sight of Cyrus still cradled in Prue's lap. Confusion mingled with pity in her face as she knelt by Prue's side. "Prudence... He still lives."

"Yes, but his magic is gone. You can restore it." Prue's words were frantic. "Please, Mama, I know you can."

"If he was dead, my magic could bring him back," Gaia said, shaking her head. "*Your* magic could bring him back. But he still lives. Life magic would do nothing for him."

"But our magic *creates*!" Prue insisted. "Can't we

simply create his magic and imbue it back into his body?"

Gaia offered a sad smile. "Our magic does not work that way, my darling. We do not choose how a life force is shaped. We merely will it into being, and our magic provides the rest."

"What does that even mean?" Prue shrieked, finding it hard to control her emotions. "You can create an entire *realm,* but you can't give him his death magic back?"

"He willingly gave it up for you, Prudence. I cannot undo that magic, or it risks sending you back to the grave."

Tears burned in Prue's eyes, and she closed them, letting sobs roll through her. "Goddess, this can't be happening. Mama, what if he doesn't wake?"

"He will. The sacrifice for his spell was his immortality. Not his life."

Prue's eyes opened at that. "What?"

"He is no longer a god."

Prue's heart twisted painfully in her chest. *No longer a god.* "So he's..." She couldn't say it.

"Your magic can rouse him, darling," Gaia said. "He is connected to you. If anyone can wake him, it's you. You do not need me for this."

Prue looked at her mother, resolve burning in her chest. "But I do. And I needed you to be free. You have given everything for me—for Mona, too. You *had* to be set free."

Gaia went perfectly still at her words. She blinked rapidly, her throat bobbing as she swallowed. When she looked at Prue again, her eyes were moist. "Thank you, my sweet child." Her voice was thick. She stretched out her hand and squeezed Prue's fingers.

Prue squeezed back and took a deep breath, looking at Cyrus once more. "How do I do this?"

"He will not be the same when he wakes," Gaia warned. "He has already been altered from this."

"I understand." Prue's voice was level with determination. She would do whatever it took to revive him. She would *not lose him.* "What do I do first? The conditions... A spell like this—"

Gaia raised a hand to cut her off. "You must not look at this like a witch. You are a goddess now. The power comes from your blood freely."

When Prue frowned, Gaia took her hand and raised a questioning brow. "May I?" Prue nodded, and Gaia pressed her fingernail into the flesh of Prue's wrist.

Prue hissed in pain, then froze as a droplet of silver blood oozed from the wound.

She had never bled *silver* before. Her blood had always been red, like any other human's. Her mouth fell open as she stared at her mother in confusion. "How?"

"It was part of the spell I put on you at birth," Gaia

said. "To hide you from Apollo. Only with your death can your goddess power be freed."

A dozen emotions coursed through Prue from this revelation. Anger that her mother had done this to her. Shock that the power of a goddess now flowed through her veins. Apprehension at the prospect of handling such power.

"You must breathe your life magic into his soul," Gaia instructed. "I cannot force it from you; it is something you must feel for yourself. Close your eyes and open the doors to your magic. It will call to him, as his power calls to you. Do not be afraid."

Prue nodded, closing her eyes and searching within herself. She remembered Cyrus's instructions when they were in Tartarus together—to use her goddess senses instead of her mortal ones. She blocked out the smells and sounds around her, instead searching within herself for that massive well of power that churned just below the surface. It was there, waiting for her.

"Open," Gaia repeated. "You are tense, Prudence. Let it out. It will not hurt you."

Prue licked her lips and took a shaky breath before forcing her body to relax. Only then did she realize how tight her limbs were. Her frame sagged, her back hunching as she exhaled, long and slow. Gold light burned from beneath her eyelids, and her eyes flew open. A glittering gold mist surrounded her, reminding her of the witchdust she was so accustomed to from her coven in Krenia.

"That is the breath of life," Gaia said quietly. "Now, direct it toward Cyrus. He will recognize you and wake."

Prue was going to ask how, but somehow, down to her very bones, she knew. Her eyes fixed on the shimmering light before her, and then she looked to Cyrus and *willed* that power into him. It felt like stretching an invisible arm toward him. Her magic swept over him, brushing delicately over his features like a soft caress. The touch stopped at his lips, gently prying them apart before the gold magic trickled into him. Color filled his face, and his eyes flew open.

They were not silver, but cerulean. Not quite as brilliant a blue as Gaia's, but still luminous.

He sat up, gasping for breath. He pressed a hand to his chest, his brows furrowing in an expression she knew so well. And yet, it looked so different on him. This man was practically a stranger. Dark hair and pale skin, free of ink and tattoos.

Not a god at all. Not anymore.

"Cyrus?" Prue asked hesitantly.

His wide eyes fixed on hers, and his head reared back. She wasn't sure what he was seeing—perhaps the gold light surrounding her, or perhaps he was merely shocked at seeing her alive.

But Gaia was right about one thing—he was not the

same as before. Not just in appearance, but in blood. His entire scent was different. She could smell his perspiration, hear his rapidly beating heart, and even sense the mortal blood flowing through his veins.

He was human.

SHATTERED
EVANDER

A BLACK STORM SURGED AROUND EVANDER, whipping at his face and burning his eyes. The wounds in his shredded wings throbbed, and he lay there, motionless on the cold floor, unable to move.

He was dying. He felt it in his bones. At long last, this realm was finally killing him.

Chaotic voices surrounded him, but he was too weak to lift his head, too weak to even care what was happening. In his heart, he knew Mona was safe. He'd heard her voice, defying Apollo. Defending *him*.

He had saved her. That was all that mattered.

Darkness crowded his vision, and he exhaled slowly, allowing it to overtake him. He could rest now.

Then one sound pierced through the haze of noises.

A sound that had his eyes opening and his body going rigid with awareness.

A soft sob.

He shouldn't have been able to hear it; not amidst the screams and cries of the people rushing about. But he knew that voice, that breath, better than he knew his own soul.

His head lifted, and fresh pain lanced through him. He moaned, his body quivering, agony pulsing through him in sickening waves. Gods, this was torture. He was going to die here. He was going to disintegrate on these marble floors.

There it was again. A shaking, shuddering gasp. A cry of despair.

Mona.

Grunting from the effort, Evander pushed up on his elbows. His torn wings dragged along the floor, weighing him down. But still he shifted, moving closer to that sound.

He needed to retract his wings. They were beyond saving, and the heavy pull of them prevented him from rising.

But gods, he was so weak, so *tired.* He couldn't summon the energy to shift forms. When Typhon had taken over, he'd expended everything. Only when Apollo had struck him did Evander finally return to his own body, and by that point, it was too late. He could do nothing but allow his wounds to bleed, to watch as his body slowly decayed.

Mona sobbed again—a ragged, desperate sound.

Evander's breathing turned sharp. He could do this. For her. For her, he would find the strength to rise, to go to her side, to give her everything he had left. Even if it was only a modicum of his former strength and power, he would give it to her.

Fire burned in his veins as he sat up. The rips in his wings widened, oozing fresh blood with each movement.

Typhon, he thought. *Typhon, I need you. Please.*

Silence.

He didn't allow himself to think it, to even consider the possibility that Typhon was dead. But down to his soul, he already knew.

A creature like Typhon could not survive a realm like this.

And Typhon was a part of Evander. The two were united as one. If Typhon died, so would Evander.

He had moments left. He couldn't waste those precious moments.

With a roar of pain, he drew forward, staggering to his feet. Blinding white light burned against his eyes, threatening to take him.

But no. He wasn't ready yet. He needed to find her.

"Mona," he rasped. Just speaking her name brought him a burst of strength. "Mona!" he shouted.

The shaking sobs stuttered in response.

Blinking through the hazy fog clouding his vision, Evander stumbled forward, following her flowery scent. Slowly, the shapes around him came into focus, and he faltered, his mouth falling open.

A dome of tree branches and shrubs surrounded the ballroom, blocking out the dark storm of Pandora's powers. Figures darted back and forth, some screaming, some shouting orders. Some had collapsed to their knees, sobbing on the floor.

And standing a few paces from him, her body stiff and unmoving, was Mona.

Evander moved toward her, his broken wings dragging behind him, threatening to pull him down. Hot blood ran in rivulets down his arms and back. At long last, he reached her, taking her hand in his. As he faced her, he took in the despair etched into her face, the tears streaming down her cheeks. Anger and frustration welled in her eyes.

"Mona," he whispered, cupping her chin. "What's happening?" His gaze roamed over her body. "Are you hurt?" He didn't see any immediate injuries, but in a realm full of gods, anything was possible.

Mona said nothing. She gritted her teeth, her nostrils flaring. Her lips moved as if she wanted to speak, but no words came out.

Evander shook his head in confusion. Was his pain

so severe that he was hallucinating? Was she actually speaking, and he just couldn't hear it?

"Can you speak?" he asked.

Her eyes closed, and more tears fell. He interpreted that as a *no.*

"Did one of the gods do this to you?"

Her eyes opened again, and fresh fury burned in her gaze.

Yes. A god did this to her, and she was enraged. Evander's blood boiled in equal anger as his claws itched to slash at whoever had attacked her.

"Are you hurt?"

Her eyes closed again.

Evander frowned, not understanding. So, a god had done this to her, but left her unharmed? Why?

Mona's gaze shifted, and Evander followed it to find Pandora standing among two other gods, her red hair in tangles around her, and her frame hunched over as if in pain.

Good, Evander thought savagely. He hoped the deceitful goddess suffered for what she had done.

He turned back to Mona, only to find her glaring fiercely at the goddess.

Then, he understood.

"Pandora did this to you?" he asked quietly.

Another sob broke free from her lips, and Evander trailed his hands along her arms, trying to soothe her, to help her in some way. But her body was immovable as stone.

"Ah," he said in realization. "Trivia's bargain. The bargain she extracted from you when you came back to the Underworld."

Mona blinked at him, her eyes filling with tears once more. Sorrow and pain flared in those green irises, and Evander wrapped his bloodied arms around her.

"It's all right," he whispered, stroking her hair. "It's all right. I won't leave you. I swear it."

Mona sobbed again, her tears dripping onto his shoulder.

The ground rumbled, and Evander's grip around her tightened. Mona made a strangled sound, and he withdrew to look at her. Her eyes flared wide with urgency. Even without her voice, Evander understood what she was conveying.

"I won't leave you," he repeated. "No matter what."

Her eyes closed, her lips trembling as they pressed together against the fresh tears coursing down her cheeks.

Evander took several deep breaths, glancing around the broken ballroom to search for anything that could help her. He was too weak to carry her. And even if he could, he had no way to activate the portal and leave this realm.

They were both trapped here. Pandora had doomed

them both.

But Evander would be damned if he would stand by and watch Mona sink into despair.

"Listen to me." He pressed his palms against her cheeks, cradling her face and forcing her to meet his gaze. With the pad of his thumb, he swept away another tear. "You are fierce. And you are not helpless. We are in this together, but Mona, you are stronger than this bargain that binds you. Just as you were stronger than the broken bond between your body and soul in the Underworld. You are a *warrior*, my love, and nothing— not even this petty vengeance from Pandora herself— can stop you. Do you hear me?"

He fixed a fearsome stare at her, his eyes boring into hers with all the intensity of the emotions he felt for her. With his gaze, he channeled all that love and admiration, the longing and passion, the energy that flowed between them, powerful enough to shatter worlds.

Because she had to know. He would not leave this realm, this existence, without her knowing.

"You are my melody," he whispered, bringing his forehead to hers. "My song cannot be sung without you."

He closed his eyes and felt her inhale a shuddering breath, her chest against his, her rapid heartbeat thrumming against him. And with the rhythm of her heart, he began to hum the song of her soul. Ignoring the chaos around them, the darting figures and shouts and crashing pillars, Evander sang for her, pouring all his remaining strength into her song.

Because in the end, it was all for her. It was *always* for her.

He was nothing without her.

And then she was humming along with him. His eyes flew open to meet hers, and defiance blazed in those beautiful green eyes. She held his stare, her expression full of light and hope.

Pandora might have forbidden Mona from speaking, but she hadn't said anything about singing.

Gradually, Mona's voice grew in volume until her mouth opened and the song burst from her lips as if it had been caged for an eternity and now, finally, it was free. Evander took a step back, giving her the space she needed. Her song filled the ballroom, echoing off the vast walls and piercing through the storm of Pandora's magic. Light bled through the dark clouds, and several people stopped to stare at Mona in shock and awe.

Through it all, Evander continued singing, falling back to the harmony that complemented her melody, letting her take the lead. It was, after all, the song of her soul.

And it was powerful.

Gold light flowed from her hands, shimmering and blazing as it illuminated the room, chasing away the shadows. It was glorious and breathtaking, and in that moment, Evander felt inadequate standing before her in his demon form, his wings shredded and his body covered in blood. He was not worthy of her. Not one bit.

From across the room, Pandora straightened, whirling to face Mona, her expression stricken. Evander wasn't sure if it was fear or bewilderment that had her gaping at Mona, but it filled him with a savage sense of pleasure.

With a deafening *boom*, Mona's song shattered the dark branches that had cocooned the crowd in the ball-room. Twigs and leaves rained from the ceiling, and the heavy thud of branches echoed.

"No!" Pandora shrieked. But she stilled, her hands falling limply by her sides as the gold light enclosed around the room, sealing them off from the darkness. The cyclone of Pandora's dark powers continued churning angrily, but the black mist had grown thinner. Weaker.

Mona's magic was chasing it away.

Pandora merely blinked at this development, her face slack with surprise. Next to her, a tall blond man roughly tugged on her elbow, jerking her out of the room and toward the crumbling staircase.

Evander only watched as she was pulled from the room. He didn't care what happened to her; judging by the fury on the blond man's face, he was not her ally.

And that was all that mattered. Pandora would serve

her punishment one way or another.

But for right now, Evander's focus was on Mona.

He turned to her, only to find her gasping, her hands pressed to her tear-stained cheeks as a startled laugh burst from her.

Evander jerked backward in shock. "M-Mona?"

She laughed again and surged toward him, wrapping him in a tight embrace, heedless of his wings or horns or the filth surrounding him. She clearly didn't care that he was a filthy demon, his skin splotchy and gray. Her breath tickled his ear as she clutched him closer, burying her face in his shoulder.

"I love you," she whispered. "I love you with every piece of my soul."

Evander's arms circled around her waist, and he found his chest was heaving with sobs. She was here. She was *free*. Something in her magic had broken the bond with Pandora. He thought of the way she had shattered those branches.

Mona's powers had obliterated Pandora's protective dome. Her magical strength surpassed that of the vengeful goddess.

Evander could only marvel at this. Only the strongest of magic could sever an unbreakable bond between gods like that.

He withdrew to look her over, his mouth open as he surveyed her. "You—You broke free?"

"I suppose I did," she said breathlessly, grinning at him. Behind them, hunks of concrete fell from the ceiling, crashing into the marble floors. "But we can discuss it later. Come on, let's get out of here!"

Mona grabbed his hand and tugged him toward the staircase. Evander followed, his torn wings dragging behind him. But somehow, his wounds no longer bothered him. It was as if singing the song with Mona had healed him somehow.

Whatever it was, he wouldn't complain. It allowed him to keep up with her pace as they darted down the stairs. Behind them, the walls cracked, and pillars collapsed in a pile of rubble. The ground continued to shake, and they quickened their steps, trying to avoid getting crushed by the crumbling palace walls.

Mona shrieked as a piece of the ceiling hurtled toward her, and Evander tucked her into his chest, tugging her out of the way just in time. Dust filled the air, stinging his eyes. After ensuring Mona was unharmed, Evander continued, his hand still clasped firmly in hers.

They reached the broken entrance doors and hurried down the cracked steps that led to the courtyard. A crowd had already gathered at the beach below, surrounding a glowing archway that Evander recognized as a portal.

"They've found a way to activate it," he said with a

relieved sigh. "Thank the gods."

"Evander, look." Mona's voice was solemn as she pointed to a figure crouched in front of the portal. Even in the dark of dusk, her fiery red hair was unmistakable.

Pandora.

She was hunched over, her fingers pressed into the ground at the foot of the portal. Next to her, the blond man stood, overseeing the process of shepherding people through. Gold light flowed from Pandora's hands, and tree branches burst from the ground on either side of her. The light of the portal flared, burning brighter, and then Evander understood.

Pandora was using her magic to power the portal.

She cried out, her back bowing under the pressure of it. The blond man murmured something to her, and she nodded, teeth gritted, and dug her hands more firmly into the sand at her feet.

"Evander," Mona said again, turning to him with eyes full of concern. "She's going to kill herself doing this."

"Why does that concern us?" Evander said coldly. "She tried to kill us both. It's her fault this is happening."

"But she's my sister."

Evander stilled at the words, sifting through his foggy memories. It took him a moment, but he finally recalled what Pandora had said when he'd confronted her in the Underworld, just before she'd pulled him through the portal: *Gaia tried to protect her children, but she could only save two. The third one was captured by Janus himself. As punishment, he imbued the child with the soul of Pandora, bringing all her pain and misery to life in a newly born vessel.*

Evander swallowed, glancing from Pandora to Mona. "We have to escape before this realm is destroyed. If we stop to help her, it could doom us both."

Mona bit her lip, considering this. "You go through. I'll find you and—"

Evander pulled her to him and pressed a rough kiss to her lips, taking a single moment to taste her thoroughly before he pulled away and fixed a fierce stare on her. "I am *not* leaving you again," he growled. "If you stay, I stay."

She nodded, her expression dazed as she caught her breath. "All right." She cleared her throat. "If my magic is strong enough to sever her bond with me, then it has to be powerful enough to help her fuel that portal."

"But if you help fuel it, how will you get through?"

Mona's eyes turned distant, and Evander recognized the calculating look flitting across her face, the way her expression lit up when an idea came to her. She looked at him with a determined glint in her eye, drawing closer to him, her fingers dancing along his collarbone, right over the spot where his moonstone necklace used to rest.

Her smile widened. "I have an idea."

SISTERS
PANDORA

PANDORA COULDN'T EVEN REGISTER HER astonishment that Mona had severed their magical bond. Whatever favor her sister owed had been obliterated by the sheer force of Mona's power.

Mona was stronger than Pandora. Stronger than the darkness that had festered inside her for years.

And yet, Pandora felt nothing. Hollow. Numb. Empty.

She had been a puppet for so long. And now she was nothing. She didn't even feel connected to her magic anymore.

Who was she? This vengeful goddess had controlled her for her entire life. And now that Pandora hoped to be free, she discovered the goddess had only tightened the chains around her.

She couldn't deny that a small part of her was relieved—proud, even—that Mona managed such an impossible feat. Because now that the dark powers had revealed their true nature and vowed to destroy *everything*, Pandora had no motivation anymore. She had thought that once Elysium fell, she would be free to be herself, to explore her own powers and magic once more. That the anger and bitterness of the goddess from before would finally be able to rest.

But no. That goddess was just getting started.

Pandora felt nothing as Sol jerked her forward, ushering her down the steps, toward the entrance doors, and past the courtyard that led to the shore below. She would be used as a power source for the portal. That was the only reason she was still alive.

She knew this. She knew Sol only needed her for one thing.

And then she would part from him forever.

She would give her life for this. But she didn't care. It was no less than she deserved.

Years she had spent manipulating and deceiving others. But in the end, she had been the biggest fool of all. *She* had been tricked. And she couldn't even be angry about it.

It was justice. And the final piece, the final act of her atonement, would be her death. The long-sought plan for revenge would die with her.

And the realms would be safe.

It was the only thing she had left to offer.

Sol's grip on her arm tightened, his fingernails digging into her flesh. But she let him. The sharpness of his grasp pierced through the fog of her mind, reminding her that this would be the last time he would touch her. The last time she would feel his hands on her skin, even if it was in anger.

At long last, she sank to her knees in the sand before the stone archway that marked the portal. She felt Sol's hard gaze on her, expectant and impatient. So, she pressed her hands into the earth at her feet, summoning her powers once more. The ground quivered, and roots and branches burst free, twining around her obediently. With a low thrum, the portal shone to life, glowing with a brilliant gold light as a beacon for those around them. A cheer erupted behind her as the deities celebrated.

They had a way to escape. Because of her.

A kernel of satisfaction welled inside Pandora at the sound. She closed her eyes, allowing herself to relish it, just for a moment.

She was doing something right. It didn't make up for everything she had done, but still. She savored it while she could.

With a deep breath, she dug her hands more fully into the sand, allowing her fingers to be submerged completely. The grains covered her skin, grating against her flesh. She homed in on that singular sensation, the roughness of those sand particles as they scraped against her.

That focus was the only thing grounding her. Because the longer she held on, the more intensely her body began to tremble as pain wracked through her. She gritted her teeth, her breaths turning sharp and labored.

But still, she held on.

The light of the portal flared brightly as she pushed more energy into it. And then, with a sharp cry, her back bowed as something sharp ratcheted through her, ripping and tearing at her insides. She bit down on a scream, plunging her fingers more deeply into the sand.

Gradually, the pain subsided. Or perhaps she only became numb to it. She wasn't sure. But whatever the reason, it became more bearable.

"Keep it going," Sol ordered. "We need to get everyone through. Understand?"

She only nodded, unable to speak. Sol gestured to someone behind her, and a figure stepped through the portal.

The light flared again, and the ground shook. Pandora let loose another cry of pain as energy rippled through her as if the portal were forcibly tearing the power from her body.

This would shred her apart, piece by piece. It would not be pleasant, or quick.

I deserve this, she thought, her teeth grinding together so intensely that her head started throbbing.

Another person stepped through, and the pain returned, slicing deep, carving through her chest.

One at a time, the residents of Elysium traveled through the portal. And all the while, Pandora held on, pushing every ounce of her strength into the earth to fuel it.

By the end, she lay limply on the ground, sand covering her body and hair, her arms shaking. Blood dripped from her nose and mouth, but she kept her fingers in the sand, determined to finish this.

Sol crouched before her, his face impassive as he stared at her. She could only blink at him, too exhausted to say anything. Too exhausted to arrange an expression on her face.

"That's everyone," he said. "Only three of us remain."

Pandora tried to speak, but no words came out. Only a hoarse gurgle escaped her lips.

Sol tilted his head. "What did you say?"

"Amara," she rasped. "The village. We have to get them out."

Sol's eyes narrowed. "You're concerned about them?" He huffed a laugh. "That's rich, considering you're the reason for their destruction. Where was this concern when you unleashed your darkness and obliterated the realm?"

"Please," Pandora croaked. "Sol, I never wanted this. It was all *her.* I can't—I couldn't—"

"Don't for a second expect me to believe you are blameless in all this," he seethed. "You aren't a slave, Trivia. You have your own magic. Your own thoughts. Your own actions. And you let *her* dictate who you are. That was your choice."

Pandora tried to shake her head, but she was too weak. At any rate, it didn't matter.

Because he was right.

She *had* had choices. And she had chosen a revenge that wasn't hers to take. In doing so, she had damned herself, condemned to a life of slavery.

It had been her own doing. She'd been free before, but she'd locked herself in a cage and tossed away the key.

She could have chosen differently.

"I've sent Alexander to bring as many villagers as he can," Sol was saying, glancing behind Pandora. "But I fear it's already too late."

Alexander. It took Pandora a moment for her brain to catch up. Vaguely, she recalled the servant she'd sent to Sol days ago when she'd been impatiently awaiting him in the library.

He knew the servant's name.

Of course he did. He wore a mask of indifference and arrogance, preaching of the gods' superiority over others, claiming he didn't care about the help at all. He'd brushed right past them without even acknowledging their presence, and Pandora had called him out on it.

But he had still seen them. Still learned their names.

"You don't need to be so aloof," Pandora said, her voice still cracking.

"What?" Sol snapped.

"You pretend not to care. But you don't have to."

Something stirred in his dark eyes as he looked at her, but she couldn't name the emotion. Before today, she thought she'd been able to read him so well. But he was an entirely different person now. They both were.

"If I care about one thing, then I'd have to care about everything," Sol said softly. Then his gaze turned icy once more. "You forced that out of me, Trivia. You *forced* me to care. To remember her. And now, I—I'm broken again. The wounds have re-opened. Because of you."

Pandora choked on a weak laugh. "You are not blameless either, Sol. *You* made that choice. Just as I did."

Sol's mouth pressed into a thin line, his eyes narrowing. But he didn't argue. He knew she spoke the truth.

Just as she had chosen revenge, because it was the easier path, he had chosen ignorance. He chose this mask, wearing it for so long that he stopped remembering who he had once been.

Until today, when everything had come crashing

back into him, smothering him with what he had suppressed for so many years.

A deafening *boom* shook the ground, and Pandora hissed against the pain of her body quivering from the impact.

"Shit." Sol was on his feet, gazing upward. "We're out of time."

Slowly, Pandora turned her head to follow his gaze, and her heart dropped to her stomach.

The palace had fallen. Hunks of rubble fell over the cliff, crashing into the ocean below.

The castle of Elysium was nothing more than ruins now.

Pandora had done this.

Sol drew closer to the portal, not even glancing back at Pandora.

"So, you'll just abandon Alexander?" she called after him. "All those villagers who worshiped you?"

Sol stilled, then glanced at her over his shoulder, his expression full of loathing. She thought she had seen hatred in his eyes before. The two of them had despised one another, after all.

But that, too, had been an act.

This, however, was raw and feral and *real*. The strength of his rage blazed in his eyes with the intensity of a thousand suns.

"If Alexander makes it, I know you'll ensure he

passes through," Sol said. "Along with anyone else he can bring with him. But when this realm falls, I'll be the only one who can guide the sun. I must step through to fulfill my responsibilities to my people."

Pandora fell silent at that. Had Apollo been killed in the destruction? Or had he fled?

For so long, she sought his demise. And now, she couldn't bring herself to care.

"I know it means nothing to you," Pandora said. "But I am truly sorry. You're right. These were my choices. I did this. And I can never atone for what I've done. But I didn't realize how strong the curse was. How strong Pandora was. I thought I would be free. I thought..." She broke off, coughing and sputtering as her breath stuck in her throat. "I thought *she* would finally be free," she finished in a low rasp. "But I was wrong."

Sol's gaze flickered, and the briefest glimmer of regret shone in his eyes. Pandora hated bringing up his lost love, reopening those wounds once more.

But this would be the last she would see of him. She had to say it.

"I wanted her to find peace," Pandora went on. "I thought this revenge would bring that to her. I'm sorry it didn't. And I'm sorry for the part I played in it."

Still, Sol said nothing. He merely continued to watch her with that unreadable gaze.

Then, without saying a word to her, he turned and

stepped through the portal.

A sob broke free, and Pandora turned her face, burying it in the sand as she wept.

She wasn't sure how long she lay there, her hands buried in the sand and her tears soaking the earth. But after a long while, she felt a hand on her shoulder.

She jerked upright, expecting someone to attack her, only to find it was *Mona.*

Pandora's mouth fell open as she stared, stunned, at the sister who she betrayed, the sister she tricked and used just like everyone else. Behind her stood Evander, still in his demon form, his torn wings sagging behind him.

"What are you doing here?" Pandora demanded. "You need to get out. *Now!*"

"I'm not leaving you," Mona said firmly.

Pandora laughed, the sound full of bitterness. "Then you're a fool."

"Perhaps I am. But I am *not* like you, Pandora. I will stay with you because you are my sister. We are blood, you and I. And no matter what you do, no matter how despicable you are, that will never change."

Pandora's heart twisted painfully at those words, digging fresh wounds into her already anguished body. "You'll die," she moaned, letting her head fall into the sand again.

"No, we won't." Mona tugged on a leather cord

hanging from her neck, pulling it out of her bodice to reveal a sliver of moonstone.

Pandora squinted at it in confusion. "What is that?"

"A totem. I've poured my magic into it. If you pour what's left of yours, it should be enough to power this portal until we can get out."

"Amara," Pandora said, coughing up more blood. "I'm not leaving until the villagers are free."

"I've already led them through the portal on that side," Mona said.

Pandora stared at her in bewilderment. "*How?*" She could only utter the one word. Here she lay, wounded and dying, barely able to fuel the portal for the dozens of deities who had already passed through. And somehow, Mona had not only managed to fuel the other portal and get an entire village to safety, but she'd had enough magic leftover to power a moonstone. *And* she was still standing, looking as regal and serene as ever.

"How do you have so much power?" Pandora whispered. She was now so exhausted she couldn't hold her head up any longer.

"Because I died," Mona said. "The three of us were bound by a powerful enchantment that kept us locked in our mortal bodies. Only upon death can our true powers be freed." She lifted her palm, where a fresh cut was leaking blood.

But not ordinary red blood. *Silver* blood.

The blood of the gods.

Pandora's heart jolted at the sight. Mona must have cast a spell with her blood to activate the second portal. Blood magic was the most powerful form of magic.

The magic of the witches.

Of course. Pandora had only been thinking of her goddess powers. But Mona was not only a goddess, but also a talented witch. She had a whole arsenal of spells at her disposal.

Pandora lifted a shaking hand to the blood still oozing from her nose. Her hand came back stained in red.

"So if I die, I'll come back stronger?" Pandora asked, unable to contain the longing in her voice.

Mona's face turned hard. "No. You'll need someone to bring you back. Someone who cares enough to sacrifice *everything.*"

Pandora slumped back onto the sand, closing her eyes. "I have no one. Only enemies."

A warm hand closed around her own. "You have *me.* You have us." Mona crouched in the sand next to her, her eyes shining with a tenderness Pandora didn't deserve. Behind her, Evander drew closer, his face a mask of stone. He didn't hold the same affection for Pandora that Mona did, but still... he was here. And that was enough.

Slowly, Pandora nodded. "All right. What do I need

to do?"

"Anything you have left, pour it into this." Mona lifted the necklace from her head and held it out toward Pandora.

"I have nothing left, Mona," Pandora sobbed. "I am empty. I am dying."

"You *do* have power left, sister," Mona said gently. "It will take everything you have. You will likely fall into unconsciousness from the effort. But you can trust that we will carry you through."

Pandora blinked blearily at her. "You'll take me through?"

Mona nodded.

Pandora had no reason to trust Mona. But she was here. Even if she had nefarious plans, even if she intended to abandon Pandora and let her die, did it really matter?

With great effort, Pandora lifted her arm and took the moonstone from Mona's grasp. It felt cool against her burning skin. She squeezed it so tightly that it dug into her palm, bringing a jolt of fresh pain.

She clung to that pain, using it to keep her awake and alert. Just for a bit longer.

If I die, then so be it, she thought grimly. *But if I live, I swear I'll be different. I'll make different choices. Revenge be damned.*

Mona's hand was on her shoulder again, squeezing

once to reassure her she wasn't alone.

Pandora sat up, her head spinning, and pressed both hands to the moonstone. She took a deep breath, closed her eyes, and unleashed *everything*. Agony split through her, peeling back layer after layer, exposing the raw and festering parts of her. Still, she pushed, releasing her power, her rage, her thirst for revenge. Everything poured from her, filling the stone pressed between her hands. It grew hot in her grasp, but still she held on, even when it scorched her palm, even when the scent of burning flesh met her nose.

A flash of white light burst against her vision, blinding her. And then she was floating, her body weightless and empty. The pain was gone, and for the briefest of moments, she thought she had truly died.

Warm hands pressed into her, and the smell of the ocean mingled with roses, tickling her nostrils.

Mona.

Pandora's eyes cracked open to find her sister holding her, clutching her against her chest. And then Evander was there, his arms encircling her. He smelled of pine and a cool river. His skin was tough, like the hide of an animal, but it wasn't unpleasant. Pandora sank into him as he lifted her. Another flash of bright light seared through her, and the world shifted, spinning and tilting as the three of them stepped through the portal, leaving Elysium to its fate.

FRAGILE

CYRUS

CYRUS HAD TO BE DREAMING. THIS COULDN'T possibly be real.

Unless he was in Tartarus. And this was his eternal punishment.

The thought made him laugh with bitterness. It would serve him right, to be damned to an eternity as this weak, fragile thing.

He had no strength. No magic. No otherworldly senses.

Gods, it was pitiful.

"Cyrus, say something."

He turned, squinting through his blurred vision. As his eyes adjusted to the darkness around him, he found an achingly familiar face peering at him, her wide, lavender eyes full of concern and relief.

"Prue?" Cyrus frowned. It wouldn't be torture if his wife was here. That didn't seem right at all.

Eyes narrowing, Cyrus surveyed his surroundings with more clarity. Gradually, awareness crept into his sluggish mind.

He was in the vault under the castle. To his left, in front of a still steaming cauldron, stood Lagos, his head tilted to one side as he scrutinized Cyrus. And behind Prue, standing with her hands clasped demurely before her, was Gaia, the goddess of the earth. He stiffened at the sight of her, his body flooding with awareness, ready for an attack.

"What the hell is she doing here?" he snapped, his voice louder than he'd intended. The last time he'd seen Gaia, he and Prue had been battling his brother, Vasileios, in the mortal realm. Gaia had been summoned to prove that Prue and Mona were the daughters of a deity.

And Prue had nearly destroyed her with her fury.

"It's all right," Prue said gently, grabbing his wrist and squeezing it reassuringly. "I summoned her. I... freed her, actually. She helped me bring you back."

His brows knitted together. "Bring me back?"

"You were unconscious. Unresponsive. I—I was worried I'd lost you." Darkness clouded Prue's eyes, and she scowled at him. "What the *hell* were you thinking, casting a spell like that?"

Cyrus's head reared back at the accusation in her tone. "You were dead, Prue! What would you have me do? What would *you* have done?"

Prue's mouth clamped shut at that, and he knew her answer. She would have done the same for him.

The thought should have softened the tight ball of rage in his chest. It should have left him warm with the thought of how much she loved him.

But it didn't.

In the recesses of his mind, he knew he should feel affection for this woman before him. He remembered loving her. He knew who she was and what experiences they had shared together.

But in this moment, all he felt was fury.

It had to be this useless, weak mortal form. Somehow, it was stifling his thoughts and emotions.

"Why did you do it," he bit out, his gaze shifting to Gaia.

Gaia's chin lifted. "She's my daughter."

"That means nothing. It certainly meant nothing when you spent her entire life lying to her."

"Cyrus," Prue warned, but Gaia lifted a hand to silence her.

"It's all right, Prudence. I deserved that. I helped her because, with her death, her true power has been unlocked. And she needed help accessing it." Gaia offered him a cold smile.

Slowly, Cyrus turned to look at Prue, who fidgeted under his gaze. "Why?" he asked again.

Prue frowned. "Why what?"

"Why am I not dead? Why am I this—this wretched *human*?" He spat the word like a filthy curse.

Prue flinched. "I don't know."

"The price was an immortal soul," Gaia said. "It looks as if the magic required was your immortality, not your entire being."

Cyrus scoffed a harsh laugh at that. "Of course. Because death would have been too easy. Instead, I have to *suffer*." He whirled on Prue. "You couldn't have just let me die?"

Her eyes narrowed. "Are you dense? Of course I couldn't. I love you, Cyrus, whether you're a human or not."

"You love me?" he sneered. "Well, that's easy for you to say. *I'm* the one who made this sacrifice to bring you back. *I'm* the one condemned to live a mortal life. I've been shoved into this sad, pathetic form, forced to watch myself wither away while you access more power than you've ever known in your entire life."

Prue's face paled. "Cyrus..." She swallowed hard. "I'm just relieved you're still alive. I was terrified that spell had killed you! Isn't it better to be here with me, even if it's without your magic?"

"Do you think I wanted this?" he seethed, gesturing

to his trembling body. A tiny voice in his mind told him to stop before he hurt her, before he said something he could never take back. But the voice was drowned out by the chaotic anger roaring in his ears. "If you think I wanted to be reduced to this wretched shell of who I once was, then you don't know me at all."

Prue's expression turned hard. "I don't care what form you take. You could be a vile, three-horned, pus-filled demon, and I wouldn't care. I need you, Cyrus."

Cyrus jabbed a finger at her. "*That's* what this is about. You just can't bear to be alone. You don't care about me at all."

Prue's head jerked back. "You are such an *ass*! We're here together now! Aren't you glad to be alive?"

"No," Cyrus snapped. "Not like this. I sacrificed myself so you could live. So you could rule and protect this realm where I couldn't. And now look at me!" He gestured to his body with a disgusted grimace. "This is *your* fault. If you hadn't been so reckless with your magic during the cave-in, I wouldn't have had to give up everything to bring you back!"

"You would have died in that cave-in, Cyrus!" Prue cried. "Are you saying you would rather be dead than here with me?"

Cyrus said nothing, still quivering with fury. But his silence answered her question.

Tears sparkled in her eyes as her expression shifted

from shock to despair to rage. In a flash, she raised her hand and slapped him across the face. His cheek burned from the impact, his head swiveling.

"Prudence," Gaia chided gently. "Remember, he is in a new form. Mortals experience a frightening array of emotions. It will take him time to adjust."

"Do not speak as if I am not present," Cyrus growled.

Gaia's eyebrows lifted, her mouth quirking in amusement. As if his anger was entertaining.

Cyrus rose to his feet, trying to ignore the way his body tilted or the heavy weight of his torso or the imbalance of his new form. Gods, it was abysmal. He hated every piece of this new, frail body. "I. Do. Not. Want. This." His voice was quiet and lethal.

Gaia ignored him and turned to Prue, placing a hand on each of her shoulders. "My darling daughter," she whispered, her expression soft and full of adoration. "Words cannot express my gratitude for what you have done for me. It is far greater than I deserve." She kissed Prue's forehead and drew back a step. "I wish I could stay."

Prue blinked at her. "You're leaving?"

"Pandora's magic will find me. I cannot bring the darkness here. The realm has suffered enough." She fixed a proud smile on Prue. "But I'm confident *you* can rebuild it."

Prue grasped Gaia's hand, her voice tinged with

desperation. "Don't leave, Mama. We can face Pandora. We are powerful enough to stand against her." Her eyes slid to Cyrus briefly, and his nostrils flared.

"We?" he repeated with a harsh laugh. "There is no *we*, Prue. I am nothing but a weak human, thanks to you. I have no power, so I don't think I'll be standing against *anyone*, least of all alongside you."

Gaia scoffed and waved her hand. "You may as well just kill him, Prudence. He is not worth your time."

"Mama," Prue hissed, her venomous eyes still fixed on Cyrus, but they were flaring with a new emotion: hurt. Cyrus tried to ignore what that emotion did to him, but he couldn't. It twisted his insides, making him feel even *more* wretched.

But the bitterness within him only grew. He couldn't stop it. Each passing moment only made him angrier, and despite the logical side of him urging him to remain silent, a powerful impulse had him speaking again.

"Death is preferable to this," he sneered. "You took my life away, Prue. Everything I once was is *gone*. Because of you."

Tears glistened in her eyes even as she glared at him.

Lagos drew forward, finally entering the conversation. "Perhaps we should leave Cyrus to process the situation. Let him get accustomed to his new vessel. I fear if the situation escalates, one of us may say something we'll regret."

"I think it's a little late for that," Prue snapped.

"My queen…" Lagos tried again.

"*Silence*," Gaia hissed suddenly.

The entire room went still. Gaia's form was rigid, her eyes flashing with warning, her nostrils flaring wide as she inhaled. "Prudence, do you sense it?"

Prue stiffened, her face draining of color. "I—What *is* that?"

Cyrus searched within himself, only to find his chest hollow. Empty. Void of any power or strength. He deflated, his frame sagging with the knowledge that he was *nothing*. Prue and Gaia sensed something he could not.

What good was he now? To Prue, to this realm, to *anyone*?

"What is it?" Lagos asked.

With great effort, Cyrus dragged himself out of his well of misery to focus on the discussion. Whatever was happening was important, and although it would be easy for him to stop caring, he was curious.

And despite the horrible things he'd said to her, he did still love his wife.

It was this new body he despised. He despised *himself.*

"Someone is here," Gaia murmured. Her face paled. "Pandora has come for me at last."

But Prue shook her head. "It's not her. I would recognize the scent of her power. This one is unfamiliar." She frowned, her eyes full of wary curiosity.

Gaia's gaze sharpened, and she uttered a soft gasp of realization before turning and sweeping from the room, her steps echoing as she raced up the staircase.

Lagos and Prue exchanged a startled look before they hurried after her. Cyrus took a breath, surveying the empty room for a moment. It would have been tempting to simply remain here. Lagos was right; perhaps Cyrus needed a moment to himself.

But the startled cries of the crowd above sent him darting after them.

Cyrus was gasping for breath when he reached the top of the staircase. The excited chatter of the demons surrounded him, and he had to elbow his way through the crowd to find Prue and Gaia. They stood at the open doors of the throne room, facing a figure who lounged casually on Cyrus's throne.

Cyrus felt his stomach drop at the sight of the man, who smirked at their approach, his gaze flicking from Gaia to Prue, and then to Cyrus. His eyes widened as he took in Cyrus's appearance. Slowly, the man stood, smoothing his brown hair, his eyes dancing with amusement.

"Well, this is a fascinating development," he said loudly.

Gaia was gripping Prue's arm tightly, her gaze fixed on the man. "What are you doing here, Apollo?"

Apollo grinned widely. "I had to see for myself if my brother was dead. Now that I've confirmed it, I've come to claim what is rightfully mine." He spread his arms wide, gesturing to the throne room at large. "This realm now belongs to me. I am the new king of the Underworld."

THE JOURNEY CONTINUES...

LEARN MORE AT

rlperez.com/salt-and-blood

NOTE TO THE READER

Thank you so much for reading! I greatly appreciate you taking the time.

If you would be so kind, please leave a review to let others know what you thought of the book!

ACKNOWLEDGMENTS

Wow! Three Ivy & Bone books! And more adventures to come. I'm overjoyed to have you on this journey with me. First and foremost, a huge thank you to YOU, dear reader, for reading and for being a part of the adventure.

I would be remiss if I didn't offer my sincere and heartfelt gratitude to Jenni, Melissa, Tori, Melanie, and Kari, my lovely beta readers. You are incredible!! Thank you for always being willing to read my stories, even in their roughest stages.

A loving thank you to my Tuesday Tribe, for listening to me vent and championing me through the tough spots.

For my ARC team, a huge hug and high five, and a virtual slice of chocolate cake. Your enthusiasm for my novels is heartwarming and touching, and I don't deserve you!!

Thank you to Blue Raven Book Covers for the gorgeous cover art, and mien.artist for the stunning character art of Sol and Pandora. Having the art ahead of time really helps inspire certain scenes, and being able to picture it brought it to life in so many ways!

From the rooftops, I want to shout my thanks to all you incredible Kickstarter backers who pledged to support the latest Ivy & Bone project! Thanks to you, these stories were able to get a face lift with the shiny, glittery hardcovers. As a baby indie author, I never would have been able to make that possible. But thanks to your contributions, I get to see my books sparkle and shine just like the worldwide bestsellers! Thank you for making my dreams come true!

And lastly, Alex, Colin, Ellie, and Isabel, you own my heart wholly and completely. Thank you for being mine, for your laughter and hugs, for your smiles on my darkest days.

ABOUT THE AUTHOR

R.L. Perez is an author, wife, mother, reader, writer, and teacher. She lives in Florida with her husband and three kids. On a regular basis, she can usually be found napping, reading, feverishly writing, revising, or watching an abundance of Netflix. More than anything, she loves spending time with her family. Her greatest joys are her children, nature, literature, and chocolate.

Subscribe to her newsletter for new releases, promotions, giveaways, and book recommendations! Get a FREE eBook when you sign up at subscribe.rlperez.com.

Manufactured by Amazon.ca
Bolton, ON